JET II

BETRAYAL

Russell Blake

First Edition

ISBN: 978-1480170438

Published by

Reprobatio Limited

FROM THE AUTHOR

JET ~ Betrayal is a work of fiction, and as such plays fast and loose with many aspects of the truth, not the least of which are the descriptions of Thailand and its sex industry. In fairness to the good Thai people, while ping pong clubs can be viewed on Youtube and Googled, they are not as prevalent near Nana as I pretend – one has to go to other districts to find them. Nor is pedophilia as common – I have been assured that most of that sort of thing takes place in Pattaya, not Bangkok, and that the police take a zero tolerance policy. Be that as it may, there is also conflicting data that argues that 40% of the prostitutes in Thailand are underage, so perhaps the truth is somewhere between the "I'm shocked to hear there is gambling going on in here" outrage of some, and the assuredly lurid and overblown claims of others. Whatever your opinion, in all underprivileged countries slavery and child prostitution are significant problems, and while my descriptions may seem like sensationalism, they are not fantasy – would that they were only my invention.

In order to maximize your enjoyment of the books, do not take my descriptions of anything as literal, remember that this is all fiction for your entertainment, park your outrage at the door, and we'll get along fine. And above all, enjoy the ride – 100% accurate or not, it's designed to move you along at warp speed, and I hope it does.

RUSSELL BLAKE

CHAPTER 1

Gordon nudged his sleeping companion. "Doug. Wake up."

Doug's chin was drooping onto his stained military green T-shirt, sweat-soaked in the muggy night heat.

Gordon elbowed him again.

Doug shuddered, raised his head, and cracked open a bleary eye. "What?"

"Shhh. Keep it down," Gordon hissed. "We don't want to alert the guards."

He shifted his camouflage-clad legs in the mud and rotting vegetation then glanced at his partner's calf, where a filthy bandage was wrapped around a festering bullet wound, the pants cut off at the knee. The rusty stain of dried blood on the dressing was alive with ants exploring the once-white gauze.

Doug was pale, his body battling infection and fever. It hadn't helped that neither of them had been fed for two days, or that they only got water every four hours. The jungle in the southern hills of Myanmar was brutal at the best of times – if their captors didn't kill them, nature soon would.

"I got my hands almost free," Gordon whispered. "Slide over here so I can work on yours."

Both men were tied to a stake hammered into the ground at the edge of a clearing, their wrists bound behind them with rope. A crude-yet-effective form of imprisonment – and it wasn't as if there were a lot of places to go. The Golden Triangle was a lawless area that ran from Myanmar to Vietnam, encompassing a swatch of Laos and northern Thailand. Other than occasional villages, where the natives lived in abject poverty, it was a sprawling patchwork of jungle and opium poppy fields.

"How?" Doug slurred, too loud for Gordon's liking.

"Shut up. Just edge over a little. And stay quiet."

Doug complied, inching his body to where Gordon could reach his wrists.

The night was dark, but a sliver of moon shining through the trees overhead provided enough light to reveal Doug's haggard features. Glancing to the right, Gordon could make out the main encampment's tents in the clearing and the few rough-hewn shacks near the tree line, close to one of the countless streams in the hills of the Shan state that bordered Laos and Thailand.

Gordon sawed at the rope with a sharp shard of bamboo he'd broken from the base of the stake. His hands were bleeding from where the jagged edge had sliced the skin – not that he cared. If they didn't escape, they would die. It was that simple.

He guessed that it was around one in the morning. The sun had set at least five hours ago, although his sense of time had become warped, he knew, from the dehydration, hunger and exposure. They'd been left out through the inevitable periodic downpours, the mountain air drying the moisture from their skin over time, bringing with it the mosquitoes that swarmed around them. He'd been bitten so often that every area of exposed skin was swollen and red, as was Doug's.

He didn't even want to think about the mosquito-borne diseases that were endemic to the area. Dengue fever, malaria, yellow fever, chikungunya…and there was typhoid, hepatitis, the plague, hemorrhagic fever and a host of other delights that could be had from drinking the water or coming into contact with the jungle denizens.

But they had bigger problems right now.

Gordon strained to hear anything from the camp. All was quiet, but that could be illusory because, day and night, random patrols of two or three men moved soundlessly into the jungle from the shelters, assault rifles slung over their shoulders. These were Shan: area tribesmen who knew the region like their own backyard – hired guns, paid to live like fugitives and act as security for the man who was a kind of God to them.

A white man.

A round eye – with incredible riches and a desire for extreme privacy, who ruled his domain like a warlord.

Gordon hadn't spotted their elusive target: the *farang* that the natives were protecting, in whose camp they were now involuntary guests. From what he could make out of the guards' hushed discussions, the man wasn't there. So even if their mission had gone to plan and they'd been able to sneak up on the camp without being captured, it would have been in vain.

He felt Doug's rope fraying from his efforts with the bamboo and kept sawing methodically. Doug slumped into unconsciousness again at some point over the next hour, and Gordon let him be. He'd need any energy he could muster soon enough.

A noise disrupted the gloom's tranquility, branches snapping, as two armed men entered the clearing from the periphery, chatting in the local dialect – the night sentries had arrived. The camp seemed calm even during the day, the men lounging around lazily with nothing much to do but cook, patrol and gamble amongst themselves. With their patron absent, there was nothing to guard. Nobody would be interested in taking on a heavily-armed group in order to confiscate their tents or guns. This slice of the world had plenty of weapons – they were more common than shoes in the rural hills.

Gordon watched through shuttered eyes as the new arrivals headed to a small fire, where another man sat nursing a Kalashnikov rifle. They gestured in unison for him to pass his bottle. He protested half-heartedly, then laughed as he handed it over. Cigarettes came out, followed by the inevitable cards, which were shuffled in preparation for another late-night redistribution of wealth.

There would be none of this kind of sloppiness once their target was back. They'd both read his dossier. It was just lucky that Gordon had gotten the rope loose on a night when security was lax. That might be the edge that kept them alive.

Although Doug's odds weren't good.

The gunshot wound in his calf had missed the bone, but infection had set in and would hobble his ability to get far. Gordon had debated slipping off without him, but he didn't have the heart. If he had been wounded, he knew Doug would have stayed with him. After all they'd been through together, Gordon owed Doug at least that much in return.

But that didn't mean his chances were favorable.

If the guards kept drinking, Gordon hoped that in an hour they could make their move and disappear into the jungle. But then what? They were days from anything remotely resembling civilization. And this wasn't the only armed group in the region. Drug smugglers, bandits, human traffickers, poachers: all flourished in the no man's land that was the Triangle, and any one of them would kill without a second's hesitation.

Not the greatest scenario, but one they wouldn't have to worry about if Gordon couldn't get their arms loose.

Twenty minutes later, he felt the final frayed edges of the bindings separate with a quiet snap and nudged Doug again.

"Hey. You're free. Cut the rest of my rope the same way I cut yours."

Doug jolted and looked at him with uncomprehending eyes.

Maybe it had been a mistake to wait after all. He was out of it. The delirium brought about by the infection had progressed too far.

"Doug. Grab this piece of bamboo. Keep your hands behind you. Don't make any sudden movements. Saw until I'm free."

Awareness flickered, and Gordon felt Doug's fingers grasping for the shard.

When the bindings finally separated and his wrists pulled apart, circulation returned to his numb hands with a harsh rush of feeling. He peered through slits at the gunmen, who had finished the bottle and were slapping down cards, cheating each other with tired familiarity, their vigil punctuated by an occasional burp or hacking cough. The guards were seventy-five yards away, and Gordon's hope was that if they crawled into the underbrush it could be hours before anyone noticed they were missing. It wasn't as though anyone had checked on them since the sun had set, and he knew from his experience over the last two nights that nobody would be by to look at them until dawn, at the earliest.

"Doug. Listen," Gordon murmured. "We're going to slide over by that clump of plants and then run for it. Can you make it?"

Doug seemed more alert now that his hands were free and there was a chance of escape.

"I think so. How do we do this?"

"I'll go first. There's so little light, they won't be able to make us out if we don't do anything stupid. Once I'm out of sight, you crawl to me, and then we'll head downhill. If we make it till daylight, we'll be able to tell by the sun what direction we're headed, and we can get to the Thai border."

Doug nodded.

With a final glance at the guards, Gordon inched down and rolled onto his stomach, then dog-crawled to the trees. Nobody noticed – no shots were fired or alarms raised. Once he made it into the brush, he turned and watched for Doug. He hoped he wasn't making a fatal mistake by taking him.

Two minutes later, Doug materialized next to him. Both of them stood, and Doug tentatively put weight on his leg. The severity of pain this caused reflected in his eyes, but he choked it down.

After a final glance at the camp, they slipped deeper into the brush, the sound of night creatures around them their accompaniment as they wordlessly wove through the thick vegetation, hoping to find a trail in the meager moonlight.

Gordon supported Doug as they plodded forward, an hour into their trek to freedom. Doug was already tiring from the ravaging his system had endured from the infection, but he trudged on without complaint. Gordon's arm burned with inflammation from where the guards had crudely carved out the implanted tracking chip, leaving a gash of tortured flesh. He could only imagine what Doug was enduring.

They fought their way through deadwood and tangles of vines until they came to a stream that meandered downhill from the camp. A game trail ran along its banks, enabling them to pick up the pace.

"Gahh. Oh, God…" Doug exclaimed as his ankle twisted on a rut, tearing at his brutalized calf muscle and bringing tears to his eyes.

"Let's take a break and rinse off that bandage. The water will make you feel better," Gordon said as Doug sank to the ground grabbing at his leg.

As Gordon unwound the gauze, Doug gasped, his breath coming in hoarse bursts.

The stink was unbearable. Like rotting meat. Discoloration ran up the veins, and the wound seeped a bloody mixture of pus. Gordon rinsed it carefully, but didn't comment on the insects that had taken up a home. The water washed them away, but Gordon wasn't kidding himself. If Doug survived he'd probably lose the leg unless there was some miracle antibiotic they could get their hands on.

"How is it? Hurts like a b—"

Gordon cocked his head to the side and raised a finger to his lips.

"What?"

"Shhh," Gordon whispered, listening. "Damn. We need to get moving. Now. Let's get you wrapped up. We don't have much time."

Gordon wrung out the bandage and hastily wound it around the gash – the bullet had passed cleanly through the calf muscle, but the subsequent infection had caused immeasurable damage.

Doug glanced at him with alarm. "What do you hear?"

"A dog."

They struggled to their feet and stepped into the stream, hoping that would eliminate their trail – although Gordon suspected that Doug's wound was emanating a strong scent.

He had no idea where his captors had gotten their hands on a dog. Probably one of the nearby villages. A few dollars would buy almost anything, even at three in the morning. Their luck had just run out.

Clouds drifted across the sky, and without warning, a downpour started, drenching the two men and further darkening their way. There was no place to take cover from the cloudburst, but getting wet was the least of their worries.

Doug stumbled several times and cried out. He'd pulled the ravaged muscle again, and this time looked like he wasn't going to be able to continue any longer.

"Just leave me," Doug hissed through clenched teeth.

"Not a chance. Come on. Pick up the pace."

"I…I can't do it. It's too–"

A burst of rifle fire tore across Doug's torso, bullets whizzing past Gordon as he instinctively threw himself to the ground. Doug spun and collapsed next to him, burbling his last breath, and then lay still. The crash of men and beast tearing through the jungle a few hundred yards away signaled that Gordon's time had run out. He wondered whether they would drag him back or simply end his ordeal with a bullet to the skull.

The rain poured down with renewed vigor, large drops pelting him, and he used the temporary cover it offered to scramble forward and put distance between himself and his pursuers. His boots slammed onto the rocky riverbed, but the torrent falling all around him drowned the sound out. His only hope now was that nobody had night vision gear, or worse, an infrared scope. If they did, he was already dead.

He followed the brook until it tumbled into an area of angry churning froth. Rapids, the stream swollen from the rain. He stepped carefully onto the exposed rocks and hopped across from one to another, hoping to make it to the other side while the downpour covered his escape.

His footing gave out, and his sole slipped on the third rock. Gordon felt himself falling, disoriented as he slammed into the water, the force of the jolt knocking the wind out of him. He shook his head to clear it and felt warm liquid streaming down his neck; when he reached around to feel the back of his skull, his hand came away with a smear of blood.

Glancing around, he climbed to his feet and jogged along the shore as the stream widened, straining to hear any followers. The muffled sound of a dog barking told him everything he needed to know. He needed to put distance between himself and his pursuers while he could. When the rain stopped, he'd be exposed – the guards were all locals recruited from the neighboring hamlets, and he had no doubt that some of them were guides for the smuggling trails that wove through the hills. His only edge now was a slim lead and the dark of night. Come morning, if he lasted that long, he'd be a dead man unless he could make it across the border into Thailand and into relative civilization.

The irony of his being the prey wasn't lost on him. This had been a seek-and-destroy mission, the target a relatively easy, if elusive, one. Gordon had carried out similar operations in Afghanistan, the Balkans and the Middle East with no complications. He was the predator. This wasn't supposed to happen.

The sound of men crashing through the trees trailed him, but at a greater distance now.

Maybe his gambit had worked. But if so, he'd need to get away from the stream soon. It had served its purpose but was too easy to follow.

A barely-discernible path forked off from the water to his right. After a moment's hesitation, he threw himself headlong down the trail, willing his legs to greater speed even as he felt light-headed from the blood loss. He'd have to stop soon and try to clot the gash or it would do the gunmen's job for them.

Shouts echoed through the jungle behind him, but far enough back to afford him a momentary glimmer of hope. If the dog had lost the scent at the stream, then they were as blind as he was, and it was a big area.

Vines tore at his skin as the trail narrowed. At that moment, he would have given anything for a machete and an M4 rifle. He would have made short work of the amateurs who were tracking him, even with just the machete.

Shots rang out in the distance, but there was no accompanying shredding of vegetation. So the armed men were now shooting at phantoms.

A stirring in one of the trees stopped him in his tracks – a pair of glowing eyes burned into him. He squinted in the dim light and then started. There on a branch was a spotted leopard, capable of taking down a deer.

The big cat hissed as it watched him edge cautiously away while maintaining eye contact so it wouldn't think he was afraid. Animals could sense fear, Gordon knew. His fight wasn't with the hungry leopard, and he didn't want to provoke it in any way. At seventy pounds, it could inflict real damage, especially in his weakened state. He backed off, but the leopard seemed intent on challenging him. It could obviously smell blood.

The two stared each other down, twenty feet apart, until the cat decided there was easier prey in the jungle and leapt gracefully onto another branch, then worked its way down to the ground before loping off into the foliage.

Exhaling a sigh of relief, Gordon resumed his push down the path, more than aware that the gunmen were still hot on his tail. He estimated by the sound of the last shots that they were a quarter mile or more away, but he wanted that to be several miles by dawn if he could manage it. As long as the dog didn't pick up his scent again, it was achievable, provided he didn't bleed to death or get eaten.

As he eased down the hill, he entered a thick layer of ground fog that hung like a cloak over the valley below. He had a rough idea of where he was, but after having been moved from where he and Doug had been captured, it was only approximate. A handheld GPS would have come in handy.

Cries from up the hill, followed by a bark, told him everything he needed to know. The dog had caught the smell of blood on the wind and was leading the men straight to him again. The baying of the hound seemed to grow louder with each passing minute. Gordon clenched his jaw and pushed on, picking up his pace to a flat-out run.

A trailing vine tripped him, and he tumbled, rolling down the slope, gathering speed as he slid down the slick side of the muddy hill. He reached out with both hands trying to slow his fall, but it was no good. Gravity had the best of him, and the rain made the surface as slippery as an ice rink.

He thudded into the base of a tree, abruptly stopping his descent, and felt something in his chest snap. At least one, possibly two, broken ribs, he guessed. The simple assignment had now become an ordeal that he doubted he would escape with his life. Blood continued to leak from his head, and his hands were shredded into hamburger. The only good news was that his slide had taken him at least another hundred yards down a steep section of the hill, which no sane follower would attempt. If he could find another trail and maintain any kind of speed, he might have a chance.

Gordon felt like he'd gone ten rounds wrestling a bear, but forced himself to his feet, breath wheezing and a band of pain stabbing into his chest with each inhalation, but as far as he could tell, he was still viable.

He shouldered through the brush, careful of where he was stepping, aware that there were other dangers besides the gunmen. Leopards, an occasional tiger, Burmese python…all of which hunted under cover of darkness. He was wounded, bleeding, unarmed, starved and exhausted, which made him vulnerable to anything that wanted to try its luck with him.

And worst of all, for the first time in his career, he'd failed.

He'd lost his partner. Been captured. Had learned nothing that he hadn't known before the disastrous sortie.

The drizzle stopped, and the trees around him watched like silent sentries as he stumbled aimlessly, searching for any sort of route that would distance him from his pursuers. Insects clicked and buzzed in the surrounding grass; an occasional rustle greeted his trudging as some unseen animal scurried away. The mud sucked at the soles of his boots, and his legs felt leaden with each step, the effects of sleep deprivation and no food taking their toll, sapping his energy even as he demanded more from his battered body.

As Gordon emerged into a small clearing, the clouds parted just enough for the moon to leer through, its ghostly glow enabling him to see a gap in the undergrowth on the other side.

Then fog drifted across the open space, closing in on the seeming mirage. Gordon staggered towards the trees, confident that he hadn't been imagining the vision. Another bark sounded in the distance from behind him, urging him forward.

There.

Just a few more yards.

For a moment, he thought he'd missed his footing, then the crackle of dry branches accompanied his body falling into the dark.

Blinding pain stabbed through him. Intense, searing agony from his abdomen, chest and legs.

Gordon's vision blurred as he gazed skyward, the moon mocking the spectacle of his body impaled on sharpened bamboo stakes in the bottom of the pit, his blood seeping black around the lethal spears in the eerie luminescence. His disembodied mind wondered whether the trap was designed for wild boar, deer, or some other delicacy. The pain receded as his consciousness seemed to float above him, observing his pathetic state, his existence brought to an abrupt end in a trench in an unnamed hellhole somewhere in a jungle God had forgotten.

Time seemed to compress as a simultaneous rush of regrets and memories overwhelmed him. Gordon's last thought was that it wasn't supposed to end this way, that he still had more to do. Even though he'd personally released many from their mortal coil and watched impassively as they died, his own passage surprised him, and he finally understood the puzzled look in the eyes of his victims when their moment had come.

With a last involuntary shudder, he strained against the stakes, then stiffened, convulsed, and went limp, his ultimate breath escaping with a wet rattle as blood filled his lungs and his heart gave up its pointless struggle to beat.

CHAPTER 2

Present Day, Omaha, Nebraska

The airport was bustling, all cool chrome and franchise restaurants hawking overpriced snacks and six-dollar coffee. Beef featured prominently in the local lexicon, and placards of cows staring in bovine wonder at the passing passengers adorned any walls that didn't tout burger specials or extra-large-sized beverages or desserts.

The air was crisp as Jet approached her rental car, toting her suitcase as she walked through the parking lot, dodging pools of water from the melting snow. She'd gotten her first look at the great state of Nebraska on approach, and her initial impression of it, and Omaha, could be summarized in one word: flat. The few hills were all of a couple hundred feet tall, rolling, covered with farmland. Large though it was, the city was set in a familiar mold, but with a decidedly American suburban feel to it. From the air, it looked like one large tract home development.

She found her Chevrolet and tossed her suitcase in the back seat before sliding behind the wheel and starting the engine. The little four cylinder motor revved as it warmed up, then settled into a monotone hum as she pulled to the exit and handed the attendant her paperwork.

The flight from Paris had been long, and the connecting leg in Chicago annoying, but she was here now. The only question was what to do next. She had an address and a name. That was it. No plan. No strategy.

She'd tried to formulate one on the plane, but she didn't know enough about the situation to be effective. The only information Jet had was the identity of the person who had been given her daughter after she'd been stolen from her at birth. She had no idea what the person or people knew or didn't know, or what David had told them as a cover story. She highly doubted that he'd told them the truth. That had never been his style. As far as they knew, the baby could have been an orphan, or had been rescued from an abusive situation.

Jet had never even seen her daughter, Hannah. She was sure she'd recognize the two-year-old, but the truth was she might not. Jet knew nothing about anything in the little girl's life since she had disappeared from the hospital following a difficult delivery – the doctor had lied, telling Jet that her baby had died during childbirth.

She didn't even know her daughter's name.

Her new name. The name given to her by the people who were the only parents she'd ever known.

Jet's eyes welled up, but she fought back the urge to cry. She was just exhausted from the ordeal of the last few days: her lover's death at the hands of Grigenko, the murderous Russian oligarch who'd sent a hit team to kill her as well. The gun battle at his yacht. A harrowing escape from France. Discovering the daughter she'd believed dead was actually alive.

She knew she was running on fumes, but she couldn't rest until she had her daughter back.

And then what?

And how?

She glanced at herself in the rearview mirror, inspecting her newly trimmed, dyed black hair and then caught a look at her eyes. They were tired. The last week had worn on her, and the stress was starting to show, even if nobody else could see it but her. She needed to rest.

But first she needed to get her daughter.

Jet fished around in her purse and retrieved a handheld GPS unit. She thumbed it on, and the little screen flickered to life. Stabbing at the tiny keyboard, she entered the street address, which she'd committed to memory, then peered at the display. According to the unit, she was seven and a half miles from the house. A quick look at the onscreen map told her that she could be there within fifteen minutes.

She swung onto the main artery that led to the outskirts of Omaha, mind racing over the possible scenarios she would find when she arrived at where her daughter had spent the last two years. Jet didn't know what to expect; her throat tightened with accumulated tension. She forced herself to relax. Getting agitated was dangerous and would serve no useful purpose.

When she arrived at the subdivision, it was as anonymous as any she'd seen, filled with identical homes built from one of three different templates – modest affairs for the middle-class working folk, who apparently made up much of Omaha. Many of the cars were medium-priced American models, and it being a mid-week afternoon, the streets were empty, with everyone either at work or picking up children from school.

Jet had never been to the United States before, so the Norman Rockwell neighborhood was inherently foreign to her, as was the sheer size of everything. The shopping plazas, the cars, the people, the roads were all big. It was as if someone had supersized the entire country. She'd never seen anything like it, but she resolved to try to fit in so as not to attract attention. Her greatest asset at this point was that she was completely off the radar – invisible, traveling on one of her alternative passports, her identity a Belgian freelance journalist.

She slowed her speed as she rolled past the address, looking over the unremarkable single-story house with practiced eyes. A fence, no doubt a backyard, two car garage, probably three bedrooms judging by the size. Absolutely nothing to distinguish it in any way from the hundreds of other tract homes on the long, quiet street.

After pulling over, she jotted down the phone number of a real estate agent whose sign was planted in the front yard of the home next door. A stroke of luck if she could get in. It would tell her everything she needed to know about floor plans, quality of any security systems, neighborhood watch groups, door and window locks.

The downside to the neighborhood was that it afforded few places to hide, and it looked like the kind of place where everyone knew one another, meaning there was no way she could easily mount a watch on the house. She'd have to get creative – there would only be one shot at getting her daughter, and she couldn't blow it.

She meandered down the street, jotting down a few more phone numbers – apparently there were a decent number of sellers, victims of the lingering financial crisis that had stretched for almost half a decade. Every other sign declared foreclosure or that the home was bank-owned – including the one next door to her target.

There was nothing more to see. Her next stop would have to be to get a disposable cell phone and then find a motel nearby. Twisting the wheel, she headed back the way she'd come, eyes darting back to the house as she passed it again. There were no obvious signs of life, but then again the blinds were closed on the front windows so it was hard to judge whether anyone was home.

A few blocks down the road, Jet pulled into a Target parking lot. She shut off the engine and popped the trunk, then transferred her suitcase to where it would be out of sight. No point in begging any thieves, although, so far, Omaha looked like a postcard for suburban safety.

Ten minutes later, she returned to the car and made a call on her new burner cell phone.

"Realty World. This is Joanie!" an overly cheerful voice chirped.

"Yes. Hello. This is Susan," Jet lied. "I'm looking at homes, and I got your number off a sign in front of a house I liked…"

"Oh, yes! A house! Well, you've come to the right place! Which one was it?"

Jet told her the address.

"Mmmm. Yes. I know the one. That's a great deal. The bank owns it. Wants to unload it as soon as possible. You can probably steal it, and they'd lend you the money to do it!"

"Well, that's good to know. I'm looking all over, but that seems to be a nice, quiet neighborhood. Is there a time when I can get in to see the place?"

"Of course. How about in an hour? Can you make it then?"

"That would be perfect."

"Susan, right? What's your last name?"

"Jacobs."

"And will your husband be with you?"

"No. The house is for me."

"Wonderful. And do you have financing in place so you can write an offer?"

Jet was rapidly growing annoyed with the pre-qualifying.

"Let's not get ahead of ourselves. There are a lot of homes out there. I plan to pay cash whenever I buy and then get a mortgage once I've bought it."

"Oh, good. I like that. You know what you want, and you're not going to waste any time."

Jet sighed. "I'll see you at the house in an hour, right?"

"Absolutely!"

Jet wondered what assertiveness training course the auto-suggesting saleswoman had gone to, and disconnected with a shake of her head. She checked her watch and confirmed that she had time to find someplace to spend the night. Someplace quiet.

Twenty minutes later, she had checked into a generic motel, two stories, with exterior room entrances and nobody watching the comings and goings of the occupants. She'd asked for the quietest spot they had, and the woman at the reception desk put her in the ground floor room at the far end of the complex. It turned out to be simple, clean and adequate, with an electronic in-room safe and wireless internet. She hastily unpacked her few possessions and locked her IDs in the safe along with most of the cash she was carrying. She'd have a better idea what she would need to source once she'd scoped out the neighbor's house.

Joanie turned out to be a mid-forties woman who precisely matched her voice. With a bouffant hairdo and an evangelical smile, she wore a pant-suit and sensible shoes and shook hands like a man, before launching into a non-stop barrage of information and questions.

As they walked through the home, Jet pretended to care about the amount of space in the kitchen, the faux granite counters, the new appliances. There was no furniture, and the carpets had been recently changed, and the interior painted, so it smelled like chemicals and stagnant air.

"Like I said. The bank is motivated. You know how that is," Joanie enthused.

"Well, it's in reasonable shape. What can you tell me about the neighborhood? Is it safe?"

"Oh, extremely. It's one of the lowest crime rates in all of Omaha!"

"That's good to know. And what about a neighborhood watch?"

"You know, I don't think they have one. There hasn't been a break-in for years. I mean, many, many years. That just doesn't happen here. You couldn't find anything safer."

"Have you shown it a lot? How long has it been on the market?"

Joanie checked the listing paperwork.

"Looks like almost five months. And no, it hasn't had a lot of traffic. Not too many folks want to move during the winter months, with the snow and storms and all. I think you could pick it up for a song."

Jet spent half an hour with the pushy agent, entertaining her high-pressure sales pitch and then decided she'd seen enough. Joanie insisted on showing her the backyard, which was in disrepair after being ignored all winter, before they finished on the front porch. She tried to get as much information out of Jet as possible, who invented a background – being transferred to open a new insurance office in town, from Seattle, looking to make a decision within a week, definitely a buyer... Joanie's eyes widened when she heard that Jet wanted to buy soon, and she redoubled her insistence that this was a perfect house for her.

"I think you should write an offer. Just a lowball, but it can't hurt, and if you get it for that...well, there are all sorts of deals, you know?"

"Joanie. Thanks for your time. I have your contact information. I'll get back in touch with you if I need to see the house again and write an–" She stopped mid-sentence as a car pulled into the driveway next door, and a woman got out, then walked to the rear passenger door and opened it.

To unstrap the toddler in the child seat.

Jet's breath caught in her throat.

The woman was medium height, a muted blonde, dressed in office clothes, and was fumbling with an overstuffed plastic shopping bag as she unclasped the buckle on the safety seat.

Joanie's incessant chattering faded into a distant tremolo as the blood rushed to Jet's ears and her heart began trip-hammering. She heard herself mumbling some vague assent to the annoying woman in response to yet another suggestion that she write something up on the house, and then time grudgingly creaked forward again, and the slow-motion state she'd found herself in for a few seconds shifted back to reality.

The blonde lifted the toddler out of the seat and set her gently on the driveway, where she stood unsteadily and then trailed the driver to the front door on the chubby, slightly wobbly legs of a healthy two-year-old.

She was absolutely beautiful.

The most gorgeous sight Jet had ever seen.

There was no mistaking her. Even from thirty feet away, she could see herself in the tiny face, the cast of the eyes, the nose. That was her daughter. Her Hannah. A flutter of Jet's essence shifted in her abdomen, a momentary recollection of the life she'd carried to term, its tiny heart beating in cadence with her own.

Transfixed though she was, Jet forced herself to look away. She didn't want to raise the smallest amount of suspicion with Joanie or do anything memorable – which was relatively safe, given all the agent could see or hear was an opportunity to make a sale, preferably today.

"Joanie, I really appreciate the tour, but I just realized the time. I have to get going to a meeting. I'll give you a call in the next day or two after I finish looking around. This house is a strong contender. It has everything I want."

Joanie visibly deflated as the words registered. Her hopes of a quick offer dashed, she tried one more time, but didn't have much enthusiasm left.

"Well, I'll be showing it more regularly once the weather turns, so if I was you, I'd act quickly. It's a creampuff and so cozy. And safe. And the bank–"

"Yes. I know. The bank is motivated – I got that loud and clear. Look, thanks so much for taking the time to show it, Joanie. I appreciate it, and I'll be touching base shortly."

Jet ventured a final sidelong glance at her daughter then turned away, pausing to shake Joanie's meaty hand before returning to her car, the world threatening to spin dizzily out of control at any second.

She slid the key into the ignition and started the engine, fighting to calm her breathing – while outwardly she was unflustered, internally it was all she could do to keep from running into the house and grabbing Hannah there and then.

But that wouldn't be a lasting solution. She needed to get to her – that was a given. But she also needed to be clever about it and cover her tracks, so once she had her back, she would have her permanently.

Jet shifted the car into gear and pulled slowly from the curb, throwing Joanie a curt wave as she drove away, mind whirling with conflicting emotions. Her daughter was mere footsteps away, healthy and beautiful, and yet Jet was forced to drive off as though she didn't exist. The unfairness of the situation rankled as she turned onto the larger street that led to the main boulevard. She had done nothing wrong, and yet her child had been stolen and given to another woman to raise – by David: the man who was her father, a man Jet loved but could never forgive for stealing Hannah away.

The bitterness of the betrayal rose in her gorge as she thought of it, and then a wave of grief washed over her as she remembered his last moments, trying to make amends for doing the unforgivable; all in the interests of keeping those he loved safe.

Jet brushed the tears of frustration from her face as she pulled to the stop sign, looking in both directions before rolling through it.

What was done was done. David was dead and was never coming back, and she was now in Nebraska and had the most important job of her life to do.

She'd found her Hannah.

Finally.

Now she needed to get her back.

In the end, the rest was noise.

Getting Hannah back was the only thing that mattered.

CHAPTER 3

Jet pulled the stolen Toyota Camry to the curb thirty yards from the house, having shut off the headlights as she inched to the curb. All the surrounding homes were dark, with the exception of a few porch lights glimmering in the shadows of midnight. She exited the vehicle, hoisted a black nylon backpack she'd bought earlier that day, and made her way to the vacant home she'd toured three days before with Joanie.

She edged to the porch and stooped, quickly finding the agent lock box and turning the combination to the numbers she'd memorized when Joanie had opened it. Her latex gloves squeaked on the slick surface as she fished inside for the key, and after unlocking the front door, she returned it to its hiding place, spinning the dial so it stopped on a random digit.

Once inside the empty house, she quickly pulled night vision goggles from the bag and put them on – courtesy of an overnight delivery from an internet vendor. She knew better than to purchase anything specialized in Omaha. Caution was an indelible part of her makeup when preparing for any kind of an operation, and rescuing her daughter was no different.

The interior of the house illuminated in the green glow of the goggles – a common commercial version that would be suitable for tonight's task – and she extracted the rest of her gear.

Jet sat cross-legged on the floor and watched the street out front for forty-five minutes, wary of any movement or signs of life. Nothing. No cars, no dog walkers. The neighborhood was completely still.

She crept to the back door and eased it open, then took cautious steps to the fence that separated the yards. Seeing nothing suspicious, she climbed over the wood slats and moved to the rear entrance of Hannah's house, ears straining for sounds of movement inside.

The lock took fifteen seconds. She slowly twisted the knob, careful not to make any sound, and when the latch freed, she pushed it open, the hinges silent from the drop of oil she'd applied to each before jimmying the lock.

The house was the twin of the vacant one next door, so she knew exactly where the master bedroom and the guest bedrooms would be. It was a better-than-even chance that Hannah would have her own room.

Her running shoes made no sound as she crept along the hall to the bedrooms. If she had any luck at all, Hannah's putative parents would sleep with their door closed. If not, and they awakened, she was prepared to deal with them, but she hoped she wouldn't have to hurt them. They were probably innocent in all this, considering how David had operated. Every player would be compartmentalized from the others, and nobody would know more than they absolutely had to.

She'd ruminated on how he had found these people, eventually deciding that it really didn't matter. Because of his work with the Mossad, David had been granted access to far greater resources than she could have imagined. The most probable scenario was that he'd arranged to have Hannah delivered to a couple waiting for an adoption. There were myriad ways of achieving anything, she knew, if enough money was thrown at a problem, and he had told her that his operational budget was vast and untraceable.

The master door was closed, so she moved to the first guest bedroom – the likeliest of the two she would have used for a children's room based on her tour of the home's twin. The lever handle opened with a click.

Inside, she saw her first problem – a transmitter that would carry any noise Hannah made to a speaker in the master bedroom. Her fingers felt for a pocket knife, and she lifted the wire with a steady hand and severed it with a single slice. Hannah stirred in her toddler bed but didn't make any noise, still sleeping, unaware of her mother only a few feet away.

Now was the moment of truth.

She leaned down and lifted Hannah, who struggled momentarily in her arms and then snuggled against Jet's neck as she held her close, still out cold. Jet was surprised how much she weighed – around thirty pounds – and for a brief second, she was struck by how little she actually knew about children and mothering.

As Hannah snuffled against her neck, Jet's heart melted.

She crept out of the house and down the side access to the Camry, removing her night vision goggles as she approached the vehicle. The streets were still quiet, empty and cold. Hannah woke up as she was being strapped into the child seat and looked at Jet with sleepy eyes, confused by why she was being transported in the middle of the night.

Jet buckled her in and smiled. Hannah reached out to her proffered hand, slapped it in a toddler's version of high five, and laughed delightedly.

"Sweetheart. I'm so glad I finally found you. I love you. Mommy loves you."

Hannah looked confused, which made sense. She was being told that Jet loved her, which she understood based on the three familiar words, but not what it meant in proximity to the assurance that Mommy also loved her.

"You want to go for a ride?"

Hannah giggled again.

"Okay, sweetheart, we're going to go for a ride. Right now."

Jet rounded the front of the car and climbed behind the wheel, then crossed the two wires she'd left dangling. The engine turned over with a purr, and she eased the vehicle down the street, waiting to turn on the headlights until she'd rounded the corner that would take them out of the subdivision.

As she drove the two miles to the industrial area where she'd left her rental car, Jet considered what she'd just done, and the hurdles she'd have to face getting Hannah out of the country. She'd need a passport and all the right paperwork. More importantly, she'd need to evade any law enforcement effort to apprehend her.

Jet had thought through all the elements of their escape with care and had calculated that they could be in Dallas after a hard ten hours of driving. There, she could find contacts who would be able to create documents for her. There were thriving underworld operations in virtually every major city that could create whatever she needed. But she had to get clear of Nebraska before daybreak, which meant she had no time to lose.

She swung onto the main road and gazed at Hannah in the back seat, her eyes already beginning to close from the rocking motion of the car. Jet realized this would be way harder with a toddler, but there was no turning back. She had her daughter. They would figure the rest out in the process.

They changed vehicles, and Jet opened the five-gallon gas can she had stowed in the trunk and doused the stolen Toyota inside and out, leaving her gloves and her shoes on the passenger seat after donning the replacement pair she'd stashed in the rental. She opened a pack of cigarettes she'd purchased for the purpose and lit one, then after puffing it until the tip glowed red in the darkness, she flicked it through the open window of the glistening Camry.

The vapor ignited with a *whump*, and within three minutes, they were back on the city streets, making their way to the motel, Hannah now asleep after the momentary excitement of the impromptu fireworks display from the car's immolation.

A police cruiser pulled alongside as she waited at a light; the patrolman glanced at her, boredom evident on his face. A housewife in a family car late at night was as unexciting as it got. The light changed, and he tromped on the gas, the engine growling as he pulled ahead. Jet smiled to herself and eased away from the signal, careful to do so at a moderate pace.

Halfway up the next block, the squad car hit its emergency lights and swung around in a screeching arc, siren blaring.

Someone must have phoned in the burning car, or the gas tank had ignited and prompted a call from nearby security guards at the warehouses in the area. Whichever, that would draw every policeman within miles, ensuring that her trip out of town would be uneventful.

The motel's lights bathed the parking lot with a fluorescent glow, and she noticed there were quite a few more cars than when she had left. None of the rooms were illuminated, suggesting everyone was asleep. She could slip into her room, grab her essentials out of the safe and be on the road within a matter of minutes. She had stolen a Chevy Equinox earlier that night and parked it next to the rental car lot, so her final task would be to transfer everything to the SUV when she dropped the car off – no point raising eyebrows by failing to return the vehicle.

"All right, sweetheart. I'll be right back. I just need to get my stuff. Be good," she crooned to Hannah, who watched her with sleepy eyes before slowly closing them again.

Jet's eyes roved over the parked cars, automatically scanning for anomalies or suspicious tells, but saw nothing. Her mind was poring over all the items she'd need to get for Hannah – diapers, food, toys, a bed, clothes – all the sundry goods that were required to care for a toddler. She would have to stop somewhere after she crossed the state line. With any luck, the police wouldn't be notified until morning, and it would take a little while for them to issue an all-points bulletin with Hannah's description and a photo. By then she would be in Kansas or Oklahoma, on her way to Texas.

She tossed her clothes into her suitcase and went into the bathroom to retrieve her hygiene kit. There was more than enough room in the bag for all of her items as well as anything Hannah would need. The safe sprang open with a beep, and she quickly emptied it, slipping one of the passports into her back pocket before changing her top to a maroon one. All black might draw attention in rural states in America's heartland, and she didn't want to be memorable in any way.

Jet glanced at her watch. She'd been inside for six minutes.

She grabbed the handle of her suitcase and shouldered her purse, then moved to the door, taking a last survey of the little room to ensure she had everything. Satisfied, she twisted the handle and stepped into the night, her suitcase rolling behind her.

Hannah was still asleep when she returned to the car, and she took care to open the trunk as quietly as possible so as not to wake her.

A spike of pain stabbed into her thigh as she was hoisting the bags into the back, and she spun around, instinctively brushing at the painful spot. Her hand felt something hard – her vision began to blur. She fought for consciousness as her knees buckled, and she slumped to the ground, her last image was of two men approaching her from a blue van parked thirty feet away, one of them carrying what looked like an air rifle.

Then the world spun, and everything went black.

CHAPTER 4

The first thing Jet registered was that she was lying on a hard slab in the dark. She turned her head and tried to move her limbs, but it was no good. She had been bound with some kind of straps.

Her fingers worked on finding some weakness in the bindings, and she struggled to slide an arm free, but the straps were secure. Whoever had done this to her had known what they were doing.

Her head pounded, sinuses screaming in pain, but she choked the discomfort back while she tried to focus. Something dripped rhythmically in the corner of the small room. Water. One drop, every ten to fifteen seconds. It smelled like mold and must and dank, fetid air.

What the hell was this?

And then panic flooded her.

Where was Hannah?

Her breathing and pulse rate spiked as she fought against the restraints, exhausting herself as she flailed in vain, trying to break free. It took every bit of operational discipline she had to talk herself down and regain her composure. Losing it wouldn't help anything. She needed to glean as much information as she could about wherever she was and wait for an opportunity.

Think. What happened?

Last thing she remembered was that she had been shot with a dart, and then everything had gone hazy.

Obviously some sort of tranquilizer.

But why? And who could have possibly known that she was at the motel? She'd been clean. No tails. She was sure of it. Nothing made any sense.

And yet here she was, bound in a dark room, imprisoned by unknown captors.

Footsteps echoed on concrete, and then metal scraped on metal. Light streamed into the room as the door at the far end opened, and a man stepped in. She could tell it was a man by his silhouette, as well as his cologne. Sickeningly sweet. Other men waited in the hall – there had been more than one set of footsteps.

The man reached to the side, and the chamber became flooded with yellow light. A lamp mounted to a collapsible tripod stood by the gray wall. She could make out paint peeling from its damp surface beyond the glare.

She had shut her eyes, pretending to be incapacitated. They might slip if they thought she was still unconscious.

"Come on. Wake up. The drug has worn off by now, so let's not waste each other's time. I know you're listening to every word, so open your eyes, and let's get down to business, shall we?" the man said. He pronounced his consonants oddly, with a slight lisp, but different. Almost like a speech impediment, the word 'so' sounding more like 'tho'.

Jet opened her eyes and regarded him.

"There. That wasn't so hard, was it? Sorry about the little bondage session, but I've been warned that you are extremely dangerous – that your entire body is literally a lethal weapon, cliché as that might sound. It seemed prudent to restrain you until we'd had a chance to chat."

"Is that what you call this? Chatting?" Jet snapped.

"Well, you'll have to forgive my manners. I've had to improvise. This was all the hospitality I could arrange at short notice. But yes, we are going to have a nice little chat, and you're going to discover how you can help me so that I can help you." The man's voice and cadence were eerily menacing, even though he was soft-spoken, almost gentle in his cadence, which was more chilling than if he had been screaming abuse at her.

"Help you? I don't have any idea who you are. Why would I want to help you? You've kidnapped me from a motel in the dead of night for God knows wha–"

"Please. Spare me. I know who you are. I know all about you. Again, don't waste my time with denials or protestations."

Jet bit her tongue.

"Let's see if this rings any bells. Your code name was Jet. You were with the Israeli intelligence service for almost six years, during which time you broke every record for effectiveness. Assassinations, kidnappings, blackmail, insurrection, false flag attacks…when the Mossad needed the dirtiest of the dirty done, you were who they sent."

Her eyes narrowed to slits. "Who are you?"

"Ah. Now we're getting somewhere. So you concede that we don't need to play around anymore? You may call me Arthur. Nice to meet you...Jet." He walked closer to her, and the lamp's glow illuminated his face. There was something wrong with it. The skin. It looked like scar tissue, like...

"Yes, it was the result of a horrible burn. Six surgeries later, and this was the best they could do. But I've learned to live with it. A friendly dose of napalm in Vietnam. A long, long time ago. I'm actually very lucky I have sight in both eyes. You can't have helped but notice that I have a hard time pronouncing some sounds, though. That's a regrettable byproduct of not having lips."

"Arthur. Fair enough. Who are you?"

"Why, can't you guess? I'm very sorry to hear about David, by the way. He was a solid fellow. An honorable man."

"You knew David?"

"Obviously. I arranged for one of my subordinates to help with information about the Russian. About Belize. I also helped him in sourcing weapons and blueprints..."

"You're his contact with the CIA?"

"Not exactly – most of the grunt work went through my underling, Terry. But I was the ultimate authority. He couldn't have done any of it without my approval."

"Why does the CIA have me tied up in a cell?"

"Now we come to the heart of the matter. Because, my dear girl, I need your help with a matter of some delicacy. A matter that is right up your street."

"Where's my daughter?"

"I was wondering when you would get to that. She's fine. I have arranged for her to be cared for by a temporary foster family – good people who will lavish her with love. I'm afraid you have caused some problems for me, and for yourself, with the original couple that raised her. I interceded and clamped a lid on the kidnapping so it doesn't go viral, but it will leak out eventually. They adore her, and the only thing they know is that she's been kidnapped. Baby Samantha, by the way. That's her name."

"That isn't what I named her."

He waved a black leather-gloved hand at her. "Call her whatever you like when this is over."

"You have no right to steal my baby. She's mine. You know it. This is wrong."

"Well, I suppose it is rather wrong, but it is the only way I could think of to have my needs met. I want you to do something for me, and I'm quite sure that you wouldn't have done it voluntarily, so I needed some leverage. I would say that having your daughter is pretty good leverage, wouldn't you?"

She struggled against the straps, then relaxed. No point in using energy she might need later.

"See? I was right. It was prudent to keep you restrained for our first discussion. Imagine how unpleasant it could have become if you'd been able to reach me."

"Unpleasant for you, perhaps. Not for me," she spat.

"True. Which is why you are perfectly suited to this job."

"What makes you think I'd do anything for the CIA?"

"I have your daughter. I have no fight with you. But I have an operation I have had nothing but trouble with, and nobody on my team seems to be able to solve my problem. But you? You could solve it, with your illustrious background."

"You kidnapped my daughter and took me captive to get me to do a job for you? You're insane. That's not how this works, and you know it."

"I do, indeed. I've been doing this for far longer than you've been alive. Trust me when I tell you that if there were any alternative, I would have let you go your merry way with your daughter, and that would have been the end of it. But extraordinary problems require extraordinary solutions, and I have need of your skills. So I have had to take an…unconventional approach. I hope you'll forgive me." Arthur executed the hint of a bow, and she could see that his hair was white and that the scar tissue ran across his entire head.

"If you hurt her…"

"I am not an animal. I have no desire to harm your daughter. If these were normal circumstances, I would have removed myself from the entire affair once David died. Yes, I know all about the fire on the Russian's boat. After considering the plans he had asked for, I guessed that his target was the yacht, and from there it was a simple matter to work out what had happened. He went dark after that night, so I suspected the worst. And then when Grigenko's jet vaporized…well, let's just say I surmised that you survived. Which created an interesting opportunity for me."

"How did you know I would come for my daughter?"

"I didn't. It was a calculated risk. But I realized that if he *had* revealed his scheme to you, it would be impossible for you to stay away – so I was willing to devote a few resources in the event that you surfaced."

"Surface. I see. And how did you track me to the hotel?"

"I had a team across the street from the house, and when they saw a strange car pull up on the street and watched you slip into the house next door, they put a tracker on the car. It wasn't hard to guess what was happening." He paused, sucking in a breath with a hiss, his tongue slurping wetly as he blotted the corner of the raw gash that comprised his mouth with a handkerchief. "And so, here we are. The two of us. I, with a proposition for you. And you, in a position to pay very close attention to it, and I would hope, predisposed to accept my proposal."

"Go to hell. I'll kill you with my bare hands. You'll never be safe."

"Perhaps. But you're the one who is tied up at the moment, if I'm not mistaken. So save the idle threats for later. I'm not asking you to fall in love with me, and I know that my actions are reprehensible. Let's just agree that you probably hate me right now, and justifiably so, might I add. That emotion is a luxury you can indulge to your heart's content later. For now, if I were you, I'd be more interested in what I needed to do to get my daughter back so I could get on with my life than in threatening me or vowing revenge."

She glared at him and said nothing.

"I have a problem. You are the solution. Solve my problem and I let you reunite with your daughter and I step forever out of your life. You're free to do whatever you like, and I'll take the secret of your existence to my grave. Consider it the price of my assistance to you and David in the Grigenko matter."

"Solve your problem," Jet repeated.

"Yes."

"Do I need to ask what the problem is?"

The eerily smooth skin of his face pulled taut in a grimace that could have been a model for a Munch painting. He was smiling.

"Why, my dear, I think it's obvious. I need you to kill someone."

CHAPTER 5

Arthur nodded at the guard outside to shut the door and then walked slowly to the foot of the steel bed she was tied to and looked her over.

"That's it? You want me to kill someone? For that you need to take my daughter and blackmail me?" Jet demanded.

"I think you would find this more palatable if you regarded it as payback for all of the help I arranged for David on his Russian issue. And as for your daughter, if you accept that I'm taking good care of her while you're otherwise occupied with this errand, it will be easier for both of us. Again, there's nothing I want more than for you to have, er, Hannah back. I can only imagine how awful it must be to have finally found her, only to have her torn away from you."

"Forgive me if I don't get all weepy at your sentiment."

"I would expect nothing less."

"So why does the CIA need me to perform a sanction for it? You have people who can take care of that sort of thing – being the best funded and largest intelligence service in the history of the world, and all."

"This is a delicate matter. We have already tried to attend to it in-house, but haven't been successful. When you showed up looking for your daughter, it created an opportunity. You specialize in a kind of work that's a dying art, I'm afraid. Ever since the Wall came down and Russia stopped being the great Satan, our skills and resources have diminished. Sure, the Chinese present a clear and present danger, and the odd foray into the Middle East has kept us in practice, but nothing to hold a candle to your achievements. You could say I'm somewhat of a fan."

"How could you possibly know about my missions with the Mossad?"

"That's one of the questions I won't be able to answer. Suffice it to say, I know what nobody is supposed to, and frankly, your résumé is as impressive as hell. I've been a player for forty years, and I've never encountered such attributes. It's truly remarkable. If you were a gymnast or a ballerina, you'd have a cabinet full of gold medals. Alas, it's a rarified talent, but one that I completely appreciate."

"Spare me."

Arthur rubbed his ruined face. "Let me tell you a story. It's one that I've never told another living person."

"Meaning all the others are dead…"

"Yes. But no matter. It's a fascinating one. It involves greed, corruption, deception, and betrayal."

"Don't they all?"

"Hmm. Three months ago, I was in charge of conducting a transaction in Asia. In its essence, it was a simple matter. The CIA arranged to fund certain factions with interests aligned with our own, whose cooperation was deemed vital. Are you familiar with Myanmar?"

"Burma. Military dictatorship. Rogue nation. What's to know?"

"Then you're probably aware that it is not considered friendly by my government. Let's just say that if you're an enemy of my enemy, you are my friend, for the moment."

"That didn't work out so well for Saddam Hussein, did it?"

"I don't make the rules. Anyway, there was a group in Myanmar that we felt were deserving of our support. But not the sort that you can go to Congress to sign off on. More discreet. To cut a long story short, one of our top agents in the region was chartered with handling the transaction. Fifty million dollars in diamonds. Untraceable. All of them easily convertible to cash. It was a simple arrangement. He was to go in, give our friends the diamonds, and then report back. But apparently, he had different ideas. The money was too large, or maybe he had just been in-country too long. He took delivery of the diamonds, but our friends never received them. And then we learned that they had been butchered in a gun battle. So it would appear that our man decided to retire and give himself a better than customary pension. Fifty million in diamonds' worth."

"So he stole your diamonds. But, come on. Fifty million is a drop in the bucket. Didn't I read that your defense department can't account for something like ten trillion dollars? Fifty million is beer money – a rounding error. There are Wall Street moguls who stole twenty times that much who are still walking around New York, who never even got charged."

"True, but the point is that we can't have our operatives stealing company property. Sends the wrong message, I think you'll agree."

"And why is it that you haven't been able to deal with this yourself?"

"To be frank, we tried on two separate occasions. Both ended disastrously. This man has decades of experience in the region and is as comfortable there as a native. He's disappeared into the jungle, where he's living like a tribal chieftain. It's proved difficult to even establish where he is on any given day. Add to that, the wrinkle that the Myanmar government is actively hostile to us, and it's a recipe for disaster."

"What happened to the last two teams that tried to take him out? What went wrong?"

"Unknown. The first operative was found in Northern Thailand. The indigenous animals had feasted on him, so there wasn't a lot left to process. Our last attempt, two men, disappeared without a trace. We've had no word from them for over a week. They had a sat phone that would work anywhere in the world, so it's safe to say they're off the table. Which brings us to you."

"I might be more receptive to this if I wasn't strapped in some prison cell."

"I need you to fully understand the gravity of the situation, and not try to harm anyone here if we untie you."

"At some point you'll need to release me."

"I think I'll feel better about that once you've had a day to think this through. For the moment, I don't believe you won't immediately try to rip my throat out. And I've grown rather fond of it in my dotage."

She glared at him. He had so far read her correctly.

"What I propose is that you take on this assignment. In return, upon its successful completion, I will give you half a million dollars – which will go a long way towards paying for your daughter's education and whatnot. You are free to choose any method you like to terminate the target, but with one caveat. I want the diamonds back. We haven't seen a flood on the market, so he still has them. Get me the diamonds and bring me his head, and you'll have your freedom as well as a handsome reward. That's the deal."

"Wow. A one percent finder's fee. That's very generous."

Arthur cocked a particularly ugly patch of scar tissue that used to be an eyebrow.

"Ah. Well, at least now we have a negotiation. Fine. I'll up the offer to two percent of anything you bring back. Up to a million dollars."

"And these straps? I'll have to go to the bathroom sooner or later."

"I'll bear that in mind."

He turned to leave. "Think this over. When I return, I will expect an answer, which will be a binding commitment."

"So help me, if you harm a hair on Hannah's head—"

"See? Still with the threats. Look. I just offered you a million dollars to do what you've done for almost free for the Mossad for years. I'll look after your daughter like she was my own while you're gone. You'll never have to worry about anything again once this is over. I strongly suggest you consider this carefully. You're not going to get a better deal. Ever."

With that, Arthur spun on his heel and knocked on the door. One of the men outside opened it, and then he was gone. She heard the bolt slide back into place, and then the footsteps moved down the hall to wherever they'd come from, leaving her alone with her thoughts.

For all his experience, Arthur had made a mistake. Two, actually. The first was that he had tipped his hand. He needed her. That gave her power over him. The second was more subtle. He'd left the light on, which gave her the ability to see. That might not have seemed like a huge advantage, but it was enough.

She set to work on maneuvering her left arm, a millimeter at a time, up towards her shoulder as she exhaled, decreasing the expansion of her ribcage to the extent possible. The skin tore against the sharp edge of the strap, but she ignored it, forced even more air out of her lungs, and pulled.

❧❦

Arthur stood in the deserted lobby of what had once been a mental institution in rural Virginia, long since abandoned and condemned for demolition. As the state fought with the federal government over the property and the ultimate use of the land, it sat empty, chain-link fence with razor wire ringing it, keeping looters and vandals out, and presenting the agency with one of several facilities where it could detain sensitive subjects in complete privacy.

Three men stood out of earshot, murmuring among themselves. All wore suits and had weapons in shoulder holsters.

He took a few more steps towards the main entrance, a glass and iron affair with two oversized doors that were scarred from decades of grim traffic entering a facility few ever left unless in a body bag. Plywood had been mounted across both glass panels to prevent breakage, and an armed guard patrolled the grounds day and night. The locals had considered the woods around it a damned place for generations, so it was natural that the facility no community wanted anywhere near it would wind up there. Built as part of Roosevelt's New Deal construction boom in the 1930s it had been shut down in 2001, the last of the patients transferred to modern hospitals, where they could get more compassionate care. Its history was one marked by questionable treatments and controversial approaches, and it had gained a certain professional notoriety in the Forties and Fifties following a propensity for performing lobotomies on a far greater percentage of its population than anywhere else in the country – fully double the national average.

A pool of rank rainwater glazed the uneven tiled floor of the foyer, and a furry form scurried into a corner as he approached. The place was perfectly suited for this sort of detainment. That it had a certain medieval quality was icing on the cake. He wanted those he was 'negotiating' with to hate and fear it, and want to be anywhere else in the world. As he was sure the woman named Jet wanted to be free of her grim imprisonment.

He flipped open his cell phone and placed a call, staring off into the near distance as he waited for it to answer.

"We have her. I gave her the ultimatum. I expect an affirmative response within the next twenty-four hours," he said quietly.

"Then what?"

"Then our friend gets his comeuppance."

"Why are you so confident in her when your best men couldn't make it happen?"

"She's…different. Hard to explain it. If anyone can pull this off, it will be her. That, and we're sort of out of options, aren't we?" Arthur observed.

"There's that."

"Which, I thought I would mention…we aren't having much success with the new group that took over since he killed the old one. Apparently they feel that there's substantially more risk associated with dealing with us than there was before. So the cost is considerably higher. Which makes it far less interesting for us."

"I understand. Perhaps they will see reason once we have rid the jungles of the white devil."

"That's our hope. Right now they're talking to others, and you know as well as I do, that if anyone else does a deal it will disrupt everything we've built. That cannot be allowed to happen," Arthur underscored.

"We are in agreement. It can't. You really think she can do this?"

"I've never met anyone I am more sure about. You know her history."

"The jungle is a different environment than the desert."

"True enough. But she's got ten times more experience than our next option. Honestly, she's scary to be in the same room with. And you know I don't scare."

"Very well. Do whatever it takes, but make it happen. We're running out of time."

"I know."

CHAPTER 6

The sound of a banshee wailing reverberated off the asylum walls and brought the guards at a run. The shrieking was horrifying, pure terror, ending with a yowl of pain and then silence.

"Move. Come on. But remember what we're dealing with. She's extremely dangerous," Fred reminded his men.

All three gripped stun guns. They were not to use deadly force if it could be helped. The orders were clear.

"What do you think happened?" Jim asked.

Fred rubbed his nose and sniffed. "Could be rats. I never thought it was a good idea to leave her down here unguarded. Some of them are the size of minivans. If a bunch of them got to her…it could be ugly."

"Or it could be some kind of a trick."

"She's lashed to the bed. You helped me do it. Nobody could get out of that. Especially not after getting shot full of rhino tranquilizer."

Fred beamed his flashlight on the rusting steel door. The area was completely quiet other than their breathing. Whatever had caused the commotion was over. The single industrial fluorescent lamp in the hallway flickered, its glow inadequate to provide more than slim illumination to the windowless space. The other four lamps had long ago stopped working, lending the area the feeling of a dungeon.

"Jim, you slide the bolt open. Carl, you go in first. I'll follow," he whispered.

The two subordinates nodded and tensed in preparation.

The bolt slid open with a *thunk*, and then Jim, who'd jerked it free, pushed the door wide, the bottom scraping on the uneven broken tile before slamming against the interior wall.

The room was dark. They could just make out the shape of the ancient bed, but it was indistinct. Carl, in the lead, reached to his side and felt for the tripod lamp. He found the stand and groped up to the control at the top and flipped the switch, but nothing happened.

Annoyed, he pointed his flashlight at the bed. The beam played across the empty surface just as a bolt of yellow swung across his field of vision and a hard metallic rectangle slammed into his head with the force of a hammer blow. Warm blood streamed freely from a gash in his forehead, and he cried out as he dropped the light. The room swirled in blackness, and he lost consciousness, sinking to the floor with a groan.

A short length of metal smacked into Fred's skull, and he went down like a bag of rocks, landing heavily at Carl's inert feet. Jim stood frozen just outside the door, staring dumbstruck into the room's inky depth, trying to process what was happening. Jet swung down from the ceiling, gripping an overhead pipe like a gymnast and propelled herself into his chest with both legs, her feet striking him with startling momentum. His stun gun clattered harmlessly by his side as he collapsed onto the cold cement floor, his ribs shattered. She watched him as he struggled for breath, then she reached down and pulled his pistol loose from his shoulder holster, pausing to inspect the Colt 1911 .45 caliber semi-automatic before tucking it into the waist of her jeans.

Fifteen seconds had passed since the door had opened, and all three agents were incapacitated. She shook her head. If this was any indication of the level of expertise at Arthur's disposal, it was no wonder he needed competent help.

The strap buckle had made an effective weapon, as the first unlucky man had discovered, and the rest of the binding straps had proved useful to provide a cradle between the exposed pipes running along the ceiling, where the sheetrock had long ago rotted away.

The man she'd body-slammed didn't look good – he was still struggling for air, flailing like a fish on the deck of a fishing boat. It was possible that one of his ribs had punctured a lung, judging by his inability to breathe, but it wasn't her problem – they were all lucky to be alive. She dragged him by the hair and dumped him in the room with his unconscious colleagues, then took a moment to consider the pile of bodies before pulling the door closed, driving the bolt home and then turning and surveying the hall. A few still-wet footprints in the accumulated dust told her which direction the men had come from.

The agent's pistol back in her hand, she crept cautiously down the hallway, past thirty doors identical to the one she'd been locked behind, towards the stairs at the far end. Light filtered in from above, and she saw a slick of greasy fluid tracing its way down the stairwell, which stank of rot and filth. Wherever this was, it had been unoccupied for a long time.

She ascended and paused at the landing, allowing her eyes to adjust to the unexpected gloom of the ground floor. All of the windows had been boarded up, and the only illumination came from an exposed incandescent bulb hanging from a workman's scaffold; motes of dust floated in orbit around the sixty-watt glow.

Jet crept to the double doors and peeked through one of the spaces between the moldy plywood. A broad driveway stretched into the distance, empty except for a black and white cat skulking near an empty fountain in the center of the plaza that served as the arrival area. A few outdoor lamps lit the immediate surfaces with a harsh white glare, but thankfully it got darker farther away from the building – if she could make it to the shadows undetected, she would have a running chance. Glancing at her watch, she saw that it was seven o'clock. So she'd lost at least almost a full day.

Whatever the time, she wasn't going to stick around and see what kind of reinforcements showed up after the men locked in the tomb below missed their check-in calls.

Jerking her pistol free, she pushed one of the oversized doors ajar a foot and slipped through the opening into the frigid evening air. She didn't see anyone, so if there was any exterior security, it was lax, unless the grounds were wired for motion or infrared – which she'd discover soon enough.

Keeping to the overgrown hedges that lined the drive, she trotted in a crouch to the massive iron gates that sealed the compound from the road beyond. A rusting chain held the barrier closed, but she was able to squeeze through the gap between the two sections, turning to take in the hulking faux-French façade of the building she'd escaped. It looked abandoned, except for the new fencing that ran just outside of the rock perimeter wall that circled the grounds.

"Hey. What are you doing here? Go on, get outta here. This is private property," a gruff man's voice yelled at her from near the left wing's entry. Jet could see that the guard was uniformed and carried a shotgun. She slipped the pistol back into her jeans and pulled her light sweater over it. He was far enough away that he wouldn't be able to make out the detail in the half-light of dusk.

"Sorry. I was just looking," she called and waved, then backed away from the entrance, turning after a few feet and jogging down the darkened road in the opposite direction.

Sensing that something was off about a woman in the middle of nowhere without any car, the guard screamed at her again.

"Hey! Wait a minute. Come back here."

She ignored him and picked up the pace, the exercise a welcome relief after being immobile for countless hours.

"I said come back here."

His voice trailed off in the distance as she ran.

Depending upon how smart he was, she could expect him to call in a suspicious person to whoever he reported to sooner than later. And then it would be a manhunt, unless the CIA wanted to keep its abduction of innocents on American soil to itself. She hoped that was the case, but couldn't bet on it.

She would need to get off the road. Soon.

Once she was out of sight of the guard, she moved onto the grassy shoulder, maintaining her speed as she raced along the roadside, the last gray light fading into the darkness of night. At the first sign of headlights she could be in the trees, which grew dense on both sides. Barring infrared gear, she could probably remain undiscovered until she could sort out her next step.

Her first priority was to find Arthur. Find Arthur and she would find Hannah.

This same man had stolen her daughter away from her twice. First working with Hannah's father, David, and now this time, for his own selfish ends.

He was about to discover that he'd been right to be scared of her when he'd been in the room, regaling her with his troubles. The instinct to keep her bound like a deadly predator had been a sound one.

One way or another, she would find him. And when she did, what she would do to him would make whatever nightmare had burned his face off seem like a Hawaiian vacation.

CHAPTER 7

Jet's footsteps thudded against the hard-packed dirt of the road shoulder. She hadn't seen a single vehicle since leaving her prison's grounds, but she knew it was just a matter of time until her captors mounted a search. Twenty minutes after escaping, she came to a clearing that housed a few rural buildings – a market, gas station and a restaurant with an attached bar, its tired neon sign blinking intermittently.

A dozen vehicles sat in the seedy lot, almost all pickup trucks. The place looked like a working man's watering hole, where after a long day on the construction site, its patrons could throw back a few to soften life's inevitable harsh blows.

Perfect for her purposes.

She slowed, checking to ensure that the pistol was completely concealed by her top. Satisfied with the result, she pushed her way through the doors and took a quick survey of the patrons. Mostly male, mostly mid-thirties to late forties, almost everyone sporting a baseball cap adorned with a heavy equipment company's logo. She moved easily to the long wood bar, most of the eyes in the room on her, and then pulled up a stool and sat down. A bald man with a flushed face and about a hundred pounds of extra bulk waddled from a corner where he'd been cleaning glasses while watching a talent program on the Seventies-era television that served as the primary point of interest.

"What'll you have, darling?"

"I'm sorry. Nothing just yet. I'm...I'm waiting for a friend."

He appraised her.

"I wouldn't leave someone like you waiting very long," he said, then returned to his position near the TV.

Jet caught a glimpse of herself in the mirror that lurked behind an army of half-empty liquor bottles that were seemingly lined up for inspection. She wiped a smudge of dirt from her cheek. All things considered, she didn't look bad for a woman who'd been kidnapped and imprisoned, had neutralized three armed guards and run at least a good three miles.

She sensed the presence of a body sidling up to her before she turned to face the man. Decent enough looking, with a day's growth of stubble and a profile starting to go to fat, but with twinkling blue eyes that hinted at some joke known only to him.

"Hello there."

Jet ignored him for a few measured seconds, then smiled. "Hello yourself."

"What are you drinking?"

"Nothing right now. I'm waiting for someone. We're supposed to meet, but I got here late, and he's not…I'm waiting for someone," she repeated.

"Barkeep! A drink on me!" he yelled to the desultory bartender, who reluctantly tore his eyes from the screen and glared over at them. "What can I get you?"

"That's very sweet, but it's not necessary…"

"Of course it is. So what's it going to be?"

She hesitated. "A light beer?"

"A light and another Seven and Seven," he called out, and then returned his attention to her face. "What's your name?"

"Alison."

"Alison," he pronounced the name slowly, rolling it in his mouth like a fine wine. "Alison. That's a beautiful name. For a beautiful woman – fortunately for me, alone in my favorite bar on the outskirts of nowhere."

"Maybe not for long. Remember, I'm waiting…"

"Then it sounds like I don't have much time."

She smiled again, wanting to encourage him. "Better work fast."

"He only brings drinks at one speed."

"Not really a race car, is he?"

"More dependable transportation."

"Like a bus."

"Or a tractor."

They both laughed easily as the bartender approached with their order.

"What's your name?"

"Jim. Jim Bassenger."

She held out her hand, and he took it in his, giving it a shake. She noted that he had large hands, the nails relatively clean; he wasn't a laborer.

"So, Alison, who's waiting for luck to walk through the door, and what brings you to this part of Virginia?"

Virginia? She racked her brain for her mental atlas. Virginia was somewhere on the east coast. She had last been in Nebraska. A long way away. Then she remembered. Langley, the CIA headquarters, was in Virginia. Of course, they would have transported her there. Where else?

"I'm headed to New York. I have some friends who invited me to come stay for a few weeks, to see if I like it." She shrugged and took a sip of her beer. "You know. Have a little adventure in my life in the big city."

"New York, huh? That's full of adventure, all right, but it's dangerous as hell, too. And really expensive."

"I've heard. But sometimes a girl's got to take a chance, right?" she said and then glanced at her watch.

"Who are you waiting for? Boyfriend? Date?"

"No. One of my friend's buddies who lives somewhere around here. She said to look him up…"

"Well, if he's not going to show, looks like I'm buying," Jim announced.

She threw him a long, appraising glance then smiled and held her beer up in toast.

"To unexpected new friends," she said.

"I'll drink to that."

Fifteen minutes later, they emerged from the bar arm in arm, and he led her to his black Dodge crew cab truck. Jim was divorced, thirty-seven, an electrician working on commercial buildings, and had a small house only four miles away. He invited her to come over to watch a movie or something, which she correctly interpreted as meaning drink too much and have sex with him, and after she finished her beer and he had knocked back two more of his favorites, they arrived at an unspoken agreement.

The big engine started with a roar, and he gunned it as they pulled onto the road, leaving a spray of gravel behind it as he let the wild horses run free. She looked out through the side window and smiled again – this was a perfect cover. A couple, in a local truck, smelling of alcohol, on their way home…she reached next to him on the seat and picked up an orange baseball cap with CAT stenciled on the front and pulled it on, reaching up to study her reflection in the rearview mirror as he drove.

"Looks good on you, baby."

She beamed at him. No wonder he was single.

He turned off the main road, and she saw a convenience store near a huddle of closed shops, its neon sign proclaiming speed and economy in blinking red and blue.

"Pull over, Jim. I need to get some stuff," she said, pointing.

He obliged and swung into one of the parking stalls.

"I'll just be a minute. I wonder if there's a pay phone?"

"Don't know. Maybe," Jim offered, sounding distinctly unenthusiastic at having his party interrupted.

"Be back in a few. Don't take off without me. I still need you to take me back to get my car at some point," she said, the implicit promise that it would be much later obvious by her tone.

His mood perked up. "I'd wait all night. But don't make me," he said, delighted that things seemed back on track.

She walked into the store and performed a quick scan. There was a rear exit by the storeroom. She approached the old man at the register and gave him her most winning smile.

"I hate to bother you, but do you have a bathroom I can use? It's kind of an emergency..."

He looked her up and down with cynical eyes, and then his expression softened.

"Emergency, huh? I would tell you to go down the road a quarter mile and use the gas station's, but it's pretty grim. Wouldn't wish that on a pack of starving dogs."

"Please? I'll only be a minute. I would really appreciate it..."

He pointed a gnarled finger at a doorway leading to the rear of the store. "Second door on the left. Don't take forever," he growled, then resumed reading his paper.

She stopped for a few moments at the bathroom, then continued to the rear exit, taking care to unlock the deadbolt as quietly as possible before easing it open and stepping into the night.

A quick glance confirmed that there were several dozen homes nearby, and she was confident that she would be able to find a vehicle she could hotwire. Jim had served his purpose – she was now at least seven miles from the hospital, so the odds of them being able to mount a coherent search were dropping with each passing minute.

A small residential street stretched fifty yards behind the shops; she darted for it, using the trees as cover. Her brief romance with Jim had come to an abrupt end. She wondered how long he'd sit out in front waiting, then switched mental gears. She needed wheels so she could put real distance between herself and the CIA goons.

Jet prowled the street, eyeing the various cars parked along the curb, and then her ears detected a sound that wasn't consistent with a rural Virginia town – the thumping of rotors in the distance. A helicopter.

The search had begun.

She moved from shadow to shadow, trying the door handles of the sorry procession of vehicles, and stopped when she came to a ten-year-old Nissan Maxima. The door opened with a squeak, and she slid behind the wheel, taking care to shut off the interior light so as not to alert anyone. She reached below the steering wheel and felt for the bundle of wires she knew would be there and then paused.

The *whump whump* of the helicopter's blades were definitely closer.

Jet resumed her project and, within a few moments, had the wires separated and was pulling at the two she would need to start the car. She got them free and quickly stripped the insulating rubber from them using her teeth, and then crossed them, causing a spark. The engine turned over, but didn't start. She was about to give it another try when some instinct caused her to look up through the windshield.

A hundred and fifty yards away she could see the blinking lights of a helicopter, hovering a few stories above the tree line.

How the hell had they found her?

The car wouldn't do her any good now if they'd narrowed her position down this closely. She threw the door open and bolted for the woods across the street, glad that her clothes were a muted color that wouldn't stand out in the night.

As she ran, she heard car engines approaching on the road she had just fled.

This was impossible.

She willed her legs to greater speed and tore through the brush, branches cracking beneath her feet as she distanced herself from her pursuers. There was no way they would be able to get her in the woods. Too dark and too much manpower required.

Up ahead, she could make out some more buildings through the trees. Houses. Another subdivision.

She altered her course and made for the closest home, and was just rounding a large tree when a car swung onto the cul-de-sac and pulled to the curb no more than thirty yards away.

Arthur opened the door of the black Lincoln and stepped out, looking directly at her position behind the tree.

"It's over. Stop wasting my time. If you ever want to see your daughter again, step away from the tree, put down the gun and move slowly towards the car," he said, his distinctively unpleasant voice straining to be heard.

She debated her slim options and then did as he instructed, placing the gun on the grass and then moving to where he stood.

A Chevrolet Suburban lurched to a halt behind the Lincoln, and two muscular men in suits emptied out of the back doors.

She raised her hands over her head and stood still as they stepped to where she waited.

Arthur watched as they forced her arms behind her, cuffed her, then walked her to the SUV. She glared at him with obvious hatred.

"My dear, save your energy. You've caused me considerable trouble this evening. That was your one chance. If you ever want to see your daughter again, you'll get with the program and knock this shit off. I'm not the enemy, or at least not yours. Now get in the truck, don't try anything, and stop this now. Do I make myself clear?"

"How did you find me?"

"Chip in the gun. New technology. You never had a chance."

She nodded and allowed herself to be led to the back seat of the Suburban.

"If I agree – how do I know that you'll keep your word about Hannah?"

"Because I have no reason not to. And because I'm quite sure you'll kill me if I don't."

She studied him.

"We agree on something."

"Yes, I suspected as much. Look, this whole escape thing was pointless. All you accomplished was to injure three of my men and piss me off. You are no closer to getting your daughter back. The truth is that there is only one road to accomplishing that, and you've been told where it leads and what you need to do. Just get that through your skull, and we'll get along better. In order to get her back, you need to pay me back for my assistance in bringing down Grigenko. Everything has a price. David knew that. I know it. Now you know it. Pay the price and go on to live happily ever after. Don't invest any more energy in these childish theatrics. They are getting you nowhere," Arthur suggested, spittle spraying occasionally from the effort of stringing so many words together.

She got into the SUV, opting for silence. He moved to within a few feet of her, and the agents discreetly moved out of earshot, the driver taking the hint and joining them.

"I need an answer now, I'm afraid. Do you help me help you, or no?"

"What if I decline?"

"Then hold onto your memory of your daughter because it's all you'll ever have of her. And then hope that you can survive in a terrorist detention camp for the next fifty years because that's where you'll be going. You'll be categorized as such by the CIA, and there will be no trial or defense."

"So much for the land of the free."

"Last time I checked, you aren't a citizen, so don't complain. You were apprehended with two passports in different names. You were on American soil for nefarious purposes. It's your word against the CIA's, and you have nobody to tell your story to. You'll be sequestered twenty-four hours a day with no access to anyone but your guards, who won't talk to you. That will be your life. That is, if I don't decide to just put a bullet in your head while you're trying to escape. The idea crossed my mind, and I'm sure I could find three volunteers back at the asylum – one of whom might die from the trauma to his lungs and the internal bleeding you caused."

"Those are the hazards of this kind of duty. You should train them better."

"Perhaps. Now I am out of time. Your answer – a million dollars and your daughter back, or incarceration and possibly worse?"

Jet sighed. There was really no choice. If she'd been able to escape, maybe…but not now.

"You win."

"I'll take that as a yes."

"It's a yes. But a couple of conditions. I don't want to go back to the basement with the rats. And I'll need a complete dossier on the target, as well as a full history of the two botched operations. And I will be responsible for coming up with a plan, with no strings or conditions. Just get the diamonds back, and terminate the target. Other than that, I answer to no one."

Arthur nodded, raising a cloth handkerchief to his mouth to blot the saliva that had begun welling in the corner. "I would expect nothing less."

"And you'll supply me with whatever resources I need to pull this off, without question."

"No. I reserve the right to question. I won't just write you a blank check."

She closed her eyes for a moment. "No interference, though. I won't be second-guessed by agendas that differ from my prime objective. I've seen that too many times, and it can get you killed."

"That's reasonable. Terminate the target, and get the diamonds back. There is no additional agenda. That's it," Arthur stated flatly.

"Then we have a deal. Once I am successful, I get my daughter back, the million dollars, and we're even. No surprises or strings. Agreed?"

"Agreed."

CHAPTER 8

The big SUV took Jet to a safe house in Manassas, Virginia, where she found a simple but comfortable two bedroom residence with a fully-stocked fridge – a marked improvement over the damp cell she'd woken up to. A CIA physician was waiting for her when she arrived, and explained to her that she would need to get a tracking chip implanted under her skin near her shoulder as part of her arrangement with Arthur. She couldn't think of any easy way to avoid it, so she sat in the offered chair and stoically allowed the doctor to insert the microchip.

The procedure only took a few minutes, and then he and the two agents that had accompanied her left, one of them advising her on the way out that they would be in a parked car only a few yards away if she needed anything.

Even though she was tired, she resolved to go through the files that sat on the dining room table, along with a laptop computer for her use. She assumed that everything she did was being watched or tracked – that would be standard procedure in a safe house. It wasn't worth trying to spot the various hidden cameras that were sure to be in every room. She couldn't do anything to disable them that wouldn't result in immediate problems, so she would have to make the best of being a virtual prisoner, albeit one with clean sheets and freshly-squeezed orange juice in the refrigerator.

Jet picked up the first folder and fell into an overstuffed reclining chair in the living room and then switched on a lamp next to it. A prominent Top Secret stamped across the top and bottom greeted her when she extracted the file.

Flipping it open, she found five photos grouped together on a contact sheet, followed by six more head shots of a Caucasian man in his early forties. Blond in some of them, brown-haired in others, a chocolate brunette in still others. Neutral features that had likely been rendered even more so by cosmetic surgery – field agents were often made to look generic so as to better blend into any situation and draw no attention. Hairstyles changed across the photos, with side parts replaced with a longish shag that gave him a vaguely bohemian look.

Most of the photos were taken from passport and official identification shots. His eyes varied in color as much as his hair, ranging from blue to green to brown.

She appraised him and saw a decent-looking, completely generic white man with no distinguishing qualities – a chameleon. Designed to be the perfect operational asset, capable of convincingly being a businessman one week, a tourist the next, a professor the following one, a journalist or doctor or attorney at whim. She supposed, somewhere there was a file at the Mossad with similar photographs of her, although David had sworn that none of the team existed in the official records. Like so much of what he'd professed, she now doubted the veracity of his assurances.

The target's name was Matthew Hawker. Matt, to his ex-colleagues. His list of aliases ran two pages.

Forty-four years old, born in Philadelphia, recruited from college after serving a stint with the American Army's ultra-elite Delta Force commandoes, his service record while in the army classified, but with a short note that he was an expert in special operations, insertions, explosives, sniping, and every kind of weapon. Scuba certified. A pilot's license dated three years after his honorable discharge. A bachelor in international business from Hampton University. Spoke fluent Vietnamese, Thai and Cantonese from having been raised abroad by parents who had been with the U.S. diplomatic corps. No further elaboration on what positions they'd held.

Hawker's first assignment in the field for the CIA had been in Cambodia, where he had been stationed undercover as a small time exporter, collecting data on strategic targets in the region and developing a network of informants. From there he moved around, to Vietnam, and then ultimately to Thailand, where he had been the most senior field agent in-country. The operations he was involved in were classified at a higher level than the file could reveal, but she could read between the lines with Myanmar right across the border. A senior field agent with these skills would have been involved in information gathering, insurgency sponsorship, and assassinations – whatever was required.

He'd been offered promotions to desk positions in Langley three times over the last four years and had declined them all. Apparently, Hawker liked to play the field. She understood the type of personality – once you lived in the parallel reality that was covert ops it was hard to ever go back to living any kind of a normal life. It was addictive, even if hazardous to one's health.

She looked at the photos again and noted that his eyes had the same flat, expressionless gaze that her photos always had. A professional skill learned early. The eyes were indeed the windows to the soul, and one of the first lessons had been that it was best to shutter them at all times.

Hawker's personal relationships were limited to casual girlfriends that never got serious – the story she knew all too well from having lived the life. You avoided entanglements and compartmentalized everything – there was no way of knowing on any particular day whether you would be redeployed the next, or have to run. It was a difficult existence where an operative was an island unto himself, isolated from all the usual connections that humans naturally sought out. For that reason, her relationship with David had been forbidden and would have provoked immediate consequences, had it ever been discovered. You could never grow close to anyone. It was dangerous, and endangered your partner. Better to keep it limited to the superficial, never growing attached.

Nothing in Hawker's background suggested anything but a model agent. There could have been no warning that he would betray the master he'd served obediently for close to two decades.

His last assignment wasn't described in the file. Which was understandable. At some point, all documentation became vague as an agent became immersed in more sensitive areas – as Arthur had intimated, in affairs that required discretion and deniability.

She pored over the information again, committing it to memory, and then stretched and yawned. It was two in the morning. The rest would have to wait till the following day.

Jet locked the front door deadbolt, slid the security chain in place and peered through the window. The two agents were hardly visible in their government sedan. She padded to the bedroom, took a quick shower and brushed her teeth – making a mental note to go shopping soon and get some clothes. Hers were due for a change.

The bed was blissfully comfortable, and she was asleep within a few minutes of her head hitting the pillow. The cameras and eavesdropping devices recorded her tossing and turning several hours later, along with a few muffled cries as her slumber was disturbed by visions of her daughter being torn from her bosom, and of a white-tufted monster covered with scar tissue tormenting her as she lost her grasp.

Jet awoke at eight and, for a few seconds, didn't know where she was. Then the prior day's events came rushing back to her, and she forced herself to roll out of bed and start the day.

She pulled open a drawer and found a pair of elastic waist running shorts that sort of fitted her and several extra-large T-shirts that didn't. She pulled one on and studied her reflection in the dresser mirror – not the height of fashion, but it would do.

The orange juice was a welcome breakfast complement to the energy bars she found in the pantry cupboard, and after consuming two, she was preparing for a run when the telephone on the kitchen wall rang.

"I trust you're up," Arthur said when she picked up the handset.

"You know I am. The cameras would have told you I was."

"I'll arrange for some clothes to be brought in while you are out on what I presume is your morning run."

"Good guess."

"Any special requests?"

"Yes. Skip the clothes, and leave a thousand dollars in cash and keys to a car. I want to select my own clothes."

"Fine on the money, but no on the car. You don't have any ID yet, including a driver's license. I can't afford for you to get into an accident and trigger any questions. I'll arrange for a driver at whatever time you like."

She glanced at her watch.

"One o'clock. I want to spend a few hours on the files before."

"That will work. Is there anything else you need?"

"If there is, I'll just announce it in a loud voice in any of the rooms. You can take it from there."

"This is only for a short while. I'm hoping you'll want to get into the field and take care of this errand."

"Is there anything else?"

"No. I'll send someone by at one."

Just the sound of his voice enraged her while simultaneously giving her the creeps. She swallowed her anger with an effort, then moved to the door and swung it open. No point in locking it with the two agents parked outside. Two new ones, she noted as she stretched, before heading down the sidewalk towards a park at the far end of the block. A male jogger took up position a hundred yards behind her as she crossed the street to the park. The agency was wasting no effort.

An hour later, she trotted back to the front door and did her cool down stretches before mounting the three steps and re-entering. A small pile of twenty and hundred dollar bills sat on the kitchen table along with a smaller T-shirt and a few hygiene items. Someone had been thinking, but it was hardly comprehensive, and she would need to stop at a pharmacy as well as a clothing store.

After another shower, she towel-dried her hair and returned her attention to the files, selecting one of the two she hadn't yet read.

This one was different. A provisional report; incomplete and filled with speculation.

Anthony Simms, age thirty-two, had been dispatched into Laos after receiving word that Hawker had taken up residence in the hills there and was employing a group of anywhere from ten to fifty armed men, depending upon the source. Simms was an experienced field agent with a ten-year history of successful sanctions in the region – in other words, an assassin who did nothing but kill. His operational background was purely one of executions. No other kind of missions.

Simms had followed up on a tip about the location of the target's base camp. He had checked in every four hours as required, but one and a half days into his trek he had gone dark. His tracking chip had placed him north of the Mekong river in an uninhabited stretch of jungle infamous for drug syndicates and smugglers. The chip had stopped transmitting at ten p.m. local time. Simms had never been heard from again. His body was found a week later near the Laos border in Thailand, badly decomposed and mostly eaten by the local animals. Final identification had only been possible through dental records.

That wasn't particularly helpful.

Other than informing her that one of the CIA's more experienced killers had made his final mistake.

She returned the file to the table and opened the second one.

This time two operatives, both from the most elite of the CIA's wet teams, had been deployed when the Thai agent in charge had gotten wind that Hawker was involved with a network of human traffickers and a slavery syndicate that supplied one of the larger prostitution networks in Bangkok.

She read the account, which described a series of seemingly unrelated bits of intelligence describing a new gang in the Golden Triangle headed by a *farang* – a white devil rumored to feast on human hearts and dance in the moonlight covered with his victims' blood. The rumors were that he was impossibly rich and had a hundred men armed with the latest weapons, and was a ghost that even the Myanmar military was terrified of.

Two men had gone in.

Never to be heard from again.

Both were seasoned combat veterans with extensive histories operating in the most dangerous environments on the planet. Africa. The Middle East. The Balkans.

They had gone into the jungle a week ago.

And disappeared without a trace three days later.

The detail of the report described a group in Bangkok that specialized in underage prostitutes and sadism, offering more extreme versions of the spectrum to an international clientele that traveled from all over the world to partake in the forbidden fruits it provided. The head of the organization was a man by the name of Lap Pu, no doubt an alias, who was almost as much of a phantom as the *farang*.

Pu was rumored to have a relationship with the white ghost, and acted as his eyes and ears in Thailand.

She read for another hour, but the Byzantine maze of relationships, rivalries and rumored allegiances was overwhelming and would require much more study if she was going to formulate any kind of coherent plan.

But one thing seemed obvious to her.

The trail began in Thailand. That was where Hawker had been based, so that was where his contacts would be. Find a weak link in his associates, and with any luck, they would lead her to him.

CHAPTER 9

After two hours of shopping, Jet was reasonably outfitted, and when she made it back to the house, she was glad she'd decided to get her own clothes. Even though she was as drip dry as they came, it was nice for things to fit correctly and not look awful.

She pushed the door open, toting three plastic clothes bags, and found herself face to face with Arthur, who was sitting in the living room sipping a diet soda through a straw – a requirement, given the state of his face.

"Ah, so you're back. Did you find everything you need?"

"I got the necessities. What are you doing here?"

"I was hoping you have come up with some preliminary thoughts about our situation."

"You mean the one where you kidnapped my daughter and are blackmailing me so I'll kill someone for you?"

He ignored that.

"No, more the question of how to find our rogue agent, and what will be required to do so."

She set the bags down and stared at him in disbelief.

"I just finished reading the last of the files before lunch. Are you kidding me?"

"You are rumored to be the best. I suppose I was overly optimistic…"

"That may be, but I'm not a magician. This could take weeks to plan. I don't have a lot of information to go on. Other than some rumors of your man having gone native, the files are thin on supporting intelligence."

"Yes, I'm aware of that. We've actually received new satellite footage, but it isn't going to be of much help. It's such a large area. And there are caves, villages, and plenty of questionable encampments set up by the smugglers, any of which could be the target or a red herring."

"I'll need a day or two to think this one through, and then I'll probably want to nose around on the ground in his old stomping grounds. Bangkok. I've never been there, so that will increase the difficulty level. Ideally you would have gotten all the information on where to find the target, and then I'd take it from there. This is a completely different situation. So, not only do I have to figure out how to get the diamonds back and take him out, but I also need to find him." She fixed him with a cold stare. "I don't have a magic wand or I'd bring Hannah back and make you disappear."

"I'll need forty-eight hours to get you an ID and put a cover in place."

"No, you won't. You'll just need to give me back my Belgian passport and identity cards. And come up with a big wad of cash to spread around so I can get some answers over there."

"Money's not a problem." He stood, looking around the small room, then moved to the door. "I have every confidence in you. But I don't have unlimited time. Sooner the better is what I'm trying to convey."

"This is the type of operation that would ordinarily take a month to think through. Assuming I had the kind of support I'm accustomed to. David was the best at what he did. But now he's gone, and you're handing me a black box and asking me to pull a rabbit out of a hat. Your last two attempts on this target failed. Have you considered that might have been a function of how ill-conceived they were?"

"Yes, I have. Which is why I brought you into this." He waved a gloved hand dismissively. "You'll figure it out. Just don't take too long."

"It's like making a baby. Still takes nine months no matter what you do or say."

He opened the door. "Point taken. Whenever you need to get in touch, call me," he said, as he reached into his jacket for a cell phone and tossed it to her.

Her eyes remained fixed on him as she snatched it out of the air.

"Will do."

Jet spent the rest of the day studying the reports, going over the satellite footage, trying to piece together a strategy. By nighttime she was worn out and seemed no closer to a breakthrough than when she'd started the day. The target had an armed encampment, but they didn't know where, other than it was in the territory of a hostile regime that was notorious for being a drug production and smuggling center. And the warlords in the heroin business there were every bit as dangerous as the Myanmar military, if not more so.

The information that the Thailand CIA team had been able to glean from informants wasn't promising, and contradicted itself in as many places as it agreed. The only thing for certain was that she would need to get to Bangkok sooner than later and do her own nosing around. Which was how the last team had discovered the lead that directed them into the jungle, even if the ultimate outcome had been disastrous.

As she lay on the bed in the dark, staring at the ceiling, a whirlwind of possible approaches ran through her mind. Eventually she closed her eyes and pushed the rush of ideas to the side, replacing them with the image of her daughter laughing delightedly in her car seat, oblivious to her role as a pawn in a deadly chess game.

Her last thoughts as she drifted to sleep were of David, confessing his betrayal as his life seeped from him on the deck of the Russian's mega-yacht, his strained apology an inadequate lullaby to accompany her slumber.

જ⊷ઙ

The following afternoon, Arthur tipped the brim of his hat in greeting and took a seat opposite Jet, who ignored the formality and cut straight to the chase.

"I want to be in Bangkok within twenty-four hours. I'll need twenty-five grand in cash, a debit card that will allow me to withdraw another seventy-five and a contact there who can get me weapons and anything else I need," Jet instructed. There was no point lingering at the safe house when all paths led to Thailand.

Arthur regarded her impassively, nodding as she outlined her requirements.

"So you are ready to get started. Good."

"My big problem is that what you've supplied is all but useless for finding the target or understanding what his true defenses are, which means I need to dig around on the ground there and see what I can stir up. And that will require time and money."

"As I said, we have money. Time isn't in such a generous supply."

"What's the rush?"

"I'm receiving pressure over this regrettable incident, and my superiors want the matter concluded. They don't have the same appreciation of the delicacy of the dynamics that we do."

"Well, there's nothing I can do about that. I'm not going to go charging into a situation I know nothing about. If you're in such a hurry, how about finding out where his camp is? Then all I need to do is figure out the logistics of the assault."

"Yes. *All you need to do.*" Arthur sighed and brushed lint from one knee of his expensive slacks. "Believe me, if I could have supplied you with more helpful intelligence, I would have. The limitations of the area are as frustrating to me as they are to you."

"With an important difference. I'm the one who is going to have to risk my life in the jungle. You're going to be monitoring it on a screen, safe, halfway across the world."

"We all have our roles in this. I shall get you everything you require and arrange for a hospitality committee upon your arrival."

"No. I want to limit the number of people who know anything about this. I'll need a satellite phone to reach you. Beyond that, I only want to meet the ranking agent in Thailand. Nobody else. You have no idea what kind of reach the target has there. He was in place for a decade. In a tightly knit society like the Asian criminal syndicates, I have to believe that he's got as good or better a network than you have. Anyone could tip him off. I'd rather not be the latest body to be discovered in a ditch somewhere."

Arthur nodded and rose with effort from the sofa, taking care to adjust the rake of the white fedora perched on his head. In the late afternoon light, he resembled nothing so much as a mottled pink moray eel in a crème-colored suit and hat. Thankfully, his reptilian eyes were shielded behind a pair of dark sunglasses.

"It shall be as you wish. I'll arrange for a first-class ticket to Thailand on the next flight out and have an operative bring over the cash and the card. The phone will be in Bangkok when you arrive. I'll leave it to you to decide where you want to stay."

"Perfect."

"Your passport and things are all there." He motioned at the small package he'd placed on the table when he'd arrived. "I do hope you're successful with this. I really don't bear you any ill will. This is strictly business, and you are helping me solve an embarrassing problem. I'll keep my end of the bargain. A million dollars and your child back, no further strings."

Jet didn't believe him for a second, but said nothing. She was sure he would try to betray her once the mission was concluded. That's how his type operated. She wondered idly whether he thought she believed him, then decided it didn't really matter.

"Well, then," Arthur said. "I suppose this will be the last time I see you until your triumphant return. Good luck. Contact me for anything you need." He stepped to the front door. "There's a contact protocol in with your ID. Blind e-mail, my dedicated scrambled line. All the usual."

"I'll be waiting for the courier," Jet said, anxious to be rid of him. She had a difficult time keeping herself from hurtling across the room and tearing out his throat when she was in his presence. If he sensed that, he showed no indication.

Jet watched as he took careful steps down to the street and slid into his waiting car, the driver holding the rear door open for him before trotting around and climbing behind the wheel. When the car pulled off, she felt a palpable sense of relief.

The package contained everything. She methodically scrutinized the contact information and committed it to memory, absently rubbing the spot on her arm where the chip had been recently implanted. She went to pack.

It would be a while before the courier would arrive, but Jet wanted to be ready at a moment's notice.

CHAPTER 10

Jet peered out through the window as the huge plane banked over the Gulf of Thailand on final approach to Bangkok Suvarnabhumi International Airport, on the outskirts of the city. The serpentine brown of the Chao Phraya River poured its polluted rush into the sea, turning the blue water gray as it pervaded the coast. One of the region's near-constant cloudbursts had just rolled through, and the runway was slick with evaporating moisture as the wheels struck the tarmac and the behemoth decelerated down the long, black strip.

A buzz of energy circulated the cabin as the jet taxied to the stainless steel and glass terminal. The flight had been a long and turbulent one, and the travelers were glad to be on the ground. About half appeared to be Thais returning home, and the others were tourists or business travelers, groggy and restless after nearly eighteen hours of flight time from Los Angeles.

Even before the flight attendants opened the fuselage door, the atmosphere had changed to the exotic. Small differences in the way the passengers interacted with each other hinted at social norms that were markedly different than in the Western world. The Thais executed small bows from the waist with their palms pressed together to each other as they terminated their in-flight discussions and reached to help with overhead bags. She had spent the flight immersed in a primer on the culture, and the *wai* was one of the first items discussed – a bow that was combination traditional greeting, farewell, and 'thank you' gesture. One of the countless ways that Thailand was different. She would need to adapt quickly to the culture if she was going to fit in.

The language would also be a problem for her. She didn't speak Thai, but her reading had assured her that many natives in larger metropolitan areas spoke English due to the massive tourism trade that catered to English-speaking visitors from New Zealand and Australia, as well as from the United States and England – many of whom came to Thailand for sex tourism – a libidinous attraction the country was infamous for.

As she waited in customs, an older Thai man approached her and *wai*'d, then began speaking to her in the native tongue, mistaking her for a local due to her features. She smiled but shrugged, and he switched to English, embarrassed, apologizing profusely. That boded well for her ability to blend in, and she hoped it would make her relatively invisible in the bustling city.

Once through immigration she collected her sparse luggage and set out for the taxi stand, where again, the attendant rattled off a question in Thai, and then, realizing his error, he switched to English before blowing on a shrill whistle and waving a car forward.

The driver placed her suitcase into the trunk and waited expectantly for direction. She told him to take her to the Dynasty Hotel, located a few hundred yards from the entrance of the Nana Plaza – one of the five major sex tourism destinations in Bangkok – and near the site of Lap Pu's main brothel. He nodded and opened her door for her, then rounded the car and jumped into the driver's seat.

Driving in Bangkok was more of a suicidal rite of passage than mere transportation. She was convinced they were going to collide with motorcycles, bicycles and other cars at least a dozen times every few blocks, and by the time they reached the hotel, she'd concluded that the locals had a death wish.

Jet checked in, noting the predominantly Caucasian male clientele, many accompanied by young Thai females. She was pleased to find that her room was nicely appointed – and quiet. Her travel had taken over twenty-six hours between getting to Los Angeles, the layover and then the Thailand flight, and because of the turbulence, she hadn't gotten much rest. She turned down the bed, unpacked her suitcase and locked her valuables in the safe, and then set out the Do Not Disturb card on her doorknob.

The Bangkok skyline was breathtakingly beautiful, with skyscrapers beaming out every color of the rainbow. The recent rain had scrubbed the city clean, for a time, and it was as radiant a jewel as any she'd seen. She took in the display from her window for a few minutes as she sipped a bottle of mineral water, and then pulled the curtains closed, ready for some serious sleep. Tomorrow would be a big day. She was supposed to touch base with Arthur in the morning and arrange a meeting with the CIA operative who ran the Bangkok station. Hopefully, he'd been productive over the last twenty-four hours while she'd been in the air.

⥽•⥼

Jet had agreed to meet Edgar, the CIA's point man, at one o'clock at Benjakiti Park, a half mile south of her hotel. When she arrived, she spent five minutes reconnoitering the rendezvous spot before moving to a cluster of trees on the edge of the expansive pond, where a group of children were playing under the watchful gazes of their mothers. She was there an hour early, wearing sunglasses and a forest green baseball cap she'd bought from a sidewalk vendor.

Dressed in jeans and mauve blouse, she blended in easily with the office workers eating lunch on the grass – she could have been a low-level clerk or a shopkeeper on her break. The rental boat pier that was the meeting place teemed with tourists, milling about and taking photographs of each other with the impressive edifices of the skyline as a backdrop.

At the agreed-upon time, a man matching the description she'd been given walked to a bench and sat down, taking off his red windbreaker and folding it by his side. He removed a bag from his satchel and unwrapped a sandwich. Jet watched as he munched on it and then walked by as he was finishing.

"The boathouse, thirty seconds," she said in English and continued ambling towards the pier.

He rolled his wrapper into a ball and dropped it into the bag, then stood and picked up his windbreaker and walked to the boathouse, Jet now out of sight. He waited expectantly, but was still surprised when she materialized behind him, seemingly out of thin air.

"Damn it. You scared me," he said with a grin, then hugged her. She returned the hug and then moved down to the rental boats, holding his hand with the abandon of a lover.

"I rented one. Come on," she said playfully, and within two minutes, they were pushing away from the dock in a floating swan-shaped contrivance, pumping the pedals with their legs.

60

Once they had traveled several dozen yards from the pier, he began speaking.

"I'm Edgar. You must be Kyra."

"Correct," she lied. "What do you have for me?"

"We've narrowed down our man Hawker's likeliest associates to Lap Pu. We think he's definitely in regular contact with him and that they meet once every few weeks up in Myanmar or Laos. Our intel says Hawker is now involved in facilitating human trafficking – girls from Laos or Myanmar, sometimes just children, for sex work in Thailand. Lap Pu has a host of bordellos here, most of them masquerading as ping pong clubs with motels or rooms available for rent by the hour."

"Ping pong clubs? That wasn't covered in the file."

Edgar explained the concept – a sex show involving everything from ping pong balls to snakes.

Jet didn't say anything, her face stony.

"And this is legal?"

"No. Not technically. But the laws aren't enforced, and bribery is rampant. Many times it's the police or politicians who own the clubs. In this case, Lap Pu pays the right people, so he's untouchable."

"And there are many of these places?"

"Tons. And the only real customers are *farangs* – white men. Thai men wouldn't be caught dead in one. It's a cultural thing."

"How noble. So the clubs are sort of a freak show for sex tourists."

Another swan boat, containing a laughing couple precariously pedaling away, veered towards them before straightening out and continuing on its way.

"Correct. And of course, there's the prostitution angle. Nothing like picking a girl after the show to help you relax…"

"How is the target involved in this?"

"It's unclear. Could be he just uses Lap Pu as his eyes and ears on the street, or could be he's helping traffic minors in the slavery trade."

"I read the report. Fully forty percent of the prostitutes are under eighteen?"

"Supposedly not, but the truth is that number might be low."

"And this is culturally acceptable?"

Edgar rubbed his face. "No. It's condemned. But the biggest customers for prostitution are actually Thai men, so what they say and what they do are two different things. The view about sex here is different. While it's not really out and out acceptable to frequent sex workers, it's tolerated, and in some cases viewed as a reasonable choice for males."

Jet digested that.

"And what about the women?"

"That's also a mixed bag. Many of the adult workers view it as a legitimate way to make money in an environment where they have no other options."

"There are always options."

"Try telling that to a fifteen-year-old with a fourth grade education who hasn't eaten in a week and is culturally expected to do everything possible to support her family. Prostitution is an economic crime, in the end, whether it's males or females. Many of these kids are starving to death wherever they live, so a life of sex work is preferable to death. It's a pretty stark reality many westerners don't understand. They can't imagine a world where there isn't a safety network to catch those at the fringes. But here, it's not the fringes. Most of the peasants in northern Thailand as well as Laos and Myanmar live in extreme poverty. It's the same everywhere human trafficking is rampant."

"I'm not from the U.S.."

"Hmm. Anyway, the attitude in Thailand is different. There isn't as much of a stigma to being a sex worker. For many, it's their only chance at making more than sustenance wages. If you have a family of brothers and sisters and two sick parents all depending on you, it's a vicious circle and the money's compelling. But anyway, let's not get hung up in the detail. The point is that Lap Pu operates some ping pong clubs, and we know which ones, and we're currently staking all of them out, so we'll know whenever he shows up."

"That's fine, but it could take too long. I'm thinking I need to get my hands dirty and start nosing around at the street level," Jet said.

"Fair enough. Arthur wanted me to tell you that he's allocated a resource for you to use. An experienced field agent who speaks perfect Thai and who has a lot of depth in sanctions."

Jet bristled. "Absolutely not. I work alone. He knows that."

"He thought you would feel that way. He gave me a message – you should call him for more detail, but this isn't negotiable. Look. I know this guy. He's extremely good, knows the lay of the land, and it will make any information-gathering way easier due to the language and also because a couple looking for some kinky fun is way more believable than a woman alone asking questions. Think it through."

Jet had to concede that he had a point. It was a far more plausible cover. But she still had no idea who she could trust and who Hawker might have compromised.

"Is he Caucasian?"

"Yes. A local would raise eyebrows. This way you could be husband and wife or girlfriend and boyfriend looking for something exotic and forbidden. A lot of couples come over looking for a little spice. It's not that unusual. But never a Thai couple – it would be socially unacceptable, or at least harder to explain, especially given that you don't *speakee speakee*."

"Who is this agent?"

"I'll introduce you tonight or tomorrow, if you like. His name's Rob Phillips. Twenty-nine, been here for six years. Smart, quick and dependable."

"How much contact did he have with Hawker?"

"None. He was in the south, Hawker ran the north. Need-to-know and all that. We don't have an annual dinner or anything for spooks. I probably wouldn't know half the people working here, and I've been the top dog since Hawker went off the reservation."

"You're sure?"

"Yes. He's clean." Edgar paused. "You take my satchel when we get out of the boat. There's a satellite phone in there, along with a Beretta, as you requested, and a butterfly knife."

Jet nodded. "Ammo?"

"Fifty rounds. I'll get you whatever else you need within twenty-four hours of you asking for it." He smiled. "We aim to deliver good service here in the Far East..."

"Silencer?"

"Yes. As you stipulated. But try not to use the Beretta here. The Thai police tend to be very anti-gun in the hands of a *farang*." Edgar hesitated. "How much do you know about Thailand and Thai culture?"

"Just what I read on the flight over."

"This is a very polite society, at least on its surface. Everyone smiles at you, and it's conflict avoidant. Nobody is direct about anything – it's considered impolite. But as a foreigner we're *farangs*. And Thais view *farangs* as fat, dumb, clumsy barbarians – which I suppose is true of many examples they see of us. It's a racist society, too, as are most. Darker skin from the north is lower class, and there is tremendous class consciousness. Lighter skin, like yours, would be viewed as superior. But if you're a foreigner, you're almost subhuman from their standpoint – although part of the weird self-hatred that's endemic to the culture is that marrying a white man or woman would be viewed as elevating one's station in life. Mainly because it's a society that worships money, and most white foreigners have more money than the average Thai."

Jet shook her head. "I'm not planning on marrying anyone here."

"I'm telling you this because you need to recognize that, in this environment, you're the minority, so you have little chance of anyone opening up to you. Even though you look like you could be part Thai, you don't speak it, so you'll be treated like a *farang*, which means that you'll be smiled at a lot but also lied to about anything that matters. It's just the way it is." Edgar increased his pace on the pedals, and Jet matched him. "If you have any problems, it will be automatically assumed that whatever happened is your fault. In any sort of situation where it's a question of a Thai or you, the Thai will win. You need to understand that you're operating at a distinct disadvantage at all times, and err on the side of caution, or this could go very badly for you before you've even begun your mission."

"I appreciate the background, and I'll watch my step, but I still don't like the idea of dead weight tagging along with me."

"Rob's not dead weight. He's anything but."

"He's a kid."

Edgar smiled grimly. "So are you."

Jet conceded the point. "I probably have more experience than the average fifty-year-old agent."

"Perhaps. Obviously, Arthur is hoping that will make a difference. Time will tell."

"Let's head over to the far shore," Jet said, and they adjusted course. "So what's your plan for meeting this Rob tonight?"

"If it's okay with you, I'd say hook up at a restaurant. A crowd. Although I know you're staying at the Dynasty. The Die-Nasty, the locals call it."

She was annoyed that he knew where she was staying, but then remembered. "That's right. The tracking chip."

"I'm the only one who has access to that info."

"Except for Arthur. And whoever is doing the actual tracking. Which is three more people than I'm comfortable with. It's a stupid idea. Invites disaster."

"I'm afraid it's not subject to debate."

"I know."

It took them six minutes to cross the pond in the swan boat, and when they bumped land Jet scooped up the satchel and stood.

"Sorry about the sandwich remnants," Edgar said. "I also stuck a cell phone in there for you. I'm speed dial number two. There are no other numbers on it."

"I guess since I'm one huge GPS tracking beacon right now, I don't need to worry about the cell phone being a liability."

"Freeing, isn't it?" Edgar's smile had no trace of genuine humor.

"I'll call later to find out where my dream date is going to take place tonight."

"Give Rob a chance. You may find that he's not so bad."

Jet stepped onto the shore and disappeared into the crowd of pedestrians moving around the water on the perimeter path.

Edgar fished a phone out of his windbreaker.

"How did it go?"

"She agreed to the meet, but I think she's suspicious."

"Of course she's suspicious. She's not an idiot," Arthur said.

"She wasn't happy."

"No, I bet she wasn't. Do you think we'll have a problem?"

"Too soon to know. I read her the riot act about the locals. I hope she's as good as you say or she's going to be eaten alive before she gets within a hundred miles of the jungle."

"She is."

CHAPTER 11

Raffle's was bursting with diners lapping up the faux-British atmosphere. Black-and-white photographs of David Niven in cinematic triumph adorned flock-papered walls that brayed a shade gaudier than the hues of the green and pleasant land it strove to emulate. An insufferably arrogant hostess showed Jet to a table, in keeping with the behavior Thais believed would be authentically representative of the UK. Jet didn't have the heart to break it to the girl that the food there was generally regarded as horrible. Let her have her moment.

A young man with neatly-trimmed hair and a deep tan stood as she approached, then waited until she took a seat before joining her. She looked around, confirming that nobody was within earshot.

"So you're Rob."

"Nice to meet you," Rob said, affecting an obviously fake smile.

"Sure it is. What have you been told about me and why I'm here?"

"Just what you would expect."

"Then you should know I don't work with a partner."

"It was mentioned."

"Yet here you are."

"Don't hold back. It's okay to let me know how you really feel."

A waiter approached and asked what she wanted to drink. She ordered a bottle of mineral water and returned her gaze to Rob. He was a good-looking young man, fit, with a deceptively ordinary face – she wouldn't have given him a second glance in a crowd. Brown hair, brown eyes, no scars or distinguishing features. Put a pair of glasses on him or a mustache and he would be a completely different person.

"It's no secret that I'm against this whole idea. But I don't have much say in it, apparently, so here we are," she observed.

"That being the case, what's for dinner?"

They considered the menu, and when the waiter returned with her drink, they ordered.

"We can't just sit here and not talk," Rob said, taking a sip of his beverage.

"Sure we can. Everyone will think we're married."

"Hmm. So, what's the first move?"

"You tell me why I should ever see you again once I leave this restaurant."

"Well, let's see: I speak Thai, know Bangkok well but am not known in the circles you'll want to travel, can hold my own in any situation...and because you have instructions to work with me."

"Rob. Let me make this as clear as I can. I have no instructions. I have a man with a melted face asking me to consider using you as an asset for a short time while I'm in Bangkok. So, sweetie? It's not the way you think it is."

The entrées arrived after a tense back and forth. They ate in silence, Rob sulking and looking almost as unhappy as Jet did. When the bill came, he paid, then Jet stood up abruptly.

"Thanks. Come on. Let's take a walk, and I'll fill you in on where I'm at."

"Yes, master."

"I think that would be 'mistress'."

They exited the restaurant and strolled side by side, and she brought him up to speed on her thoughts. Once she'd finished, he nodded.

"I agree with the thinking that I can help on this. If we pose as a couple looking to swing, we'll have an easier time in the clubs. In the meanwhile, we can put feelers out to all the informants and spread some money around through Edgar. When we get a lead, we can start hanging out at whichever one of his places Lap Pu is at, and then play it by ear. Unless you have a better idea," he said.

"I'm not sure how else we're going to find him. It's not like we can just blunder in and start asking where we can find a slavery kingpin who knows a white devil somewhere in the northern jungle."

"Then it's decided. I'll be your boyfriend, and hopefully, Edgar will have something for us soon. Once he does, we can play it by ear and see what else surfaces."

She still didn't like it, but as she'd listened to herself telling Rob about her strategy, it had sounded increasingly tenuous. Perhaps he could prove helpful after all.

"How do I reach you when I have more info?" he asked.

She fished the cell phone from her pocket and gave him the number.

"Now take me to Nana and show me around. I want to get a feel of the place."

The streets were teeming with drunken tourists as they neared the infamous Nana Plaza – three stories of establishments catering to the sex trade. They passed several girls, who looked barely thirteen, in short skirts and six-inch heels, teetering around as they chattered at passing prospects. "Hey, sexy man. Hey, big man. What you looking for? Come on, sexy man."

A ten-year-old boy, an emaciated street urchin, smiled shyly at them as they passed. She watched out of the corner of her eye as an older Caucasian man slowed and stopped to chat with him, then they walked off together in the opposite direction.

"Hey, big man. Want a ladyboy tonight? Who knows how to love you up right?" a young street hustler murmured to them as he leaned in to Rob. "Check it out. Crying game. *Kathoey.* Ladyboy?" He gestured at four stunning young women who, apparently, were transgender. One of the beauties blew him a kiss as the others tittered.

"Looks like you've found some fans."

"There's something for everyone here. But I don't swing that way."

"Are they all men?"

"Depends. Some have had the ultimate operation, some haven't. But they all started off as men."

"What's the attraction?"

"You got me. I guess sexuality can be complicated. I'd have thought if you wanted a guy, you'd just go with a guy, but obviously not. They're actually viewed as a third sex by many of the locals."

"Is there anything off limits here?"

"Not really. Welcome to Thailand."

They approached Nana, and the crowd got thicker; sidewalk peddlers touted knockoff purses and pirated DVDs as brown uniformed police filtered through the throng as a deterrent to violence or theft. Australian accents echoed off the bar fronts as groups of rowdy partygoers bellowed drunkenly at each other, to the mingled invitations to come in and have a drink from the hundreds of bar girls dressed as provocatively as possible in the interests of luring customers.

"The joints look pretty shabby," Jet observed. Perhaps at one time decades ago it had been a hotspot, but Nana had an air of decay about it – of an aging debutante long since past her prime, but still clinging to her partying ways.

"They are. Same with Soi Cowboy – one of the other big sex districts. Both Nana and Cowboy have seen better days, and now with the economic downturn, many of the bars are losing money."

"Wow. So even the whoremongers are feeling the pinch?"

"I'm sensing a distinct lack of sympathy."

Bar after bar with young Asian women beckoning to anyone walking by to sample their wares blinked with neon desperation in the perspiring night. Jet and Rob moved past the currency exchange and took the escalator to the first floor, where the motifs catered to every possible depravity – bondage and S&M, ladyboys, schoolgirl playpals, and straight go-go bars.

"The real kink is on the top floor," Rob explained, "and at the private clubs in the area. Ping pong shows. That's what our man Lap Pu specializes in, along with prostitution."

They cruised the plaza and the surrounding streets, where everything imaginable was for sale.

"I had an acquaintance tell me that if I wanted a knock-off Chinese-manufactured Benz that looked like the real thing right down to the last detail, he could get me one. There are literally no limits here."

She looked around at the hookers of all shapes and sizes. "How much worse could it get than this?"

"Much. You'll see once we start hitting his clubs. They have shows in the front and whorehouses in the back. But it doesn't stop there. Even though the official stance is that child prostitution is vigorously prosecuted, it's well known that it goes on every day, and Lap Pu is one of the big names in the business."

After another half hour wandering the streets, fending off propositions every few feet, she was done. "I think I've seen about enough for one night." A man had just leaned towards them and made a distinctive popping sound with his mouth and inquired in English if they were interested in ping pong. Jet thought she would never be able to hear the words again without imagining his leering face, discolored teeth and wisps of black mustache framing his popping mouth.

"All right. You're lucky it's a Tuesday. If this was a weekend, it would be three times more crowded."

"What about disease? AIDS has to be rampant."

"It's on the increase. For about a decade, condoms were mandatory for sex workers, but that's become more relaxed as the economy has tightened. Some of the girls will do anything for a few more baht, and they wind up paying the ultimate price. Same for the boys. It's an ugly situation all around."

"How much does a sex worker make?"

"I think the going rate is anywhere from two thousand baht to five thousand baht. Depends on where you get them. In dollars, that's anywhere from fifty dollars to couple of hundred, again, depending on where you pick them up and how long you stay with them. A lot of the tourists come here and want a girlfriend experience, a situation where she'll stay with them for however long they want, twenty-four hours a day, and lay by the pool, go to dinner, the whole works. That costs more."

"So maybe they can take home thirty to forty thousand dollars a year?"

"Again, depends. I'm not an expert at this, but what I've heard is that it's a big piece of the Thai economy. Imagine if your options were making five or six hundred dollars a month as a bilingual schoolteacher, for instance. Starting to see where the financial driver is here?"

She was tired from the multitude of experiences and psychically drained by the exposure to so much corruption. Bangkok was a black hole, a dwarf star for energy. At the moment, it was hard to imagine that anything good existed in the world.

Jet said goodnight, and Rob promised to get in touch as soon as he knew something. They parted ways on the sidewalk in front of the Nana hotel, a multitude of older male tourists laughing loudly as they exited, on their way to the sex mall for a night of abandon.

Her hotel was only a two-minute walk, and she'd never been so happy in her life to be back in a small room with working air-conditioning and a sturdy lock so she could hose off the accumulated filth that seemed to have coated her entire being – and wake up to a new day that wasn't steeped in toxicity.

CHAPTER 12

Rob's voice sounded excited on the cell phone the following afternoon. "We've got a lead."

"What is it?"

"Lap Pu sighting late last night at his largest club. An informant slipped us the tip. Apparently, he's got some meetings tomorrow night."

"That's great news. Whose informant?"

"Friend of one of the bouncers. Works club security on the evening shift. Saw the great man himself at midnight with an entourage. Overheard him agreeing to get together tonight and meet tomorrow. So we have two nights, at least."

"How long since his last trip north?"

"It should be time for another one within the next week. He disappears for a week at a time. Nobody knows what he's doing."

"What do you suggest for tonight?"

"We meet up for dinner at nine, eat, then go to the club and throw some money around. I noticed you didn't drink last night. Do you have a problem with alcohol? Because it would help if you could throw a few back in the bar."

"No problem. I just don't like it very much."

"Have any preferences for dinner?"

"Anyplace but British cuisine."

"I'll call you later."

Rob hung up, and she returned to her table, where a slew of photographs of the man known as Lap Pu were spread out on the table, courtesy of Edgar.

The dossier on Lap Pu proffered a paucity of real insight. Fifty-something years old, a Bangkok native, started out life with a couple of his family's markets, gravitated to the sex trade in the late Seventies. Opened a bar in Soi Cowboy, then another in Phatong, and from there moved up the food chain until he was a major player in the business. Lived a lavish lifestyle, with homes all over the country, including several resorts on Phuket. Friendly with every administration, he had never been arrested and was considered a stand-up fellow. Except for the rumors that he was one of the top sex slavers in Bangkok and had an elaborate network of smugglers moving females from Myanmar and Laos to Thailand, many underage. But like so much in Thailand, rumored truths were not an impediment to his prosperity, and he had kept his nose clean – or at least as clean as someone in the sex trade in Thailand could.

His main enterprises were brothels catering to specialized tastes, the kinkier the better. Ping pong shows, ladyboys, every sort of domination and submission, groups…if you could imagine it, chances are that Pu offered it in one of his establishments.

The last team that had disappeared had followed Pu into the jungles at the northernmost edge of Thailand. But that was Jet's only hope of finding their target. Other than Pu, the CIA had nothing, and even with him they hadn't gotten far.

She opened the safe, extracted the Beretta and stripped it, studying the various components to verify it was in good shape. It looked almost brand new. The silencer was new, showing no evidence of having ever been used. The magazine held fifteen 9mm rounds, with enough stopping power to handle most urban situations, provided that she didn't require accuracy over fifty yards.

The problem was that it was unwieldy and problematic to conceal with the silencer, so discretion would have to take a back seat to practicality. She retrieved the butterfly knife and expertly flipped it open, confirming that the blade was razor sharp. Pacing the room, she flicked it open, closed, open, closed in a reassuring motion as she thought through the permutations of scenarios.

Rob seemed as competent as anyone she'd met with the American intelligence service, but she was still uncomfortable going into the field with a partner. If he did anything stupid or unpredictable, it could be disastrous. She would need to keep a close eye on him – her daughter's ultimate future depended upon this mission going successfully, and she couldn't afford any slips.

As Jet reassembled the pistol, she decided that she would carry it in her purse without the silencer. If there was any shooting, then it wouldn't be a secret – she'd take that risk. There was actually far greater chance that her purse would be stolen than her getting into a gun battle, she knew, and reminded herself to keep it glued to her, especially once in the club.

She debated calling Edgar to request a more compact weapon, and decided that it was warranted.

"I need it as small as they come. But not a .22. Has to have some heft," she instructed over the phone.

"Let me see what I can get on short notice. Shouldn't be a problem. How about something clandestine – if I can get a disguised weapon will that help?"

She described her likely evening's agenda, and he grunted.

"Let's see what the spy armory can come up with. I have a few ideas. I'll call as soon as I know something. Is it okay if I send it along with Rob, or should we meet before?"

"I think I'd like some time with whatever you get, so we need to meet."

"I'll call within an hour. The park work for you again?"

"Always."

❧❦

Four hours later, Jet was back in her room studying the two pieces Edgar had slipped her. The first was a Sig Sauer P238 sub-compact pistol with a six round magazine, five and a half inches long and easily concealed. Accuracy would be considerably lower than the Beretta, due to the shorter barrel, but in a club it would be effective enough. She hefted it and was surprised by how light the evil-looking little weapon was.

The second item was what appeared to be a working Nokia cell phone, but with an undocumented feature – it held three .32 caliber rounds which could be fired using the center select button after punching the call button. Edgar had told her that it would only be effective for ten to twelve feet, but it might come in useful in an emergency situation.

She shook out a tiny micro-transmitter from a plastic bag and inspected it, then powered on the cell phone gun, which had another feature: it could track the chip up to a distance of fifteen miles. The screen illuminated, and a street map popped up with a red dot glowing. It showed her position accurately, and Edgar had said it was the latest technology – good to within one foot. Civilian GPS was only accurate within eight yards. Military GPS could get that down to under three yards with dual frequency technology, and with augmentation it could get down to sub one-foot accuracy, but that would require a team tracking the chip at Langley and then forwarding on the information, which was inefficient and cumbersome. Better to be able to track him real-time on the phone.

She had no firm plan, or really any idea what to expect going into the club. They knew he would be there, but beyond that it was a question mark.

Rob met her at a Thai restaurant a few blocks from the club, and they ate a light dinner as they watched the locals traverse the teeming streets and vendors hawking trinkets and pirated goods. A group of bar girls who worked as prostitutes at one of the myriad nearby go-go bars walked by, laughing.

"They don't look like they're older than fifteen," Jet commented, taking a bite of her *Kaeng phet pet yang* – duck in red curry.

"They're older. Asian women tend to look younger. It's genetics. Most of the bars do regular checks for underage workers, so the mainstream ones are strict about it."

"I don't know. They don't look it."

"Many of them dress and do their makeup so as to appear younger. It's a more desirable look here."

"Why is that? I mean, I get the whole idea of youth being attractive. But, come on. There's youth, and then there's borderline children."

"It's the market. I don't get it, either. But many of the patrons of the sex trade are Thai men, and they like them young. Probably has to do with the woman being unspoiled and youthful," Rob speculated, chewing on a shrimp.

"Unspoiled? Come on. If you're a hooker, servicing God knows how many men per night in a go-go bar, isn't that a stretch? I mean, I can rationalize as well as anyone, but please…"

Rob held his hands up. "I agree. But I don't make the rules. That's what sells, and the market is what the market is."

"So it's a society of pedophiles."

"Not necessarily, although there's certainly plenty of that to go around. It's more about some twisted male fantasies about having sex with the teenage girls you could have had in your youth. Even though most of the men that come here know full well that these girls are eighteen and up, they're buying into an illusion. There are whole clubs that offer nothing but schoolgirl-themed sex workers. It's a big business. And the Japanese eat that up. Their society is rigid and based on control and rules, so they come here and want the forbidden. Even if it's all an act."

"Hmmm. It just seems wrong. I mean, I've been all over the world, and I've never seen anything like this. And I'm not exactly innocent – I've been in a lot of horrible places. But it seems to me that this whole civilization is based on selling youthful sex to fat, red-faced white men."

"You aren't that far off, except that again, Thai men are huge consumers."

They ate in silence, dissonant music blaring from a tinny speaker in the far corner of the restaurant, and then another group of bar girls ambled by on their way to work.

"They all have darker skin. Is that also what the market wants, or is that just me?"

"Most are from Isaan, in the north. The skin is darker up that way. That's one of the reasons Thais consider the typical women that *farangs* favor to be low class. Darker skin is associated with poverty, which is the worst sin you can commit here. Being poor. The average annual income of someone in Isaan is four hundred dollars a year," Rob explained.

"So they come here to make that in a week. Or in some cases, in a few days."

"Exactly. Like I said yesterday, it's economics. Always." He took another mouthful of noodles and shrimp. "What's the plan for this evening?"

"Edgar said that you were going to be briefed before you came to dinner on the latest from the club. He's got a guy outside on the street. What did he tell you?" Jet asked.

"The bouncer is working tonight, and he said they expect Lap Pu in later. Beyond that, we have nothing new."

"I was thinking we spend some time there and see if there's an opportunity to plant a tracking device on him, or at worst, on his car. I don't like my odds of being able to follow him from the club."

"He has a number of homes. Nobody's really sure how many."

"But the only one we're concerned about right now is wherever he's staying."

"It's a long shot. But I suppose it's as good as any."

They finished their dinner and paid, then moved out into the bustle of the streets. Two blocks south, they rounded a corner and found themselves facing a blinking neon cat, sporting a top hat and a lascivious grin.

A man approached them from the darkened doorway.

"Ping pong show. Very nice. Best in Bangkok. Anything you want. Girls. Boys. Come on in. Cold beer."

Jet exchanged a look with Rob that appeared unconvinced.

"I don't know…"

"Top Cat famous all over world. Anything you want. I get for you. Anything." He offered them a leer that promised that indeed, anything that could be imagined could be found in the Top Cat.

"Can we just look around?"

"Of course. Come in. Drink cold beer. Look at all the ladies, the show. Come. Come now, sexy lady. Come to the Top Cat."

She took Rob's hand, raised an eyebrow and nodded. Rob played along, and they moved into the doorway. Two large bouncers stood immediately in front of a black velvet curtain. Music boomed from behind it. Rap. The street hawker nodded at them, and the larger of the pair pulled the curtain aside with a hand the size of a ham.

Rob led, and within two seconds, a hostess wearing what appeared to be a gladiator outfit crafted from black vinyl latched onto them and led them to a booth near the raised stage. The club was half full, all tourists, ninety-five percent male. At least forty young women wearing little but smiles lounged around, chatting in pairs and threesomes, their more fortunate co-workers having already found willing companions for the next hour among the men gathered around the stage.

They took a seat, and the gladiator asked them what they wanted to drink. Rob held up two fingers.

"Singha," he yelled over the music, ordering the most popular beer in Thailand.

She departed on stripper heels, and Jet took in the club. It was larger than she'd expected – looked like it could hold several hundred people. Lighting was limited to red, which was appropriate, and was dim, with barely enough to make out the other clubgoers. She supposed that was typical.

The beer arrived within seconds, very cold. Rob paid for them. They'd agreed he would be the money for the night – in keeping with their cover as a couple on holiday looking for something exotic.

The music changed, and the stage lights illuminated with a flourish. There was no introduction. A young woman mounted the stairs to hooting applause, and then held up a foot-and-a-half-long metal tube, brandishing it like a baton. More cheers.

Rob leaned close to her ear.

"Darts. See the balloons around the stage?"

"You're kidding."

"Nope."

"How the hell…"

Any questions she had, or had never even considered, were answered over the next five minutes.

Three more women joined the dart performer after the display was over. It was time for ping pong. Jet watched in amazement as paddles were distributed to the men nearest the stage, and then the game began in earnest.

Her eyes scanned the room as the show continued, and she spotted an older woman with a child near one of the doorways leading to the rear of the building. The little girl couldn't have been more than twelve and was dressed in a short skirt and a tube top, exposing her adolescent frame and skinny appendages. The woman grabbed her by the arm and was yelling at her, pointing at the crowd, and the little girl nodded, tears streaming down her face.

The woman's face contorted in frustration, and her hand whipped out like a striking cobra, slapping the child so hard her head smacked against the wall. Jet's stomach broiled with anger, but she bit it back, her face displaying no emotion even as she stifled the urge to leap up and flatten the woman.

Another cheer greeted the final salvo of ping pong balls, and then a tired-looking MC climbed up on the stage and announced in broken English that there would be plenty more entertainment coming up shortly, and that everyone should take a well-deserved relaxation break and find some way to amuse themselves while waiting for the continuation of the show.

The matronly woman who had hit the child approached them.

"Why you here? What you want? You want a girl? Two? Maybe a boy?"

Rob shook his head, but Jet reached out and gripped his arm.

"We're actually looking for something a little more…exotic," she said, hesitating on the last word.

"Ahh. Ladyboy? You wanna ladyboy?"

"Mmm, no. What else do you have?"

The mama-san's eyes narrowed to slits. Jet could see her calculating, looking them over, trying to assess how much money they might have.

"I get you anything you want. Anything." She put an emphasis on anything.

Jet leaned in close to her and whispered in her ear.

She recoiled and then gave Jet a smile.

"That's not cheap."

"I didn't expect a bargain."

"Maybe I can get that for you."

"I saw a little girl over by the bathroom. She would do," Jet said.

"Oh, you have good taste, but very expensive. She just in. Unspoiled." The woman's English had suddenly improved now that this was a negotiation. Three minutes later, they had agreed on a price for a room in the back and an hour with the girl.

Jet murmured into Rob's ear, his face blank, and then he nodded and took her hand, following the woman into the back of the club.

The room was larger than she would have thought, and featured a small bathroom with a shower and a bed with fresh linen. Mirrors on the walls gave it a funhouse feel, which she was sure was unintentional. She did a quick inspection to ensure there were no cameras or listening devices, pulling the mirrors away from the wall to confirm they weren't two-way, then turned to Rob.

"What the hell are you doing? Why get a child? Have you lost your mind?" he demanded.

"Shh. I have my reasons. Now don't say anything more until they bring her."

Two minutes later, there was a light knock at the door, and then the child opened it, eyes averted, and she stepped into the room. Jet moved to the door and locked it. She knew the club would have a key, but they would only open it if it was an emergency. The girl was on her own.

She moved to the edge of the bed and then looked up at Jet, whose heart lurched. Beautiful brown eyes gazed at her, terrified but resigned, and then she began pulling her dress over her head.

"No. No. Rob. Tell her she doesn't have to do anything. Tell her," Jet whispered.

Rob fired off a rapid fire burst of Thai, and the girl looked confused. She stopped trying to disrobe and looked at Jet quizzically. Rob turned to Jet. "Now what?"

"Ask her what her name is."

Rob did so.

Jet could barely hear her response. Rob repeated it.

"Lawan. It means beautiful in Thai."

"How old is she, and how long has she been here?"

Rob asked, and the girl murmured another soft few words.

"She says she's almost eleven and she's been here for a week."

"How did she get here?"

More discussion.

"Her father sold her to some men, who brought her to Bangkok."

"Sold her?"

"She says they were hungry for many days. So her father did what he had to in order to keep everyone alive."

Jet bit back the cold fury that was threatening to explode from her.

"What has her week been like?"

The discussion lasted ten minutes, with Lawan describing the trip south, then being put to work in the club. As she went on, Jet seethed with rage. The little girl had been bought and sold like an animal. Even dogs were treated better. She slept on a mat in a tiny back room with several other children who were in similar circumstances. Lawan was the youngest. The others were twelve and thirteen, a boy and a girl. Lawan said she didn't like either of them. They had emotional problems – the little boy was always angry, and the girl didn't communicate.

"Tell her that we just want to talk to her. She doesn't have to do anything. I want to know what she's seen here, and everything about her," Jet said, sitting on the bed after pacing the floor while listening to Lawan's account.

Rob translated, and they spent the rest of the hour talking to her, listening to a story that was as tragic as it was commonplace.

"What can we do, Rob? How can we get the police involved? This has to be stopped."

"I'll ask Edgar, but my hunch is that, given the amount of protection Lap Pu has, they will have disappeared by the time anyone gets around to conducting a raid, assuming that any raid ever took place. This is one of those sad truisms of life here. Sometimes there isn't anything you can do. It's sickening, but true."

"That's not good enough. There's always something you can do."

"I know, but reality is that as horrible as this is, it's not part of our mission. You know that. We need to concentrate on the objective."

He was right. She knew it. This was a distraction they couldn't afford. The logic of it was clear. But sometimes logic wasn't everything.

"Rob, I want you to tell her that we're sorry she is here, and that I'll be back to help her at some point. I don't know how, but I will."

"I'm not going to tell her that. She'll tell someone eventually, and then they'll just move her, and that will be it. And not to be redundant, but again, that's not our mission."

She counted to ten, calming herself.

"You're right, Rob. I'm sorry. It just makes me crazy to see this."

"I know. It's not doing anything for me, either."

Jet got onto her knees, and Lawan came to her. She held the little girl's trembling frame for a brief eternity, and when Lawan stepped away, a tear rolled down her cherubic cheek. Jet's eyes moistened, but she shook it off and stood.

"Tell her that if anyone asks, all we wanted her to do was watch us. Think she can manage that?" Jet asked.

"I doubt anyone will ask, but okay, I'll tell her."

Precisely one hour after Lawan had arrived, another knock sounded at the door. She shuffled to the knob and unlocked it, and then threw Jet one final look, a combination of sadness, fear and misery. Jet took a deep breath and steeled herself. The *mama-san* entered and looked at the bed, which they had rumpled so it look used, and then inquired whether they would want anything more. Rob told her that no, everything was good. As they were leaving the rear area, two beefy bodyguards in double-breasted suits moved towards them down the wide hall, and they stepped aside. The goons brushed past them, trailed by a diminutive man in his late fifties, thick silver hair slicked back with gel, wearing a burgundy silk jacket and black slacks. Lap Pu was instantly recognizable from the photos she'd seen, but she didn't blink when their eyes locked for a fleeting second. She turned to Rob and laughed, then whispered something, smiling. Pu's gaze drifted past her, and then another guard brought up the rear, the bulge of his weapon straining the material of his suit.

Once back in the booth, Rob ordered another beer for them both and then leaned forward, as if telling Jet a joke.

"That was about as close as you could ask to get. But it looks like he's got the troops with him. Good luck getting a tracking chip on him. That was a swell idea, but now…well, it looks pretty much impossible."

"Nothing's impossible. But I agree that now's not the time. We need to find his car and figure out a way to get the chip on it so we can find his house. I'll need a distraction. Here's where you earn your keep. Got any ideas?" she asked.

"I think we–"

The waitress interrupted them with two more cold beers, and by the time she'd collected payment, the music started blaring again. Time for more of the show.

They sat watching another half hour of seemingly impossible acts, each more depraved than the last. Halfway through the festivities, Rob proposed something that could work. It would take perfect timing, but it was their best chance. As the show wound down to a smattering of tired applause, he pulled out his cell phone and called Edgar.

CHAPTER 13

Rob and Jet exited the club and wove their way drunkenly down the street, turning the corner on the alley that ran behind it. A gleaming black Mercedes sedan sat by the seedy emporium's back door, the driver standing by the hood, smoking a cigarette. Jet laughed at some witticism Rob had uttered, and they stopped, she leaning against the brick wall as he moved close and kissed her.

Two men darted into the alley, one with a knife and the other with a chain, and before the couple could disengage, the shorter one slammed Rob in the back with the chain, screaming at him in Thai to give him his wallet. His companion repeated the demand in a guttural voice, and Jet backed away from them as Rob stood, aggressively facing the two.

They began circling him, the assailant with the chain swinging it over his head in a threatening manner as the one with the knife tried to flank him. Jet ran towards the Mercedes, eyes wide with fear.

"Help. Please. Help us," she screamed in English, and then the two men attacked Rob in a flurry of motion.

The driver wanted no part of the scuffle, even when the woman begged him. He shook his head. Rob broke into a run and sprinted down the alley towards him. The driver shrugged away as Rob stumbled, falling to the ground, and Jet took cover behind the car. The men gave chase, and then seeing the driver, yelled at him.

"Move along, dog dick. Or you'll be next," the larger man growled at him from twenty feet away.

"That's right, shitbird. This isn't your fight. Get your candy-ass out of here or you'll be sorry," the smaller mugger snarled, with an ominous rattle of his chain.

The driver pulled a gun from his shoulder holster and held it aloft for the two men to see. A Nighthawk Custom chrome-plated .45. The two Thais stopped their advance and stood frozen before slowly backing away, then turned and broke for the alley mouth.

Jet removed the chewing gum from her mouth and stuck it below the back bumper and sank the tracking chip into it.

She stood and ran to Rob, who had paused near the wall of the building opposite the car, and threw her arms around him.

"Honey. Are you okay?"

"Oh, God. They almost killed us." He turned to face the driver. "Thank you so much," he said in English, and then repeated it in mangled Thai.

The driver waved him off, annoyed. Stupid *farangs*. What did they expect, drunk in this neighborhood? Idiots. He looked down in disgust at his half-smoked cigarette soaking in a puddle by his feet. Perfectly good smoke wasted.

"Thanks again," Jet cooed, and then she and Rob continued down the alley away from the attackers and the club, the driver's angry gaze following them until they reached the next street and turned the corner.

"The signal's strong. We have a winner," Jet said, holding the phone up so Rob could see the blinking red light.

"I'll get a car. We'll want to follow him, right?"

"Sure. Although I don't want to get close enough to risk alerting him. We'll have to be careful. Let's not get ahead of ourselves and screw this up."

"Agreed. So what's the plan once we have him at his house?"

"We'll put it under twenty-four-hour watch. We have no idea how long it will be before Pu makes his next trip north, so this could take a while. You want me to contact Edgar about vehicles and a surveillance team, or will you?" Jet asked.

"I'll take care of it. Give me a few minutes. I'll go get my car so we're ready to go."

Rob walked off towards the hotel district, leaving Jet waiting in front of a section of stalls selling Coach purses and Prada sunglasses, all made on the Chinese/Cambodian border and a hundredth of the price of the real thing. There was plenty of foot traffic; the area buzzed with activity.

Bangkok came alive at night, when the population emptied into the streets for the seemingly endless celebration that was its natural state.

Four drunk Australian men in their late twenties staggered down the sidewalk, laughing boisterously and holding a loud, off-color conversation about their prior night's adventures. When one of them caught sight of Jet, he nudged his buddy and approached her.

"How much?" he asked with an inebriated smile.

She just shrugged, playing dumb. As good a time as any to try blending in as a local.

"Come on, honey. How much to give us a rub and tug? All four of us. You'll like it. The lads and I are 'me so hohny'."

She pointed at her throat and shook her head, then turned away from them, returning her attention to the purses.

She felt his meaty hand grab her arm and try to swing her around.

"Don't give me that—"

Jet pivoted and delivered a brutal strike to his abdomen, knocking the wind out of him with an *oof*. She supported him as he fell against her, his knees buckling, and then she pushed his dead weight into the arms of his mates.

The remaining three stood stunned, and then the largest, wearing an orange rugby shirt, rushed her.

"Try that kung fu shit on me, you bi—"

The kick to his groin was so fast, he had no time to register it before he went down with a gasp, knocking a bin of Luis Vuitton clutches onto the sidewalk as he fell. The shopkeeper came running at the sound to find two of the four men sprawled on the sidewalk. The final two didn't seem to have any appetite for more Jet and backed away from her a few steps.

She executed a small *wai* with a smile, then turned and sashayed away, wary of any pursuit. There was none, the inebriated bullies now occupied with trying to get free of the shopkeeper, who was demanding payment for the wet purses. That would keep them busy for a while —Thai vendors were as tenacious as lampreys: if they thought you owed them something, they would tie you up for hours, screaming and threatening to call the police. Any time there was a disagreement between a Thai and a foreigner, the brown-clad cops would invariably side with the Thai, so they never hesitated to avail themselves of that option. The Aussies were screwed.

She could see why the locals both despised foreigners and courted them. They came with boatloads of money the population desperately needed, and exchanged it for the national product – easy, cheap sex with attractive, willing partners. But they were an ill-behaved bunch, arrogant, loud and unrefined, and so, behind the ever-present Thai courtesy lurked a simmering hatred bred of generations of being used as the westerners' outhouse. The altercation with the four men had been a typical one. Drunk, loutish oafs assuming that any woman on the street was a sex worker, and thus theirs to do with as they liked – the only sticking point being an agreed-upon price. There was no way they would act like that at home.

It felt good to get rid of some of the anger that had been welling inside her since her time with Lawan. There had been a number of non-violent ways she could have extracted herself from the altercation with the four men, but the truth was that she wanted to hit someone, to hurt them. The little girl's situation was beyond awful, and there was nothing she could do about it. Jet knew there were thousands of similar children being brutalized all around her that night, but for whatever reason, she'd been touched by Lawan and couldn't shake her.

Rob had been prudent, but that didn't mean that he was right. She understood the danger and recklessness of getting involved in trying to save the world. But the memory of Lawan's innocent face and the look of helpless despair in her eyes stayed with her. Somebody had to do something. And the only one who seemed to care was Jet.

A Nissan pulled alongside her at the curb, and Rob's voice called from the window.

"Hop in."

She swung the door open and slid into the passenger seat, the tracking phone glowing in her hand.

"Did you talk to Edgar?"

"Yup. He'll have two more vehicles at our disposal within an hour, and a surveillance team in place within two."

"So now we wait. It might be a long night."

"Most are."

CHAPTER 14

Tuk tuks roared by their position a block from the club, the three-wheeled conveyances ferried tourists from one den of iniquity to another. A seemingly endless parade of buzzing motor scooters made kamikaze runs in and out of the speeding traffic, their pilots seemingly fearless, immune to the effects of any ill-timed braking or a swinging fender. Sirens pierced the night as the ambulances mobilized to scrape up what was left of the riders who had timed it wrong.

"There are literally hundreds of accidents every day with the bikes and scooters," Rob said, reading her mind.

"But everyone drives like they're insane."

"It's part of the local charm."

"Reminds me of Rome. Or New Delhi."

"Hmm. Never been."

"You haven't missed much. Especially India. It's a different world."

"I've been confining my travels to Asia." Then Rob clammed up. He obviously didn't feel like sharing any further, so Jet let it go. She wasn't particularly interested, anyway.

"You're still thinking about the little girl, aren't you?" he asked, after a time.

"Why do you say that?"

"I can see it in your eyes."

"Maybe."

"It's a despicable situation, but we can't get involved. The risks are too great. And I didn't sign up for that."

"I know."

An uncomfortable silence settled between them, which was fine by her. She wasn't in a mood to talk.

They had been sitting for two and a half hours and could just make out the front of the club, occasional patrons appearing out of the night and wandering inside – always Caucasians.

"Thais only go to the ping pong clubs if they're taking foreign guests out on the town. Otherwise it's not their thing."

"I know. Edgar told me. Seems like that's about the only perversion that's not their thing. Sex with children, no problem. Ladyboys galore, bring it on. But ping pong. Heaven forbid…"

"Not everyone condones sex with minors."

"Yeah, I can see the loathing and disgust the proprietors and customers at the club displayed. Touching."

Rob didn't pursue it.

"Hey. He's moving. Look." She held the phone up, and they watched as the blinking red dot began inching away from them.

"Hold on."

Rob started the engine and swung into traffic, narrowly missing a tuk tuk that appeared out of nowhere from behind a double-parked car. The driver swore in Thai and made a universal gesture of displeasure at Rob, who grinned and then gunned the gas.

"He's two blocks west. Make a left at the next street and you'll be behind him."

Rob edged over, cutting off a van that rebuffed him with an angry honk, and then swerved around a stationary taxi before making the left onto the larger boulevard.

"Okay. We're three blocks back. See if you can get us within a couple, but not too close. I don't want to queer this by getting right up on him," she instructed.

They jockeyed back and forth until they were two hundred yards back, then settled into a tracking pace that stayed even with Lap Pu's car.

"Look. You can see his taillights up by that truck. This is close enough," she said.

"Yes, master. Oops. *Mistress*." He stressed the sibilance mischievously.

Twenty minutes later, the Mercedes swung onto a residential street with high-rise condominium buildings towering on both sides. The driver reached up and hit a remote control, and an electronic gate rose. They watched as the Mercedes moved into the underground parking garage, and then the barrier descended.

"Let's see what we can get on this building. I want everything possible. Blueprints, a list of residents, you name it. My bet is a guy like Lap Pu won't be in a one bedroom. Probably one of the larger units, possibly the penthouse."

"I'll send the request to Edgar. Now what?"

"Now? Now we wait. Let's get the surveillance team in place."

Rob nodded and made the call.

᠅

The following day at one p.m., Pu left his condo with an entourage of bodyguards. The watchers followed him to a large traditional Thai restaurant, where he met with a group of business associates for two hours. In the meantime, Edgar got Jet the plans for the building, and they quickly pinpointed Pu's likely condo – a four-bedroom, forty-two-hundred-square-foot unit that occupied a third of the penthouse. His neighbors were a prominent real estate developer and a television celebrity.

The downside was, that on first blush, the condo seemed impenetrable, at least without getting caught. To breach it and shoot her way out would not have been a problem, but for any sort of stealth approach, it posed a host of issues.

She studied the diagram and felt a tingle of anticipation. There was always a way. It would just be up to her to find it.

Three hours later, she had devised a scheme. It would be risky and involve an element of luck, but then again, most of her life had been like that, so she wasn't dissuaded. The building had a weakness, as did his condo.

Jet picked up her phone and called Edgar, taking two minutes to describe what she would need by six o'clock that evening.

᠅

Pu looked out over the Bangkok skyline, its lights twinkling like a holiday pageant as far as his eye could see. It had been dark for almost an hour, and he stood in his silk bathrobe, smoking a Lucky Seven cigarette as he gazed out at his empire, a crystal tumbler of single malt scotch in his hand. The television murmured in the background, the news blinking images of the world's daily atrocities at the back of his head as he contemplated the night sky.

A trace of jasmine lingered in the bedroom from where his new favorite, Suchin, had spent a frolicking two hours with him, having only recently departed. She was a delight, barely eighteen, exceptionally beautiful and smart. But a conniver, he could tell, always trying to calculate how to best exploit any given situation.

He didn't mind. That was her role. He was money and power, she was beauty and grace, but she wanted what he had to offer more than he needed what she could provide. And so the dance without end went, the pirouettes and *pas de chevals* artful, if obligatory.

He had never harbored any desire to settle down after his wife died in a car accident eighteen years ago, struck down without warning in the prime of her life. Companionship was easy to find when you were a rich sex industry magnate in Bangkok, and he had a virtually endless stream of eager friends to share his bed and table. It might be a shallow life, but it had its pluses, he mused, blowing a white cloud of nicotine at the uncaring ceiling.

Pu tossed back the last of his scotch and stretched, enjoying the familiar burn of the smoky nectar as he cracked his neck and then stubbed out his cigarette. He glanced at his watch. It was time to rinse off and then gear up for dinner, followed by the inevitable meetings that were a part of managing his network of businesses.

He padded to his nightstand and unclasped the stainless steel Rolex Submariner that he'd been wearing for a decade – preferring it to the more ostentatious styles worn by his peers, whose platinum Masterpieces and Presidents screamed wealth to anyone interested. Pu preferred a low-key appearance. He knew how much money he had, and he didn't need to proclaim it to the world. Leave that to the younger peacocks intent on fanning mating displays with their feathered finery. At fifty-nine, he didn't have any need to prove anything to anyone – the only benefit from growing older he could see.

He placed the watch next to his empty glass and dropped the cigarette butt into it, the ember hissed out in the dregs, a few drops he had neglected but nonetheless came to good use. With a final look at the skyscrapers stretching endlessly into the distance, he turned and moved into his mammoth master bath suite, custom-designed to his taste by one of Bangkok's top firms and lovingly crafted from the finest Italian marble – one of his few indulgences, to be savored in private.

Jet watched the scene on the screen of the PDA she clutched in her hand, twenty feet above Pu's balcony on the roof of the thirty-two-story building, a warm sea breeze caressing her features as she followed his progress into the bathroom. With a final glance at the image, she reeled up the fiber-optic camera she'd lowered into place and zipped it in her windbreaker pocket before stepping off the building edge into nothingness.

Six seconds later, she had rappelled down to the terrace and was sliding the glass door open – it being a safe bet that Pu wouldn't lock it that high in the sky. She knew he had a complement of bodyguards in the front room, but nobody would be expecting an intruder from above, much less a black-clad female ninja.

Without wasting a second, she made for the nightstand and scooped up the Rolex before moving soundlessly to the corner of the room and dropping into a crouch.

She pulled a tool out of her pants pocket, affixed it to the case back, and turned. The waterproof casing gave with a jolt. After placing the watch on the polished granite floor, she retrieved a small plastic bag containing the micro-transmitter, which could be tracked by satellite as well as with a handheld device – much like the one she'd been implanted with.

The chip fitted perfectly, the dot of super glue holding it firmly in place on the inside of the case back. A tiny battery with six months' life was incorporated into the circuitry.

Jet's ears strained for any suspicious sounds as she reassembled the watch, locking the back into place with a snick. She looked at her own watch and saw that she had been in the condo for ninety seconds.

She rose and replaced the Rolex on the nightstand, listening as the old sex lord finished his shower, and inched to the door again. She stepped out onto the terrace, and just as she was closing the door, she heard the water shut off.

When Jet reached the railing's edge, she snapped herself back into the hanging harness and began winching herself up, but the damned contraption caught with a lurch and stopped winding.

A flicker of motion caught the corner of Pu's eye from the terrace as he emerged from the bathroom with a plush green towel wrapped around his slight frame.

A moth fluttered against the glass and then flew off into the sky in pursuit of more hospitable surroundings. Pu watched its unsteady flight for a few seconds and then turned, scooped up his watch and put it back onto his wrist before returning to brush his hair and shave.

Jet clambered over the roof edge, panting from the exertion of pulling herself up the two stories using only her arms, having given up on the winch after a few frustrating seconds. She lay in place for several moments, gazing up into the night sky at the glowing tapestry of stars, and then willed herself to her feet, carefully coiling the line.

Holding a micro cell to her ear, she dialed Rob.

"Mission accomplished."

"I'll alert Edgar. He'll have it tracked from headquarters and follow it via a remote link in his office. When should I pick you up?"

"Give me five minutes. I'll duck out the service entrance. Anyone in sight?"

"Negative. All quiet."

"I'll be down in a few."

"Roger that," Rob finished, and then the line went dead.

CHAPTER 15

Rob and Jet entered the club again, after a different smarmy hawker had pulled them in from the street. They followed the same gladiator girl to the same booth as the prior night.

The festivities were in full roar, with cries of drunken delight from a contingent of mid-thirty-year-old men, all wearing the same red T-shirts.

Rob edged closer to her. "Bachelor party."

"Lucky bride. I wonder if the groom is going to tell her how he spent his time? My guess is he'll leave out the sex tourism part."

"It's an imperfect world."

"I'll say."

Pu entered a few minutes later, which they were expecting, based on the signal from his car. They'd pulled into a parking spot only minutes ahead of him.

It was the same routine as the night before, his entourage of hired muscle leading the way back to his offices, trailed by several Thai men who had business with him. Jet noted the way his eyes roved over everyone in the club, lingering on her for a fraction of a second before continuing. Did he remember her from the prior night? She felt a momentary chill and took a sip of her beer. Their cover was to be seen in the club, a debauched couple out for wild times, so it didn't really matter if he recalled her or not. But it still gave her the willies, for some reason.

The grand finale onstage was greeted by a cheer from the bachelor party. A slim female performer bowed theatrically and winked at the groom, his friends cheering him on as she gave him a salacious smirk and gestured at the rooms in the rear with her head. He stood with a shrug to much back slapping and took her hand, following her into the shadows as the music blared back to full roar – a twenty-year-old Snoop Dog rap groove with an ominous beat.

"I want to talk to the *mama-san*," Jet announced.

Alarm flashed across Rob's face. "Why?"

"I just do. Do you think she speaks English?"

"It's a bad idea. A really bad idea."

"I've been thinking about it all day. It's not such a bad idea. It would actually be in keeping with our cover as a rich, spoiled couple."

"What are you going to do?"

"You don't want to know."

"You're going to blow our cover."

"No, I won't. Trust me on this."

Before he could argue any more, she stood and made for the back of the club. The *mama-san* was waiting like a meaty specter just inside of the doorway.

"What you want? Anything you want," she began, then recognized Jet from the night before. "Ah. You back. You want more?"

"I want to talk to you."

"Talk? What about?" she inquired suspiciously.

"The little girl."

"Oh, sure. You want I send her to you? Finest kind. Cutie…"

"No. I want to make you a proposal."

"Proposal? I no understand."

"I want to buy her."

"You know the price. Same as last night."

"No. Not for an hour. I want to buy her."

The woman's eyes widened for a nano-second and then narrowed. "Buy?"

Jet nodded. "That's right."

"I no can sell her. Not mine."

"Then let me talk to whoever can."

"Impossible. He busy-busy."

"I think he'd be interested in making a lot of money, don't you?"

She eyed Jet shrewdly. "You give me tip, I ask. Okay? Good tip, I ask harder."

Jet pulled a wad of cash from her front jean pocket and peeled off a fifty-dollar bill.

"Go ask real hard, and there's another one if you come back with a yes."

She snatched the bill, and it disappeared into the folds of her dress, and then the woman trundled down the long hall to the far door, a pair of armed bodyguards framing it. After a brief discussion, she ducked inside, and then two minutes later emerged with a big smile.

"I ask very hard. Told him you nice lady. He see you now."

Jet slipped her another fifty and moved past her, taking her time to walk down the hall. The bodyguards stopped her and did a fast search, lingering a little longer than necessary on her breasts and bottom, but she didn't bat an eye. The stouter of the two pawed the door open and gestured for her to go inside.

The suite was huge, occupying at least a quarter of the total club area. Pu excused himself from his discussion with the two men he'd arrived with and motioned for her to accompany him to his adjacent private office. She took a seat in front of his hand-carved desk, and he closed the door behind him before plopping down in the black leather executive chair.

"What you want?" he demanded.

"I want to buy the girl."

"She not for sale. That not how things work. You go home now," he snapped.

"I want her for myself. I'll pay good money. How much?"

"You police?"

"No."

"Reporter?"

"No."

"Who are you?"

"Someone who wants to give you a lot of cash for the girl. Tonight. Easiest money you ever made."

"She not for sale," Pu repeated, but in a tone that left the door open.

"What did you pay for her? Five hundred dollars? A thousand?"

"None of your business."

"I'll give you ten thousand dollars for her. Right now."

Pu acted insulted. "No way. Bye-bye, lady. Talk over. Enjoy a drink on me." His English was improving.

"Fifteen thousand. In your hand. You're never going to make that much."

"You no understand the economics, do you? She good for two hundred thousand dollars over next two to three years. Then she too old, but still good for hundred an hour." He reached over and stabbed at the oversized keys of a calculator and then held the screen up so she could see it. There were a lot of zeroes.

"She no for sale. Have a nice night. We done," Pu said dismissively, then rose.

"Twenty-five thousand dollars tonight for the girl. You can buy twenty like her for that."

"Not like her. She special."

"You know that's a good deal."

"Then you go buy twenty. You no hear so good. Talk over. Bye-bye." He depressed a button on the underside of his desk, and one of the bodyguards appeared within seconds. "Show nice lady out. Bye-bye, nice lady."

"You'll be sorry you didn't take the money."

"Sure I will. Remember, next beer on me."

The oversized thug grabbed her arm, and she shrugged free, debating whether to cripple him, and then acquiesced. Her objective wasn't to cause a spectacle. Jet forced herself to think of Hannah. That was the long term plan. *Think of your daughter*, she commanded herself.

A girl in a schoolgirl uniform, who appeared to be all of sixteen, was climbing the stairs to the stage, a Burmese python draped around her shoulders. Jet hurried to Rob, who sensed something was badly wrong.

"Let's get out of here. Now," she demanded.

"Why? What happened?"

"I'll tell you in the car."

The gladiator appeared as if by magic next to them with two beers on a tray. "Compliments of the management," she said in a squeaky voice and then placed the drinks on their table. Onstage, the girl was walking around, brandishing the snake, which was a juvenile, barely four feet long. The crowd whooped, and the men in the bachelor party stamped their feet.

"Let's go," Jet repeated.

"Sit and drink your beer. Calm your ass down. You're making a scene," he said evenly and then raised his beer in a toast across the room to the bartendress, who for no reason either of them could fathom was wearing a

Santa hat in addition to a red negligee. She winked at them and returned to wiping down the bar with a rag.

"I'm behaving consistently with our cover."

"What did you do?" He took another sip.

"I made an offer to buy Lawan."

He almost blew his beer through his nose.

"You what? Are you out of your mind? So you met Pu? Talked to him?"

"I want to help her. Somebody has to."

"Not you. You don't have to. That's not your job. It isn't why you're here." He took a breath. "How did it go?"

"Not so well. He refused."

"What did you offer?"

"Twenty-five."

"Twenty-five hundred dollars? You're low."

"Twenty-five thousand."

"You're insane. For a girl you just met."

"For a human being in trouble."

"I gather he wasn't interested?"

"Correct. By his calculations, she's worth a half million to him."

Rob whistled. "Wow."

"Yes. Apparently, the money in child sex abuse is big."

He drained his beer. "Okay. I agree we should get out of here. But you've just made it very difficult for us to come back. Ever."

"It doesn't matter now. We have the tracker in his watch. As far as I'm concerned, I never want to see this shithole again." The schoolgirl was now performing a provocative dance with the snake, to the delight of the spectators, the music having slowed to a pulsing Middle Eastern beat, presumably evocative of snake charmers.

Jet pushed to her feet. "Come on. I'm done with this."

Rob followed her to the exit after flipping two hundred baht onto the table. They were just pushing the curtain aside as a moan went up from the crowd.

"You leaving now? You miss the best part!" the street hustler admonished at the exit and then stepped out of Jet's way when he caught a glimpse of her eyes.

Rob shrugged at him.

"Touch me, I break your arm," she warned the man, who backed slowly away, his hands held high.

"Okay. Have a good night, lovebirds," he sang with a cackle and then spun, off in search of more prospects.

"You handled that well," Rob said as her boot heels snicked against the sidewalk.

"Don't talk to me. I need a minute."

"Sure thing. You just about blew our entire operation, but no sweat. Take some 'me' time. Why not?"

She threw him a black look and then slowed.

"I'm sorry."

"You should be. I thought you were pro. Mind telling me what the hell was pro about any of that?"

"I figured it wouldn't hurt. And it could have worked. Anyway, it was worth a try. No harm done. So we don't go back to the club. Our job there is finished, anyway."

Rob sighed. "I suppose it is."

They resumed walking again and crossed the street to the next block. Tonight, the area was quieter than the prior evening, with only a few tuk tuks roaming the road in search of fares.

Neither of them had much to say. At the mouth of the alley where they'd parked, she hesitated. The area was as black as the night, the overhead light on the building by the car having burned out while they were inside. She was just about to warn Rob that something was wrong when a figure rushed out from the shadows and lunged at her with a knife.

CHAPTER 16

Jet spun to the side and pitched her purse at the assailant's head as she simultaneously blocked another blow from a second man who'd swung a hatchet at her shoulder. A third grunted as Rob executed a flying kick that caught him in the chest, snapping several ribs with a crack; he crashed against the wall, his machete falling harmlessly into the gutter. A fourth attacker stabbed at Rob with a wicked-looking stiletto, but he parried it and landed a series of rapid strikes against the man's neck.

A gunshot rang out from down the alley, and Jet heard the distinctive sound of a bullet whiz by her left ear as she ducked, fishing into her purse as she dodged another swing of the hatchet. The knife wielder slashed at her, and she jumped back, tossing her purse to the side as she freed her pistol. She heard Rob grunt as the stiletto sliced his ribs, and then she slammed the butt of her gun into the side of the hatchet man's head, dazing him.

The man with the knife lunged at her again, just as another shot boomed and a slug ricocheted off the brick wall beside her. She brought her weapon up and fired, blowing half the knife fighter's face off, and then shot the hatchet man twice, point blank in the chest. Even as he was falling, she dropped to the ground and fired two more rounds down the alley at where she'd seen the shooter's muzzle flash. Another shot rang out, grazing her leg, and she fired her final round at where she'd seen movement twenty yards away. If she'd had her Beretta, she'd have hit the shooter, but with the Sig Sauer it was dicey.

She heard a *thunk* from behind her and rolled to see Rob leaning against the wall, the gore-crusted machete in hand, his two attackers dead on the pavement. She grabbed her purse off the ground and launched herself at the alley mouth.

"Move!" she yelled, and then tore off without waiting for him. She rounded the corner as more shots followed her, blood streaming down her leg from where the bullet had grazed her quadriceps. Rob was behind her and was also oozing blood: from his abdomen. Jet slowed her pace.

"How bad is it?"

"I'll live," he hissed. "You?"

"Same here. You have a gun?"

"Nope. Too dangerous carrying one in the club."

"Good thing I was packing."

He nodded. "Still got at least one shooter back there."

"I know. In here," she cried, then ducked down a pedestrian shopping area, the startled strollers backing away from the blood-sodden pair.

They continued running another two blocks, and then she slowed, taking cover in the shadows of a darkened building.

"What the hell was that?" Rob asked, gasping for air.

"Ambush. But question is who?"

"Lap Pu?"

"But why?"

"The kid?"

"Makes no sense. Could have been because of the money I flashed around, but that didn't feel like a robbery. More like a hit."

Rob frowned. "But if it was a hit, why the amateurs? Why not just gun us down by the car?"

"Good question. Did you notice that they were all pretty rough-looking? Not city rough. Outdoor rough. Their skin was like leather. I've seen that on Bedouins…"

"What now?"

She pulled some Kleenex from her purse; after tearing three loose for herself and pressing them against her leg, she handed Rob the packet.

"We need to get out of here."

"I'll call Edgar," Rob said, pulling his phone free of his shirt pocket.

A twinge of anxiety tickled Jet's stomach, but she couldn't place what was causing it. She nodded to Rob, and he dialed Edgar's number. After a few terse sentences, he hung up.

"There'll be a car here within ten minutes. White Yaris."

"And a doctor?"

"Already arranged. We'll go straight there and get patched up."

"So now all we need to do is stay alive till help gets here," Jet said, eyes scanning the dark street. A motorcycle putted by, two locals astride it, laughing together as they bounced down the road.

When the Yaris pulled to the curb and flashed its lights, they hurried to it and slid in without a word. The driver was rolling away before they'd slammed the doors, his eyes roving in the rearview mirror, on the lookout for threats.

"Nice shooting back there," Rob said in a low voice.

"Not too bad yourself with the Slingblade impression."

"What I really want to do is direct."

The little car purred along, and Jet stared out through the tinted window, lost in thought. Whoever had attacked them had known exactly where they would be, so it couldn't have been Lap Pu – they'd gotten there before him, so at best he would have had to follow them.

The implications weren't positive.

Someone knew their every movement.

Someone who wanted them dead.

❦

"We'll dress this and stitch it up, and you'll be as right as ninepence," the doctor, a wizened British man, assured her with a nod.

She winced as he sutured her but didn't make a sound.

"Now, then. Let's take a look at that stab wound, young man" he said, motioning for Jet to get off the exam table.

"Do you have a sink?" she asked. "I need to rinse out my pants. Blood and all."

"Other room. Take your time. All right, then. What have we got here?" he asked Rob, who merely sat on the table and pulled his shirt up.

The doctor peered at the gash and flushed it out with antiseptic, Rob's sharp intake of breath hissing as the pain hit.

"Well, it's messy, but superficial. A few stitches for you, and the drama will be over. Hold still," the old man instructed, then blotted the injury with gauze before threading the hooked needle. "You're lucky I hadn't polished off the second half of the Balentines I'd started on. As it is, steadies the hand and soothes the spirit."

Rob ignored the banter, preferring to suffer the ministrations in silence.

"There. No worse for wear, I'd say. Just watch for swelling or redness. I'll give you both a five-day course of antibiotics, purely precautionary, to stave off infection. I dare say you'll be fine. Do try to avoid getting stabbed or shot, though. Bloody inconvenient to have to open the office near midnight."

"Thanks, Doc. I'll keep that in mind." Rob began buttoning up his bloodstained shirt.

"No, no. You can't go out like that. Here, let me see if I have a spare in the closet. I'm sure I do. If not, at least an exam coat." The doctor opened an en suite door and rummaged around before emerging with a gaudy Hawaiian print rayon shirt with dancing dogs cavorting all over it. "Ah. One of my favorites. I'll be sorry to see it go. Wear it in good health. World's going to the dogs, and so forth…"

He handed it to Rob, who eyed it skeptically before pulling off his more conservative one. Jet returned wearing her jeans as he donned the dog shirt and strained to button it across the chest. The result was absurd, and when he faced the mirror, he joined Jet in laughing at his reflection.

"Looks brilliant, young man. Magic, really," the doctor said without a trace of a smile.

"I wonder if they make a set of matching pants?" Rob remarked drily.

Their business with the doctor concluded, they descended the stairs to the street, where the Yaris was parked out front, the driver napping behind the wheel.

Rob pounded on the window. "Come on, wake up, you lazy…"

"Run," Jet whispered and then spun, tearing back up the stairs.

Rob stood by the car for a second, unsure of what was happening, and then ducked and darted for the front door just as a shot gouged a chunk of plaster out of the entry foyer wall by his head. He was a third of the way up the stairs when the glass door behind him exploded, showering him with tiny glittering shards. He scrambled the rest of the way to the landing and heard the sound of running footsteps from the street below, then darted down the hall to where Jet had sprinted for the doctor's office. He was just through the door and twisting the deadbolt shut when rounds thudded into the steel. The doctor gaped around, panicked.

"Is there another way out of here?" Jet asked in a low voice.

He nodded, pointing. "Back exit. What on earth is going on here?"

"Come with us. It's not safe. They killed the driver," Jet explained, then threw the back door open. A raw concrete landing led to another metal door that was bolted shut. She caught Rob's eye.

"They tracked us here. Go down the back stairs. I'll be with you in a second."

The front door groaned on its hinges as the attackers threw their weight against it. Rob nodded, grabbed the doctor by the arm, and led him to the rear stairs. Jet dashed to the drawers and opened them, finding what she wanted in the second one. She grabbed some gauze, a small plastic bottle and the paper-sheathed disposable scalpel and then ran for the stairwell, where she could hear Rob and the doctor clumping down to the ground level.

If they were lucky, they would have a minute or two before their pursuers began looking for another way in. Her only hope was that it wasn't a large team. If it was, they were screwed.

Rob and the doctor were waiting at the bottom of the stairs.

She thrust the scalpel at the doctor.

"Quick. You need to cut this thing out. Now." She unbuttoned her top and slid a sleeve off, pointing to the spot where the chip had been imbedded just a few days earlier.

"What am I cutting out?" he asked, hands shaking as he fumbled with the paper wrapper.

"A microchip. Tiny. But you have about twenty seconds to get it or we're all dead."

She gritted her teeth as he sliced her flesh open over the small bump and probed around with the sharp tip of the blade until he extracted the shiny silver disk. Thick, red blood dripped from the incision, but she ignored it.

"Blot it and glue it. Rob. Take this chip, and throw it back up the stairs."

The doctor wiped away the blood, then squirted Dermabond into the incision and pressed the two sides together. He took his hand away ten seconds later, and she clenched the wound, applying pressure.

"Get ready to run," she whispered to the doctor, who nodded. She pulled her blouse back on and buttoned it, the gash now sealed tight.

When Rob returned, she opened the rear door, peering into the half dark of the service way that ran along the backs of the buildings. There was no sign of life.

A crash echoed from upstairs – the attackers had knocked the doctor's front door down.

"Now," she said and bolted, Rob and the old man trailing her.

As they neared the end of the block, the hulking outline of a construction project loomed on her left – an older building that was being renovated. A chain-link fence circled it, but there looked like enough room at the gate for her to squeeze in.

"Can you make it?" she asked Rob and the winded physician.

"We'll have to."

Jet went first and slid into the gap, clutching her purse as she beckoned them to follow. "Hurry."

Rob went next, his dog shirt tearing as he struggled to get through. He finally made it, then held out his hand for the doctor.

"Come on. Now."

The old man wedged himself into the gap and then stopped, his white exam coat snagged by the raw wire jutting from the fence.

"Tear it. Let's go," Rob urged, as his eyes swiveled down the alley.

Three men toting assault rifles emerged from the doctor's building, gun barrels sweeping the street.

The doctor gasped at the sight of the gunmen and renewed his efforts to get free, but the only thing he accomplished was to make the fence rattle, drawing the gunmen's attention.

The night exploded with the stutter of automatic weapons, and the doctor's body jerked spasmodically as a succession of white-hot rounds tore through him. Rob ducked back into the building where Jet was waiting and shook his head.

She turned and mounted the concrete steps to the second floor. It was gutted, empty except for a workbench, with no place to hide, so she continued to the next level, Rob behind her.

They heard their pursuers trying to pry the doctor's corpse from where it blocked the gate, and then another blast of gunfire shattered the night as one of the men shot the padlock off.

Jet pointed at a far window and then broke for it. Peering over the edge, she calculated the distance to the next building and then backed away from the empty aperture before hurling herself through it feet first.

She landed in a pile of broken glass. She'd kicked through the window and was lying on the floor of a darkened office.

"Jump," she hissed at Rob, who was still standing in the other building, then she sprang to her feet and took off into the space beyond, looking for an exit or something that could be used as a weapon.

Rob pounded after her and found her at a stairwell.

"They're right behind us," he rasped.

"I know. If we go down, we run the risk that one of them stayed on the street."

"So what do we do?"

She cocked her head and pointed.

"We go up."

CHAPTER 17

A crashing sound reverberated through the empty building from below as the gunmen leapt across the chasm and landed on the glass. Jet and Rob took care to climb the stairs to the roof as silently as possible, hoping that their pursuers would think they had made the predictable choice and had gone down to the ground level.

The door to the roof was old and rusting from years of exposure to the salt air and the elements. Jet listened, finger held to her lips, for sounds from two stories below and was rewarded by a door opening and then footsteps moving stealthily down the concrete stairs. When they had faded, she shouldered the roof door open.

The rusty hinges springing wide sounded like a grenade detonating to her ear.

A door slammed beneath them, and the clump of boots ascended steadily from below.

She reached into her purse and withdrew the phone she'd gotten from Edgar and keyed the sequence that would convert it into a gun.

"Go see if there's a fire escape or a building we can jump to," she whispered. "I have three shots in this thing, and it should stall them when I start shooting. But that will only last so long. If we don't get off this roof, we're dead."

He took off across the roof as she held the door ajar. Three yards of range wasn't ideal, but maybe she wouldn't need that much.

She sensed rather than heard the lead man, and a second after his gun barrel came into view, she depressed the fire button, and the little phone popped like a small pistol, the shell bouncing to the side through a sliding port. She heard a grunt of surprised pain and then gunfire filled the stairwell. Jet threw the door shut, allowing the fire to ricochet back on the shooters. Hopefully at least one stray would hit them, further adding to the sense that she was shooting back. She knew from experience that things could get weird fast in a firefight, and perceptions could play tricks on you. That was her only bet at this point.

"Over here!" Rob called. "There's a building next to us we can get to. It's a story lower, but I think we can make it."

Jet leapt to her feet and ran to him, took one glance over the side, and then backed up and tore off at full speed in the direction of the edge.

Jet seemed to hang suspended in the air for a few seconds, then she hit the roof of the next building, rolled to absorb the impact, and sprang to her feet.

"Come on. Do it!" she yelled at him, and a moment later, Rob sailed into space, tucking and rolling in the same manner when he landed. The shooting from the stairwell had stopped, so Jet guessed that the gunmen had either figured out that she was no longer there, or had sprayed so many slugs into the space that the ricochets had laid waste to them and they were lying wounded or dead on the stairs.

"Look. There's a fire escape," Jet said, moving to a ladder that extended from the building's edge below. "It looks solid. I'm going down."

She swung her leg over and dropped below the roofline. Rob trotted to the edge and followed her, but just as his head was dipping out of sight, he saw two men with rifles on the roof of the other building.

"Slide down. Fast as you can. They're on the roof. It will only be a few seconds before they're here shooting down at us."

Jet was still two stories above the street and, after weighing her options, kicked in the window of a second-story office and climbed in.

"We can make it to the street once they follow us inside," she said as he hung on the ladder outside the window.

"No. Let's split up. That will make them do the same thing, or it will allow one of us to get away clean."

"No—"

But by the time she had shaken her head, he was gone.

Jet heard his soles drop to the ground a few moments later and then the sound of running. She didn't wait to see if he would make it. Since he had made the decision to go his separate way, she owed it to both of them to do whatever it took to escape.

Then the shooting started.

She froze, then made an instantaneous decision. If the gunmen split up, that meant only one would come after her. And there were few fights she couldn't win one-on-one. Even if both of them came, if she could pick her environment, they were as good as dead.

The ladder creaked as the two men lowered themselves, weapons hanging over their shoulders. One man's leg was bleeding from where a stray round had hit him, but he was still pushing himself even as crimson drops leached from the wound and fell to the sidewalk below. The lower man made a hand signal as he reached the broken window and then unstrapped his rifle, leading with it as he strained with his leg for the ledge. He winced with effort as he pulled himself into the darkened room, peering around warily.

His partner followed him in, and they exchanged a glance in the gloom, both men straining for the slightest sound in spite of their ears ringing from the gunfire. A ricochet had killed their companion in the stairwell so they were being especially cautious, their mission having been a disaster so far.

The lead man pointed to the doorway with two fingers. The other man nodded before stepping over the glass and inching cautiously towards it. Sirens keened in the far distance, and they knew that they were now on borrowed time. Even in Bangkok, the police would show up for a full-on gun battle.

Once through the door, there was almost no light, so they waited a few seconds for their eyes to adjust. A scraping came from further in the depths of the offices. The lead man pointed at the light switch. His partner shook his head. Light would make them sitting ducks. Right now they had the same darkness to contend with as their adversary.

They moved down the hall, pushing doors open with their gun barrels, ready for anything, and then the noise became clearer. Rhythmic. Like a machine of some sort.

From the next office down.

The lead man tapped his temple with his hand and pointed at the door. A bead of sweat rolled down his face and crept into his eye, causing him to blink the burn away. His partner stood by the side of the doorjamb and eased the knob to the right, then threw it open and rolled into the room.

An old copy machine was churning away, its internal scanning arm clattering each time it fulfilled its journey across the screen and hit the carriage-stop. The lead man followed his partner into the room, gun at the ready, but the machine was the only occupant.

The sirens grew louder. It wouldn't be long.

Somehow their target had gotten away.

And now they were faced with an impossible choice. Keep searching the building and face certain arrest, or escape to fight another day but have to report back that they had failed in their mission.

The second gunman turned to look at his partner for guidance.

From downstairs, a door slammed, confirming their worst suspicions. They were now alone in the building, their quarry gone, leaving them to the police.

The lead man lifted a cell phone to his ear and murmured a few words into it, instructing the car to circle around and pick them up in the alley. Hopefully, they would be able to outrun the police. If not, they would have to fight it out. Capture was not an option.

They wound their way back to the fire escape and prepared to climb down the two stories to the street, shouldering their rifles, edging around the brittle glass shards on the linoleum floor.

The lead man's eye disintegrated as the sharp crack of the .32 caliber round shattered the silence in the small room, and he dropped like a sack of wet mud, blood seeping down his face as he fell. His partner fumbled with his rifle and then gurgled as a stalk of bamboo plunged through his back, the sharp shaft exiting his chest. He looked down in puzzled surprise at the skewer that impaled him and managed a half turn of his head before his legs buckled and he sank to the floor.

Jet stood behind him, watching him shudder, and then reached down and lifted his rifle free. A Kalashnikov. She popped the magazine out and checked it – the weight told her it was half full. After slapping it back into the rifle, she pulled the strap onto her shoulder and looked out over the fire escape, where she had lain in wait after circling back around while the two men had been distracted by the Xerox machine.

Headlights illuminated the small alley as a car pulled to a stop a few feet past the fire escape. The driver's gaze swept the dank service area in a panic – the police would be on top of them in only a few more moments. It would be a miracle if they were able to get out alive.

The roof collapsed on the driver, and the windshield shattered into a snowy starburst of safety glass as the lead man's head struck it, seeming to stare sightlessly through one good eye at him before sliding off the roof and onto the hood. The driver screamed in shock, and then bullets tore the cabin apart, slugs ripping him to pieces as the deadly hail from above shredded the thin metal.

Jet watched as gas trickled from the car's ruptured fuel tank before dropping to the ground next to it and jogging away from the clamor of the approaching police.

Two blocks from the scene of the gunfight, she slowed to a walk. The three squad cars that passed her didn't give her a second glance. The officers were looking for armed hostiles, not a nice Thai woman walking home from a nearby nightspot.

She removed the battery from her cell phone and tossed the sim chip aside, having memorized the two numbers on it. However she had been tracked, she was now taking no chances. She had to assume the worst – that she was completely compromised. The question was how, and who had come after her.

A tuk tuk picked her up three minutes later. She dropped into the back with a sigh before giving the driver instructions to take her to the Nana mall. She would pick up some new clothes at the perennially open market stalls in the neighborhood, change in a bathroom, and then figure out whether her room was compromised. If so, she had a real problem. If not, she would be moving to a new hotel within minutes, and her whereabouts would become a mystery to everyone but her.

CHAPTER 18

A rainstorm whipped the treetops near the large boulevard that fronted the mall Arthur liked to use as his getaway from Langley when things became too stressful, or he had to make some private calls and didn't want to have them go through the CIA switchboard. He sat in a red vinyl booth at a retro-Fifties coffee shop, the waitresses dressed in sock hop garb in keeping with the theme. The soda fountain was already doing a good business even at ten a.m., a tribute to the quality of the shakes as well as the lack of concern over caloric intake that its patrons shared.

Arthur took a sip of his rich brew and glanced around the diner to confirm he was alone. The waitresses were used to him so nobody stared at the horror that was his face. A small thing, but one he appreciated, and he always tipped generously by way of thanks. He reached into his jacket and extracted a cell phone with a scrambler module incorporated in it.

The voice on the other end answered within moments. "So what's the word?"

"The operative's in place, and we're waiting to follow the contact."

"That's great. Hopefully this will be over soon, and we'll have our diamonds back."

"Well, there's also a wrinkle. I got a call a few hours ago that someone attacked them."

"What do you mean, someone attacked them? Who? What was the result?"

Arthur took another sip, what passed for his lips drooling fluid onto the saucer – an eventuality he was prepared for with plentiful napkins. No matter how hard he tried he couldn't get used to drinking hot coffee through a straw. It was just another of life's plentiful challenges.

"Information is coming in, but the good news is that the operative wasn't harmed, so other than some logistical hurdles, we're still all systems go."

"And who mounted the attack?"

"Unknown at this time. One disturbing piece of information I'm thinking you can look into, though. I don't want to use any agency assets – it appears we have a leak. It seems that the operative was tracked. That points to what we've long suspected – someone inside who has access to the positioning feed. It would also explain why our last two forays were unsuccessful. If they had the tracking data…"

"…they knew exactly where to find them. I got it. I'll have my tech look into who has been accessing the feeds. That should be knowable."

"When you find out…"

"I know. We'll arrange for an accident."

"Leave that to me," Arthur said softly.

"Of course."

"On the other front, we're hearing that our customary suppliers are now in discussions with a Russian group about taking over distribution into the Eastern Seaboard and Europe. I won't belabor how bad it will be for us if they get their hands on that much heroin. It would disrupt the entire pricing structure."

"I don't need to tell you how much product we are already committed to from Afghanistan. Any significant drop in the market price would be disastrous."

"I have faith that this operative will solve the problem for us."

"Let's hope you're right."

Arthur sighed. "We may want to consider a backup approach if she fails."

"There is no backup. She can't fail. We don't have any other options."

"I'll start thinking of some. While I believe she will be successful, I don't want to bet the farm on it," Arthur said.

"Do that."

Arthur hung up. In addition to his formal role with the agency, he'd also been involved in the small circle of defense department and CIA personnel that controlled much of the worldwide narcotics trafficking for twenty-seven years and counting, eventually securing a central role in the scheme as his predecessors had retired or died. It had made him a very rich man, but also carried with it responsibilities. Like ensuring that no criminal syndicates stepped in and cut into the supply chain. Pricing on many drugs was as artificial as the value of most currencies, and if the Russians hit the street with heroin that was half the price of his, that would cause a disastrous downward spiral in profits as his network had to meet that pricing to move product.

He finished the dregs of his cup, wiped his face, put a five-dollar bill on the table for the two-dollar coffee, then stood and made his way to the door, ignoring the stares from the few interested patrons near the front entrance. He'd long grown accustomed to being a freak, a monster, the thing of childhood nightmares. There was nothing he could do about it but try to live as normally as possible. Assuming one believed that being one of the top CIA black ops managers was deemed normal.

Looking up at the sky from beneath the awning, he opened his umbrella and pushed out into the storm, his car and driver waiting for him in the red zone a scant twenty yards away.

A contingency plan was prudent, he knew. The attack on the woman was fair warning. Something more was in play than they understood.

And Arthur hated surprises.

❧⸙❧

Edgar sat with his back to the wall in the main dining room of an Italian restaurant, two hundred yards from the Nana complex, stirring his iced tea and watching the customers arrive for an early lunch. He checked his watch. Ten minutes late. He took a drink of the concoction and studied the menu absently.

Jet appeared out of nowhere and took the seat across from him, facing the window. Edgar's face betrayed nothing, although she could tell he was again surprised at her arrival.

"Came in through the back?" he asked.

"Seemed prudent."

He studied her. "What happened? I saw some reports on the news…"

"I won."

"That's it?"

"Pretty much sums it up, don't you think?"

He didn't respond.

The waiter brought her a menu, and she ordered a bottle of mineral water. Once he had departed, Edgar put his menu down.

"Who were they?"

"Don't know. But they were tenacious. Amateur in the end, but tenacious just the same."

"You got away clean? No injuries?"

"I'm good to go. Rob?"

"He has a sore ankle from the jump on the roof, and he lost some skin on the fire escape, but other than that, tip top."

The waiter arrived and set a bottle of water in front of her, then took their order and left them to their discussion.

"Why did you cut out the tracking chip?"

"Self-preservation. I was traced," Jet stated flatly.

"That's impossible...unless..."

"What?"

"There was a rumor. That's all it was."

"Are we playing twenty questions? Tell me."

He rubbed his face, looking tired for the first time. "About Hawker. Nobody was sure about who could be trusted when he went rogue. But one of the rumors was that he had someone at headquarters...someone at Langley. Nothing ever came of it, but that would be the only explanation."

"Assuming that it was him."

"Who else would it be?"

"I don't know, but I don't like the way any of this is shaping up. Nothing is as it seems."

"Welcome to Thailand. You get used to that in everything here. Wheels within wheels. A Russian doll. Always another layer."

She fixed him with a hard stare. "Shit. Do you have a tracking chip?"

His eyes widened. "No. I'm not...I'm not active in that way..."

Jet nodded. "And Rob?"

"Yes."

"Lose it. Bad idea. Maybe conceptually, it's a positive for a control freak, but as you can see, in practice it's just another way to get yourself killed."

"Noted."

"And what's the latest with Lap Pu?"

"Surveillance says it looks like he's wrapping up his business here. So we can expect him to make a move at any time."

"Then I'm going to need to get some supplies. I made a list." She slipped a piece of paper across to him. He opened it, read quickly, then nodded.

"I'll need to check on the MTAR. What's your second choice?"

"FN P90. Although I prefer the MTAR with a laser sight and suppressor. In 9mm."

"I'm thinking I can get one flown in. It may take a day."

"Then I hope we have one," she said.

"Worst case, I know we have some M4s with laser sights and suppressors."

"Bulkier. In a pinch that would work, I suppose. But if you want to keep a girl happy, get the MTAR and a few hundred rounds of ammo."

"Hmm. No problem on the night vision goggles. Infrared might be tricky. Let me see what I can do."

"I didn't make out that list as suggestions. If I'm going into the jungle, then I'll need to be properly equipped. Unlike the last teams, I have no intention of being road kill."

"Which brings me to the part you're not going to like."

Jet's eyes narrowed.

"Headquarters feels it would be a good idea for you to work with Rob when you go after Lap Pu."

She took a gulp of water and frowned. "Absolutely not. He's not in the same league as I am. Don't get me wrong. He's not bad, but he's not me. And that could get me killed. So forget about it. I don't work with a partner. Arthur knows that."

"He sensed there might be some problems. Asked you to call today."

"Arthur can screw himself."

"Yes, well, perhaps. But he still needs you to get in touch."

The food arrived, and they dug in. Her chicken picata was indifferently prepared with some traces of odd spices. The Thai version, she supposed.

"What else?"

"We may not have a lot of warning when Pu takes off, so I'd stay alert."

She gave him a glum look. "Really. Stay alert. I'll try to do that. But until you have my list in hand, I can't go anywhere, unless you're thinking I should go into the jungle with only a KA-BAR and a smile."

"Point taken. It will be my top priority. In fact…" He flipped out his phone and typed in the list, pausing occasionally to take a bite of lasagna. "…There. By the time I get back to my office, I'll have a line on all of it."

When she'd eaten half of her uninspiring meal, she pushed back from the table.

"I'm going. Thanks for lunch. I'll contact Arthur."

"How will I get in touch with you?"

"I'll call you at five. Let's hope that Pu stays put one more night."

CHAPTER 19

"Forget it. I'm not going to do it. That wasn't our deal." Jet's voice was quiet, and yet had an edge to it. She peered absently around the internet café from her position in the glass internet phone booth.

"I'm afraid that circumstances have changed. This isn't negotiable. Rob will accompany you and assist in whatever way you need, but he is going with you," Arthur said.

"What part of 'no' are you having trouble with?" She could hear his breath coming in harsh rasps on the other end of the line.

"What part of 'you'll do as you're told or never see your daughter again' are you unclear about?"

Jet seethed. She'd been expecting this, waiting for it, but it still took all of her willpower to keep from hanging up and jumping on the first plane to the United States to hunt him down and kill him.

"We have a problem, Arthur. You're breaking your word. That makes me think you'll also break your word when the time comes to give me Hannah. I guess we could call this a crisis of confidence. And you really don't want a crisis of confidence."

"Look. I heard all about your run-in with the gunmen. I also know that it was Rob's quick thinking – his decision to split up when you wanted to stay together – that was largely responsible for both of you getting away."

"Ha! Is that what he told you? Please. I suppose it escaped you that I single-handedly dealt with both of the remaining shooters and the driver without big strong Rob to keep me from breaking a nail."

"Be that as it may, you are both going to go into the jungle and bring me the target's head. Do that and you will get your daughter back. There's an easy way and a hard way to do this. I would strongly suggest you do it the easy way."

"No. I'm not going to play ball any more. This is over now. I'll figure out how to get my daughter back without you. I hope you sleep with one eye open because you're going to need to," she said, prepared to hang up.

"Stupid mistake. I'll have you on every Interpol terminal in the world within five minutes. You want to play with me? Get ready to spend the rest of your short life in some hellhole of a jail being serial raped by the guards. While your daughter grows up never knowing you – maybe develops a drug problem, runs away, winds up working the streets. Push me and I'll make it happen. Think I won't? Try me."

Jet took a few beats to slow down her racing thoughts. There were other ways of handling the situation besides going to war with Arthur. She'd believed he would back down, but he hadn't, and now she was at the brink. Not a place she wanted to be.

"If you want the diamonds back and the target terminated, you'll do it my way," she said.

Arthur's tone softened perceptibly. "I am doing it your way. Only you'll have Rob with you. Look, you can use him to carry the gear for all I care. But take him. He may even prove helpful with the locals once you're in the brush. Last time I checked, your Thai wasn't going to win any awards."

She realized that she had no negotiating power if he was willing to throw her under the bus to win a power struggle. Her strategy had depended upon him wanting the diamonds back more than he wanted to get his way. She'd just gotten an important lesson in how his mind worked.

"Fine. But you're to instruct him that he answers to me, and that means if I tell him to do something, it's an order. I don't need someone who disobeys me whenever he thinks his opinion is superior. He did that when he split up, and that's a dangerous trait. I won't tolerate it. I'll shoot him myself if he does it again. Do you read me?" she fumed.

"I do, and I'll convey the message. Remember that he's an experienced field operative in his own right. A lot of experience."

"So were the two teams you sent in before me, right? They're dead. Forgive me if I'm not bowled over by that hit rate."

"Touché."

"You sucked me into this because you need my expertise. If you thought you could have used your own people successfully, you would have. So don't hamstring me with dead weight. I'm playing this to win. And I mean what I say about shooting him myself."

"I understand." Arthur paused, and she heard what passed for his lips smacking. "Then we have an agreement?"

"We do. But I want to reiterate what I said earlier. If you try to screw me, I will hunt you down. Nothing in the world will save you. I hope you believe me."

"Oh, I do. Believe me I do."

"I'll call Rob after I call Edgar," Jet concluded, then punched the off button and exited the booth, returning to the front counter of the internet café to pay for her time. She didn't want to chance using cell phones to call him. She knew how easily a cell could be triangulated over a period of more than a minute. A cell would be fine with a calling card for short duration calls to Rob or Edgar, but she wasn't going to chance it with Arthur. She didn't trust him as far as she could throw him.

∂∘∘⬧

The sidewalks were filled with office workers going home for the evening as Edgar waited for Jet in his car in a parking lot near Nana. She'd called at five, as agreed, and they had arranged a meet for six-thirty, so she could get her kit. Street vendors held baskets of food aloft to the teeming multitudes, offering delicacies such as snake and fried, seasoned beetle – all for a nominal amount.

Jet's knock on the passenger-side window caused him to start. He unlocked the door.

"Nice ride," she said, surveying the nine-year-old Kia sedan's fading interior as she slipped into the seat next to him. "Drive."

"Where?"

"To the park. I'll keep an eye out for any tail. I didn't see any watchers on approach, but let's be sure, shall we?"

Edgar eased out of the stall and paid the attendant, then pulled into the gridlocked traffic, the little Kia's motor threatening to stall as he mistimed the clutch. The taxi he cut off honked a short, percussive toot. Edgar waved and shrugged. Jet studied him with a doubtful smirk, then resumed her watch in the side mirror. If someone had them under surveillance, they would have had their work cut out, unless they were doing so on foot.

Five minutes later, they'd advanced one block.

"We could probably crawl faster than we'll get there in the car," Edgar complained.

"Maybe so, but I have my reasons. Did you get everything?"

"Yes. It's all in a duffle in the trunk. I have to admit that two of the items raised eyebrows. We don't see a lot of call for those. Anyway, we had to go with the P90. I couldn't get my hands on the MTAR in time. But I have one coming, by tomorrow, if he's still around."

"Big if."

"I know."

"Any more word on that?"

"Nothing new. He's still at the condo as of now."

"I'll need a car when he bolts. And I might not have much time. Can you get me one that's clean?"

"I already have one waiting."

"No tracker on it – or in any of this gear, right?"

"Correct. Sort of would defeat the purpose at this point."

She fiddled with the air-conditioning vent, pointing it at her face.

"Arthur convinced me to give Rob a chance. Tell him I'll be calling him within the next few hours on his cell. Did he get his chip removed?"

"After we had our chat. He's clean now. Although I think it's more likely that they tracked one of your phones than the chip. By the way, I have Rob's, along with yours. We had one of our assets on the police force go and collect it at the doctor's. I presume you'll want it in the car with Rob?"

"Correct. That way anyone tracking us will think we're following Pu, which I think they probably expect at this point if the attack came from them. I would bet money they're tracking the chips. If my instinct's right, the other teams were dead before they ever left Bangkok."

"I still don't think they are, but this is your show."

"That's right. It is," she said and left it at that.

They crawled along, tuk tuks and motorcycles roaring past them like swarms of metal locusts, vendors darting in and out of the endless rows of cars with every imaginable type of merchandise. The streets had converted into a giant moving market, which she found somehow fitting. She watched for any surveillance for another ten minutes and, finally satisfied that they were clean, patted Edgar's leg.

"Pop the trunk. I'm going to walk."

"What? Right here?"

"Yes. Pop it now. I'll get in touch soon."

With that, she opened the door and stepped out into traffic, quickly rounding the fender and pulling the black duffle bag out of the trunk. She slammed the lid closed and, without looking back, darted between a delivery truck and a taxi, then veered around a motor scooter, and was gone.

CHAPTER 20

"Happy to see me?" Rob asked.

"Ecstatic."

He motioned to the duffle. "You have everything in that?"

"Yup. Let's roll."

It was two a.m., and they'd gotten word from the surveillance team that Pu had departed his club half an hour earlier, but instead of returning home, the car had headed north. Rob had picked her up near Nana and was haring up the expressway, trying to catch up. The signal had slowed near Don Muang airport, and they were closing the distance when Rob's phone rang. Edgar told them that the car signal had returned to downtown, but the watch signal was now headed north again.

"How long until you're at the airport?" Edgar asked.

"Five minutes," Rob replied.

"He's on highway one headed north. I instructed the surveillance car to stick with him until he either stops or you catch up to them. If you're five minutes from the airport, they're still around fifteen miles ahead of you, so I'd put my foot into it," Edgar advised. "They'll hand off the tracker once you're close to them. They're in a white Jetta with a frog decal on the back bumper." He gave them the license number.

"All right. I'm signing off. I'll call you once we're in sight."

The speedometer climbed until they were doing ninety miles per hour, racing along the nearly deserted freeway into the hinterlands. After they had passed the airport, the lights of Bangkok faded in the rearview mirror, replaced by the haphazard illumination of the smaller towns and convenience stops along the freeway.

An hour later, they saw the Jetta as they were approaching Ban It. Rob called Edgar, who instructed them to pull off at the next exit and do the swap.

The handoff took seconds, and soon they were back on the road, the signal blinking bright on the handheld tracker Edgar had arranged for them.

"Looks like he's about a mile and a half ahead," Jet said. "I'd get to within a mile of him then settle in for the duration."

"This is going to be a long night. The last team tailed him all the way to the Myanmar border before he crossed over and ditched the car. That's many, many hours of driving."

"Want to bet he's not driving himself?"

"I think that's a given."

"Why wouldn't he fly?" Jet asked.

"Good question. Best we could tell, he doesn't want any record of his coming and going. Even a private plane would create a record, these days. It isn't like it was ten years ago. Automation isn't the smuggler's friend."

"And yet he didn't have any problems getting Lawan to Bangkok, so it can't be that foolproof," she said.

"I didn't say it was perfect. I said it was harder than it used to be. Anyway, that's my guess. Or maybe he's afraid of planes. Who knows?"

"No point in speculating."

Rob nodded. "True. What do you think the chances are they try to hit us on the road?"

"Nil. Why would they, when as far as they know, we're coming right to them? Assuming it was this group that was after us, I'd wait until we were on their turf. Wouldn't you?"

"Sure, but what do you mean assuming it was them? Who else would it be?"

"I don't know. I just know something about all of this isn't adding up," she said, then sank into silence for a minute. "How rested are you?"

"I'm fine. If he's going to drive straight through, we should switch off in around six hours. I can easily make it till then," Rob assured her.

"Then you take the first shift." Jet adjusted her seat into a fully reclined position and closed her eyes.

When she awoke, they were at a fuel stop in Mueng Tak. The warm light of morning was beaming through the windshield. She looked at her watch.

"Eight thirty?" Jet asked.

"Yes. They stopped a quarter mile away. Probably grabbing something to eat."

"Sounds like a good idea."

"How about an energy bar and some fruit juice?"

"You read my mind. I'll take over driving now. How far are we from the border?"

"Eight hours. The roads will get more squirrely the farther north we go," Rob warned.

"So we'll get there before dusk?"

"We should."

"Sounds like someone is hoping to make a night crossing."

"How unexpected."

"What if he has an ATV waiting for him somewhere in the jungle? I think you need to call Edgar and arrange for something, just in case."

"Already ahead of you," Rob said. "We've got two horses waiting for us at Mae Sai. They can have them wherever we need them if we give them enough lead time."

"Sounds like you've thought of everything. That scares me," Jet muttered.

Rob smiled. "Occasionally we can do something right, as hard as that is for you to believe."

"Yeah. Like bury your dead."

She walked around to the driver's side and got behind the wheel, then reached over and unwrapped an energy bar while Rob paid for the gas and got their drinks.

The road became curvier as they proceeded north, and Rob had a hard time resting as they swung around the turns. The day ground on inexorably, and at three o'clock, they switched again.

At six, the red dot slowed four miles south of Mae Sai, the border town that was the major crossing point into Myanmar, and then came to a stop.

"What's he doing?"

"Looks like he's stopping."

"Why?"

"Probably plans to cross into Myanmar over in the hills. There are temples and dirt roads up there, and the patrols are lackadaisical, to say the least. What do you want to bet some army troops are paid to be anywhere but there when he crosses?"

"Makes sense. I guess we'll find out soon enough whether he's got an ATV or a horse, or if he's going to do it on foot."

"From what I know about this area, it will be a horse. The mountains here are nearly impassible in large sections. Think very low tech. But what puzzles me is that this isn't really very close to where we lost our teams. It was a lot further north, in the jungles surrounding the Mekong river. This is still jungle, but more hill tribe country."

"Are there any roads?"

"Not really."

"Maybe there's your answer. Not a bad place to disappear, I'd guess."

Pu's red dot stayed stationary until it got dark. Rob's cell had no reception, so he called Edgar using the satellite phone and gave him their position. Edgar called them back five minutes later and told them that he would have the horses there within an hour.

"Looks like it's going to be a long one," Rob observed.

Jet ignored him, thinking through their next step. She didn't like that he seemed chatty. That didn't bode well. A talkative assassin was one with dim survival prospects. He apparently took the hint, got out of the car and busied himself with his gear, preparing for the night to come.

An old farm truck arrived, towing an ancient trailer with a makeshift railing that had two medium-sized horses, already saddled, tethered to it. Rob handled the discussion with the tiny man, who jumped from behind the wheel to get the horses unloaded. Jet continued watching the glowing dot, two miles north of them. Pu was waiting for nightfall. She handed Rob the baggie containing the two GPS chips and murmured terse instructions, which he repeated to the old man in Thai. The man nodded and put the chips in his shirt pocket before climbing back into the truck and pulling away. He would toss them into the backs of two different trucks as he drove back through town, so anyone tracking them would think they had separated and were looking for Pu, having lost his trail. Anyone watching would be expecting visual surveillance, not a tracking device in Pu's watch. All the better to lead them on a goose chase, at least for a little while.

Fog rolled over the mountains as the sun sank into the hills, and before long they were enshrouded in an eerie netherworld, blanketed in white, unable to see more than fifty yards. At eight o'clock, the dot on their tracking device began moving.

Jet leapt to her feet. "We're on. He's mobile."

"Let's watch his speed. That will tell us everything we need to know," Rob suggested.

After a few minutes studying the screen, she looked up at him.

"He's walking."

"Then that's what we do."

"Yes, but we're bringing the horses. He might have one waiting across the border. We don't know how far he's traveling, so we should expect that he'll have a guide on the Myanmar side."

Jet moved to the trunk and pulled her gear out. Rob pointed at a long, flat, black nylon case.

"Is that what I think it is?"

"Depends on what you think it is."

"You know how to use it?"

"Do I look like I'm in the mood to experiment?"

She tossed him a smaller case. "This is for you. Idiot proof."

He opened it and peeked inside. "Very nice. Thanks."

They hastily packed their kits into the saddlebags and mounted up, then made for the northern summit of the mountain, taking care to have their night vision goggles ready. The thickening fog provided a cloak of muffled silence. After a mile of easing along a trail, Jet dismounted.

"What?"

"Shhh. I want to walk them from here on out. We're only about a mile behind him. I don't want to get any closer. One stray whinny or snort will give us away."

"Okay," Rob whispered, aware that voices would carry once all the background noise of civilization faded. He dropped to the ground and reached into his bag for the goggles, but Jet shook her head.

"Battery life is going to be an issue. Only one of us at a time with the night vision gear. I'll go first."

"We have several spare batteries."

She spun to face him. "Rob. Don't question me, or imagine that you have a better idea. You're here to support me, against my will. Now, please, do as I say without a hint of anything but complete approval, or you're out, right here, and won't be going any further. Do you understand?"

He balked, then nodded. "Yes, ma'am."

"That's better."

She flipped her goggles into place and switched them on, and the coalescing gloom suddenly illuminated in neon green. The fog still limited their visibility, but at least she could make out the trail.

"Follow me," she said, taking her horse by the bridle and leading it forward into the darkness.

They would be over the first crest within half an hour at their current speed: in Myanmar, traveling through an area of the country where heroin traffickers and slavers prowled the jungles, and death was as sudden and common as the fog that enveloped them.

CHAPTER 21

Three hours into their surrealistic trek, Pu's red dot began moving faster.

"Looks like he's got transportation of some sort," Jet whispered.

"I don't hear any motors, so you were right. Has to be a horse. How far ahead of us is he now?"

"About a mile and a half. But that's fine. I don't want to get right up on him. He can't keep this pace up forever, so my guess is that he'll be wherever he's headed by morning. At his new rate of speed, that would take us...thirty-five to forty miles northwest. In the middle of nowhere."

A cloudburst interrupted their discussion, soaking them both and turning the trail into a muddy slog before it stopped raining as abruptly as it had started. Shortly afterwards, the mosquitoes came out. After spraying herself down with repellant, Jet tossed the plastic bottle to Rob.

"You'll want to douse yourself."

"I know. Nasty stuff roaming around here."

They waited until Pu was two miles ahead of them, then mounted up, urging the horses to a trot, which was all they could safely manage in the misty murk. An hour later, they were descending the summit, well inside Myanmar. There wasn't a sign of another human, only the sound of creatures going about their nocturnal rounds.

The red dot began to venture deeper into the treacherous hill country, the fog thickening as they proceeded. Another shower of warm rain arrived with a clap of thunder, but this time the downpour didn't stop, adding to the discomfort of the trek.

The first rays of dawn were cutting through the clouds when the dot stopped moving. Jet held up a hand and pulled her horse up short, then dropped out of the saddle, still holding the tracking device. She moved to Rob and whispered to him.

"Bingo. He's stopped. I think we're there. This must be one of Hawker's camps."

"I'll call it in to Edgar. He'll want to know the location."

She glared at him. "You'll do no such thing. Everything about this has been sketchy since the start. I don't want anyone knowing where we are or what progress we've made until we've secured the target and successfully concluded the mission. Are we clear on that?"

"I have my orders."

"Your first order is not to argue or question mine. So help me, if you so much as look crosswise at me or do anything I haven't given permission for, you'll be my first kill out here. Look at me. Do I look like I'm joking? Do not under any circumstances call Edgar or anyone else. Give me the phone. Now."

Rob dismounted and retrieved the phone, then handed it to her. "I guess we've made it this far and we're still alive. I'll follow your lead. Seems like that's better than the last two teams did."

"Exactly. Something stinks in all of this, but I don't know where. If the target has a mole in CIA headquarters, we have no idea what information is being relayed to him. I'm taking no chances."

He looked up at the drizzling sky. "It would be nice if it stopped raining. This is pretty miserable."

"It could work to our advantage. The sound will mask any noise we make, within reason. Let's get to within a mile of Pu and stake out a camp, and then I want to do some reconnaissance – see what we're up against. If they have patrols, I doubt very much they'll be straying beyond that range. There's no point if they're not looking for a specific target or expecting any unusual risk." She glanced at him. "We'll walk the horses from here."

"At least we can see now. That's a plus."

"Yes and no. We can also be seen."

They traversed a creek and came to a cliff face a hundred yards off the trail with several small caves at its base, carved out by the rain-swollen stream cascading down the mountain. After finding a relatively shallow area, they crossed, submerging to their waists, the current strong and constant.

The caverns were little more than indentations in the rock face, but would serve to shelter them from the worst of the rain, and the sun, should it ever break through. After ensuring the horses drank their fill, they set up camp, and quickly ate and washed down some bottled water. Jet unpacked her saddlebags, setting her weapons carefully to one side, and Rob did the same. Glancing at the screen of the tracker, she zoomed out and superimposed a satellite photo of the area over it. All she could see was a sea of green. That would be little or no help.

"I'm going to poke around. Stay here. Don't leave the camp," she ordered, then wiped black streaks on her face and neck, and tossed him the tube. "This will cut any reflection."

"What do I do in the meantime, seeing as you're excluding me from all the action?"

She gestured with her head at the black case she had given him earlier. "Practice with that. You'll want to be good with it by the time I get back."

He grunted noncommittally.

Jet sheathed her combat knife, slid two throwing knives into her web belt, checked her Beretta to ensure the silencer was screwed tightly in place, and then slid the strap of the P90 over her shoulder.

"Let's hope I don't need to use any of this," she said and then disappeared into the brush in the direction of the trail that led straight to where Pu's transmitter was signaling from.

It took forty-five minutes to get to the camp's perimeter, the intermittent rain making the path slippery as it wound through the mountains. She halted at an area overlooking a ragged clearing next to a small stream and nestled herself into a hollow spot between two large plants and peered through her binoculars at the rustic dwellings below.

❧❦

Six hours later, Jet reappeared soundlessly near the cave.

"What did you find?" Rob asked.

"Pu's there. So's the target. He's unmistakable, although he's got a beard now. The bad news is, I counted twenty armed men. They look like hill tribesmen. Shan."

"What kind of arms?"

"Kalashnikovs. AK-47s."

"That figures. Probably made in China. Knockoffs, but still deadly. Plentifully available around here, and a big favorite with the hill people as well as the heroin traffickers."

"They looked like they know how to use them. Those are the same weapons carried by the gunmen who were after us in Bangkok."

"Could mean something, or not. There are so many of those floating around, they're practically the national gun of the Golden Triangle. A lot of them make their way to Thailand, too. Although the ones that are sold legally there are .22 caliber."

"The ones the gunmen had were the standard 7.62mm."

"Not surprising they have illegal weapons," Rob observed, "given that they murdered the doctor with them and then tried to kill us. So, what else do you have?"

"I took some photos. Here, take a look. There are five buildings, huts, really. A central fire pit, what looks like a primitive cooking area, and a latrine. I saw a few solar panels by one of the huts, so I'm guessing that's the target – Hawker's. The rest are probably the guards'."

Rob peered at the tiny camera's screen and nodded.

Jet knelt down, picked up a branch, and brushed away some dead leaves before sketching a rough diagram in the muddy dirt. The rain had lightened up to a steady drizzle, punctuated by occasional half-hour dry spells; they were in one of the lulls between showers. She had quickly become accustomed to the perpetual moisture, and now didn't even register that she was soaked through.

"There's a stream here. The target's hut is here. These are the others. Firepit here."

Rob studied the outline, then crouched beside her. "How far across would you say it is? How many yards from this point to the stream?" He tapped a finger on one of the squares she'd drawn.

"No more than fifty."

He stood and wiped his forehead. "So what's next?"

"We'll wait until nightfall. It looked to me like Pu was planning on staying at least overnight. His guide has tied the horses up and taken the saddles off."

"Wonder why he comes out here every few weeks?"

"I have no idea. But there were no children or females, so it's not to get slaves." She checked the time. "We have about six hours before it gets dark. Let's make the most of it. Rest for five hours, then we'll get into position while we can still see."

"I presume you have some ideas about how to take on twenty heavily armed men?"

"I thought you'd never ask."

CHAPTER 22

"Shit. He's moving," Jet muttered, forcing herself to stand. The rain was still pelting them whenever a gust blew a sheet into the meager shelter of the cave, and it was coming down in torrents, limiting visibility and making for a miserable afternoon. She stared at the blip on her screen, now crawling steadily away from their position. They had been planning to get under way in another hour, but Pu heading out changed everything.

"We have to go after him. What if he's with the target?" Rob whispered, frustration evident in his tone.

"Looks like they're moving east now."

"On horseback?"

"Hard to tell. But I think we have to assume so. Let's get going. Mount up."

They hurriedly repacked their saddlebags, Jet processing furiously. This was the last thing she wanted – a moving target, no time to formulate a plan, and nightfall rapidly approaching. If the stakes had been anything besides her daughter, she would have aborted the operation at this point and simply watched and waited for a good opportunity. Unfortunately, she didn't have that luxury, so instead she brushed water from her horse's face and patted his neck. "Come on, boy. Time to put you to work again."

She swung herself into the saddle and waited for Rob, whose horse was less cooperative. After another minute of struggling with the reluctant beast, he was ready. Jet pulled the rein to the right and nudged her horse into motion, and soon they were trotting down the path, checking the tracking screen every few minutes.

"We need to pick up the pace. They're heading at a right angle from the camp. Let's hope that we can find a route that parallels their path, or we're screwed," she said, eyeing the vegetation for any promising signs.

Ten minutes later, they came across a game trail that led off in the rough direction of their quarry. Jet ducked and urged her steed forward. Branches scratched at them as they fought their way through the brush, and then the undergrowth became sparser, and they could move more easily. A brook burbled just ahead of them, and they saw another trail paralleling it. Jet was operating purely on instinct now, trying to close the distance so they could engage. It hadn't looked like the camp was getting ready to move, so this was probably only a portion of the gunmen accompanying Pu, and possibly, the target. That was the only good news in all of this.

"How far now?" Rob whispered, pulling alongside her as the horses instinctively followed the creek.

"Less than half a mile."

"Then what?"

"If Hawker's with Pu, then obviously we take him alive. The rest of them I don't care about."

"So shoot first and ask questions later?"

"But spare Hawker. He's the priority."

A bird took flight from a tree ahead of them, flapping its wings noisily. Jet stopped and held up a hand, head cocked to the side, listening. She craned her neck, trying to see ahead of them, but the rain made it almost impossible. After checking the screen again, she turned to face Rob.

"Dismount," she hissed, already in motion.

"Why?" Rob whispered, dropping to the ground.

"Something's wrong. I don't like this."

"What?"

"I don't know." She clutched the P90 in her right hand as she held the reins with her left. "Follow me."

They inched forward through the tangle of vegetation, Jet's senses tingling, her horse's hooves squishing in the mud behind her. The stream veered to the left, and they crept along it, the water bubbling as it passed over the smooth round rocks beneath.

The trees parted, and the outline of a building shrouded in mist loomed in the near distance, its roof curved at the corners in a highly stylized fashion. They could see that the structure was an old Buddhist temple, now fallen on hard times and in a state of neglect. The disrepair became obvious as they approached it; what must have been, at one time, a remote outpost for the devout long abandoned to the elements, the faithful having moved on to less ethereal pursuits.

Rob's horse snorted, a percussive sound that broke the eerie silence. Jet's gelding pulled against the reins, stopping her, and then gunfire shattered the dusk.

Bullets tore into the frenzied animal, narrowly missing her. She loosed the reins and returned fire at the surrounding trees. The horse stumbled a few paces before going down hard, mortally wounded. Jet sprinted to the temple, firing as she ran. She heard Rob's distinctive M4 belching burst after burst as she threw herself through the temple doorway, rolling as slugs pounded into the floor next to her.

Rob's form lunged into the safety of the temple just as a round tore through his upper left shoulder, eliciting a grunt, but he still clenched the rifle in his right hand. He spun and fired at the muzzle flashes of the un-silenced Kalashnikovs and was rewarded by several cries of wounded men.

Jet emptied her magazine in a sweeping arc at the attackers and then jettisoned it, slapping a new one home and firing again.

"I'm hit," Rob hissed through clenched teeth. "I could use some help with a new magazine."

"How bad is it?" she asked, not taking her eyes off the scene outside, then taking careful aim and squeezing off another burst. She heard a crash in the bushes. A body falling.

"I'm still here. Can you change me out?" he asked, thumbing the magazine release.

She edged towards him and pulled one of the three remaining magazines from his cargo pants pocket and slipped it into his rifle with a snick, then returned her attention to the attackers.

"How many do you make?" she whispered.

"My guess? No more than ten. Problem is they're on both sides. *Were* on both sides. I think we may have gotten at least four of them, so the odds are looking better. Shit. I wish we had a field first aid kit in here. I'm losing blood."

"We have one in my saddlebag. Let's just mop these clowns up, and I'll get you taken care of." Jet shot at an area where the vegetation was moving as a gunman tried to edge closer. Her volley hit him, and he reflexively gripped the trigger on his rifle as he fell, sending rounds whizzing overhead into the trees.

A shower of wood shards fell into the temple from where slugs pounded the window opening she'd just vacated, the shots revealing another shooter sixty yards away. Rob let loose two bursts in the attacker's direction and heard a cry.

"If they're smart, they'll try to circle around and get us from behind. You got this side?" she asked, squinting outside in the rapidly dwindling light.

"Sure. Pull one more magazine out and put it by my side. I can manage it one-handed once it's out."

She slid over and did as he asked, then pulled his pistol free of his belt holster. "If you run low on ammo, let them get into range and give them a taste of this."

He nodded and tried a grin, then coughed, blood streaming down his arm. "Go get 'em," he said, squeezing off another few rounds with the M4.

Jet crawled to the back of the temple and peered through the slits in the walls, patiently waiting for a tell from the jungle beyond. She didn't have to wait long. A rustling of bodies moving through the brush drew six more rounds from her weapon, and then more inbound fire assailed her from a dozen yards farther away. She emptied the rest of her magazine at the area and then drew her pistol. The remainder of her P90 magazines were in the saddlebags. But with only two or three gunmen left, it wouldn't matter.

Rob's assault rifle chattered as he sighted another hostile, and then there was a pause, the attackers' guns having fallen silent.

"What do you think?" Rob called to her in a stage whisper.

"Shhh."

It was hard to make out anything over the hissing of the rain, but she sensed that there was more danger lurking in the brush. She crawled over to where a piece of broken pottery lay near a corner of the room and picked it up, then moved to the far window and tossed it into the encroaching jungle.

A hail of bullets found it two seconds later, from off to the left. She sighted carefully down her Beretta and squeezed off three shots, spacing them a foot apart to allow for some decay over the sixty yards of distance. The Beretta's maximum effective range was fifty yards, but she'd worked wonders with one at up to eighty. Not stellar, but still effective enough to be deadly.

"You see anything on your side?" she whispered to Rob.

"Negative."

"Want to switch weapons for a few minutes? I want to try to get up onto the roof."

"Sure. I feel like I'm outgunning the poor slobs at this point with an M4 against some Chinese pop guns, anyway."

She sidled next to him and ejected the magazine from the M4, replacing Rob's half-full one with the last full one.

"There can't be too many left," she reasoned. "They seem to have lost their stomach for a fight."

"Let's hope so. Go do your worst," Rob said, then returned to scrutinizing the periphery. "It'll be dark within another fifteen minutes. At that point, if we can reach the saddlebags, we'll have night vision, and then we can go rabbit hunting."

"Good point. But by then they'll be dead."

"Big talker."

She eyed the area of the roof near the far wall; a section of it had caved in long ago, bird droppings and decay surrounded the base, with rainwater streaming in from above. If the lateral supports on the walls were still good, she might be able to make it…

Jet slung the M4 strap over her shoulder and started climbing, using the same techniques she did when rock climbing. Her fingers reached and found a hold, then she pulled herself higher, the other hand and her feet probing for a new cranny.

She poked her head above the roof and then pulled herself up and out, praying that the structure wouldn't collapse beneath her. Tree branches weaved across most of the gap, and she used their cover to camouflage her position.

The M4's flash suppressor and silencer were good, but not magic, and the little rifle still made considerable noise, so once she started shooting, she could expect to draw fire to her position. She looked at the entangled branches, calculating whether they appeared to be able to hold her weight, and thought that they would.

Rob was right. It would be dark in no time. She could use that to her advantage.

Sounds of motion caught her attention from the game trail at the farthest reach of the temple's grounds, and she squinted, barely able to make out two men trotting away, rifles held to their chests like newborn babies.

She held her breath, waiting for signs of any more gunmen, but that was it.

Reaching out, she gripped the branches and pulled herself towards the tree's trunk, the roof dropping away beneath her in jumbled fragments as it disintegrated. She found herself suspended in mid-air, the branches now her sole support in the gloom, and she steadily inched to the trunk before lowering her feet to the next tier of branches.

The two surviving men's eyes were adjusting to the darkness when the first groaned and stumbled forward, tumbling into his companion before hitting the ground, a knife handle jutting from between his shoulder blades. His partner froze and then spun, to be confronted by a black-faced ghost pointing a wicked-looking barrel at him from twenty feet away.

Jet could see the second of hesitation in his eyes before he brought his weapon up, and had already pulled the trigger and loosed three rounds by the time the impulse to shoot her had travelled from his brain to his hands. His chest exploded, and he dropped his rifle as he flew backwards. She was already lowering herself to one knee, anticipating further attacks, but the night was still.

She crawled to the first dead man and retrieved her throwing knife, wiping it clean on his filthy shirt before rolling him out of the way and scooping up his AK-47. She moved to the other man and quickly searched him and found another full magazine, which she slid into her back pocket before edging back into the brush.

A gunshot echoed through the trees, and she pirouetted to face the temple just in time to see another tribesman collapse twenty yards from the front entrance.

She waited, listening, but the jungle had fallen silent except for the soft sibilance of rainfall.

৵৽৹

"Do you think we got them all?" Rob's voice was weak and cracked at the end of the question.

"I'm pretty sure of it," she replied, swabbing Rob's wound before applying the pressure dressing. There was a lot of blood pooled around him. An awful lot of blood, and his shirt was soaked. She bound the dressing in place with gauze, then stood, inspecting him.

"You going to make it?"

He nodded, but his normally tanned skin looked peaked.

"We're going to have to get you out of here. Can you walk?"

"Sure. At least for a while. But I'm not going to be much help with Pu or the target."

"That's okay. You were just slowing me down, anyway. Now I can get something done."

"Ten to one is hardly a fair fight."

"I'll say. Poor bastards."

"You really think you can take them?"

She smiled, the black smeared across her face making her profile appear ghoulish in the darkening temple. He could hardly make her out, but she was wearing her night vision goggles to attend to him, so she could see everything. Which is why she thought his chances of living another twenty-four hours were slim, based on the amount of blood on the temple floor.

"I can let you in on a little secret, since we're such good friends now. I've done far more difficult jobs with way tougher adversaries than a bunch of natives with pea shooters. This will be a cakewalk. I just hope that Hawker's still there. Even ten miles away, they might have heard the gunshots."

"The rain would muffle a lot of it. That's a fair distance."

"Yeah, but luck hasn't exactly been on our side today, has it?"

She reached out a hand and helped him up, then supported him with her shoulder as they limped to the temple door.

"What happened to the tracking chip?" Rob asked.

"It shows as being here. So one of the gunmen had it. This was a setup. They were on to us."

"Which points to someone in the agency helping Hawker."

"Yes. But that's not my problem. I'm sure Edgar can sort it out. Right now I need to concentrate on getting across the finish line."

Shots thudded into Rob's torso as they negotiated the four stairs from the temple entrance. Jet dropped to the ground, clawing her Beretta free of its holster as his body absorbed round after round. She could see the shooter with her night vision goggles, but sighting the pistol with them on was a more difficult proposition. She erred on the side of caution and fired six shots, four of which missed their mark.

The final two punched into the gunman's chest, and he spun giddily in a spray of crimson before slumping into a heap. Jet rolled away from Rob and reached over to check for a pulse. Nothing. She closed his sightless eyes with a steady hand and then bolted up, racing for her horse's inert form, where she'd left the P90 when she'd gotten the first aid kit.

When she reached the dead animal, she emptied out the saddlebag, then slapped a new magazine into the weapon, slid the other into the pocket of her cargo pants, and shouldered her backpack and the rectangular nylon case before running into the night, her boots thumping against the wet clay as the rain slanted into her.

CHAPTER 23

A cruel wind blew sheets of rain across the clearing, lashing the treetops with a sullen fury. The brooding clouds denied the twilight glow of the hunter's moon to the huddle of guards, on alert after their compatriots failed to check in or return from their ambush at the abandoned temple high on the distant mountain.

"Take two men and do a patrol. Come on. I have a bad feeling about this," Thet, the leader of the tribesmen, ordered the guard sitting by the struggling flames of the fire, which had a piece of sheet metal suspended over it to deflect the rain.

"Come on. It's pouring. Don't make me go out in this," the younger man whined, clutching a tarp over his head in an effort to stay dry, as he eyed the older man with cautious fear mixed with annoyance.

"It's not a request. Do it. Now. Take Maung and Htet and check the perimeter." Thet's voice had an edge. He wasn't used to having his instructions questioned.

"Fine. I'll go get them. But everything's probably okay. What do you want to bet that their radio got soaked in this, and that's why they didn't check in? It's happened before…"

"Thanks for the theories. I'll have to remember that when I'm getting ready to retire to Bangkok with a harem of bar girls. You're a deep thinker, wasted on this kind of duty." Thet cuffed him gruffly. "Now get your ass on patrol. I don't want to say it again."

The young man stood and tried to take the tarp, but Thet shook his head. "Grab slickers. That's why the boss brought them for us."

The guards had yet to become accustomed to some of the technological advances that the crazy *farang* had introduced into their simple lives. Rain gear, flashlights, solar panels, all unimaginable luxuries that had been foreign to them until he'd arrived and assembled a small private army. Every man had grown up in the surrounding hill villages and had earned their livings in the harsh environment, either farming or working for the drug syndicates that effectively ruled the region.

They had all learned to field strip a Kalashnikov before they'd hit puberty, and had killed before their voices had changed. It was a brutal life in Myanmar: a poor country with a totalitarian military dictatorship that treated its population like subjects, and in which meager hierarchy the Shan hill tribes comprised the bottom rung – lower than human. There were no schools, no hospitals, no power plants or telephone lines. Only the hills and whatever they could coax from the ground – usually opium or food crops.

Before the white devil had arrived, Thet had made thirty dollars a month working as protection for a drug trafficking group. Now he made a hundred and fifty. The prospect of a wild increase in fortune made it easy to recruit the most aggressive and deadly of his brethren, who had literally fought over the right to work the security detail for a hundred dollars a month. He'd limited the group to twenty hardened fellow Shan fighters, and whenever they lost one to disease or a skirmish with one of the roaming groups of traffickers, he had ten begging to take the fallen man's place.

The seven men he had sent to Bangkok to help the sex slaver with his problem had been his best, and he would miss them. Pu had brought news of their passing along with a warning to expect another attack – the third in the last month and a half. Thet had lost a total of twelve fighters since he had started working for the *farang*, but didn't question it. Life was uncertain at the best of times, and a big payday carried with it certain risks. The average male lived sixty-seven years in Myanmar, but in the Shan region it dropped to fifty-five, and that didn't take into account the far lower expectancy of those working for the drug runners. But as a farmer, he might make fifteen dollars a month, twenty if he was lucky, and the syndicates paid thirty for a much easier day's work. When he'd been offered the princely sum by the round eye, he'd thought the man insane, but he had come to appreciate that he was not only shrewd, but also skilled in the ways of the world.

Thet watched as the bedraggled patrol trudged to the edge of the clearing and entered the jungle, a flashlight illuminating their way. This was only one of the white man's camps, and they moved every two weeks, melting into the jungle only to reappear elsewhere the next day. Laos, Myanmar, Cambodia…the geography made no difference to him. It was all jungle and hills. But he was becoming a rich man as the *farang*'s security chief, so he was fiercely loyal to him, lest his meal ticket disappear, forcing him to go back to risking his life every day with a drug network, or have to be a protection worker for the slavers that routinely bought the more attractive children from the impoverished locals.

Whatever his benefactor had done to require this level of protection didn't matter to Thet, nor to his men. Nobody knew, although there were constant rumors and speculation – that he had murdered his family, or was running from a rival criminal syndicate, or had deserted from some army and was a wanted man. Whatever the case, he was Pu's friend, and Pu had been doing business in the region forever. That was good enough for Thet.

He hugged his rifle closer as he eyed the rain distrustfully.

There was evil afoot in the night. He could feel it.

⧉

The men swept the jungle in front of them with their weapons, the bravado they had displayed back in the camp now faded into a dull acceptance of getting soaked while their peers slept. But they weren't paid to be comfortable. They collected their money to keep the white man safe, and that is what they would do, even in the middle of a torrential downpour. The rain pelted their unfamiliar rain gear with wet *thwacks* as they edged along the trail that ran in a rough oval around the clearing.

"Ack—"

The man bringing up the rear pitched forward face-first into the mud, a bloody shaft protruding from his chest. By the time the other two had registered that he hadn't tripped, the guard in front of him had been similarly impaled and dropped his rifle, clawing at the razor-sharp point that had appeared as if by magic from his sternum. The third man was raising his rifle defensively when an arrow skewered him through his left eye, and he collapsed without getting a single shot off, having never seen his killer or heard anything besides the briefest of whistling as the arrow sliced the air on its trajectory to his brain.

Jet stepped cautiously towards the corpses, another arrow nocked, and kicked the flashlight into the underbrush before melting back into the brush, her night vision goggles and black face paint lending her the appearance of a nightmare demon with attitude.

Three down. That left seven or so to go.

She had considered letting the rest of the gunmen come to her and picking them off in the jungle, but didn't want to alert the target that he was under attack. If he disappeared, she might never find him again. This was her only chance, so she had decided to bring the battle into the camp before the remainder of his entourage knew what hit them.

She adjusted the black leather quiver, still full of arrows, so that it wouldn't impair her ability to get the P90 into play and then turned towards the camp, the sleeping men's fates all but sealed.

ॐ

Thet was restless. The men had been gone for too long. The buzz of anxiety that roiled in his gut was growing, and his survival instinct was warning him to wake the men.

He was preparing to rise and walk to the first hut when a blinding shriek of pain shot through his right lung, and he found himself gasping for breath as he fumbled with his rifle. A second silver shaft caught a stray bit of light from the flickering fire before slicing through his throat. Thet keeled backwards off the rock he was seated on, dead before he hit the ground.

Jet crept towards the dark buildings, their outlines glowing in her goggles, and then froze when she heard the tarp draped across one of the doorways crackle and an arm emerged. She pulled the bowstring back to her ear and waited for the man to show himself, and watched as a guard exited, scratching himself, and then darted through the rain for the latrine.

The arrow caught him mid-stride ten feet from the building, and he gurgled as he fell, then moaned before laying still. She hoped that nobody had heard him, but then saw the tarp pull back again, and another figure exited, holding a rifle.

In a fluid motion she pulled another arrow from the quiver, nocked it, and sent it whistling towards his head. The arrow caught him in the jaw and stabbed through his mouth, protruding through the back of his head and imbedding itself in the wooden wall behind him. He screamed, a jarring, raw sound, prompting Jet to launch another shaft at him, this one piercing his heart.

But the damage had been done. The scream had alerted the other fighters. After a brief pause, two more came barreling through the door, and the tarp on the building next to it flew aside, and a rifle barrel poked out. Instantly weighing her options, she retreated, gliding into the shadows at the jungle's edge. The smudge of the fire provided dim illumination, but it was a scant flicker within the heart of the downpour and not enough to give her away.

Jet watched as four remaining guards moved out of the buildings in a huddle that bristled with gun barrels. She nocked another arrow. They were really making it almost too easy.

By the time any of the men could react, two were dead or dying. The remaining two fired blindly in a panic, desperately sweeping the jungle around them with their weapons, but Jet was already on the move and was sliding behind their huts even as they emptied their guns in vain.

The smaller of the pair realized his mistake as his weapon clicked empty – in their haste to take on their attackers they hadn't thought to bring spare magazines.

When an arrow severed his spinal cord, he tumbled into the second man, whose life, in turn, was extinguished by the shaft's companion two seconds later.

A figure tore out of the doorway of one of the remaining buildings, running as hard as he could for the stream. Jet followed his progress, with the softness of the arrow's flight next to her cheek, and then, adjusting for his speed and the distance, released the bowstring with a twang.

She watched as the man dropped, having almost made it to the jungle's edge.

Jet waited, ears alert for any threats, but heard nothing. She could make out the outlines of the buildings as clear as day through the goggles and saw no one.

Then the tarp of a hut drew open, and Hawker stepped out, hands in the air.

"I'm unarmed," he called in English, and then in Thai.

She studied him, waiting for any trick.

He took another step forward, rain streaming down his face. "I repeat. I'm unarmed."

Jet scanned the surrounding structures warily but saw nothing. With a fluid motion, she dropped the bow and shrugged the quiver off, placing it and the P90 on the ground beside her, then un-holstered the silenced Beretta and moved to the first building, ignoring Hawker for the moment. She peered through the back window and confirmed that it was empty, then repeated the process on the next two.

"Move towards the fire," she called and saw the surprise play across his face upon hearing her voice. It never ceased to amaze her how many men believed that their violent world was only inhabited by males.

He took cautious, plodding steps, his bare feet squishing on the muddy ground, before stopping ten feet from the subdued flames.

Hawker studied Thet's corpse with interest. "Arrows? You used arrows?"

Jet could have sworn she saw the beginnings of a smile. Just a trace, fleeting, then gone.

She moved towards him, gun trained on his head, and watched as he registered her on the periphery of his vision.

"Keep your hands above your head."

"I will."

She reached to the small of her back and withdrew a pair of black anodized handcuffs, then tossed them at his feet, her pistol unwavering.

"Put those on."

"Hands in front or behind?"

"Do you think I'm an idiot? Behind. Turn so I can see you putting them on. Don't try anything or I'll blow a kneecap off, and then it's going to be really painful for you to ride out of here."

"Is that what you're thinking we'll do? Ride out of here? That'll be kind of hard with no horses, won't it?"

"The cuffs," she said.

"Okay. Here we go."

"Nice and slow."

"The only way I know." He lowered his arms, knelt to scoop up the cuffs, and stood, holding them out so she could see them.

"Night vision. Of course. Should have known," he muttered to himself, then slid a cuff open and secured it around his wrist.

"Now the other one."

"I hope I get points for courtesy and cooperation." He locked the cuff in place, then waggled his fingers. "There. I'm no longer a menace to society."

She inched closer to him. "Now turn around."

He complied, peering through the gloom at her. "Holy shit. Is it just you? You did all this?"

"How many did you think it would take?"

He shook his head. "Unbelievable. You want a job?"

"Very funny. Now we're going to head over to the horses. Think you can manage that?"

"Sure. But why? Am I going to give them a eulogy?"

She looked past him to the creek. Both animals were down. The wild shots from the two frantic guards had hit them.

"Damn. Looks like we're walking out, then."

His eyes moved, and he looked over her shoulder, past her. She didn't fall for it.

"Don't bother. That's the oldest trick in the world," she said, her gun pointing steadily at him.

"I think you should reconsider your perspective of old dogs and their tricks," he said, and this time he did smile.

"Not a chance. Now before we go any further, where are the diamonds?"

"You think I'd have them in a hut in the middle of nowhere?"

"Where are they?"

"Well, two of them are right behind you," he said.

"I told you. Stop screwing around, wasting my time. It won't work."

"Oh, I think this time it will. Don't you, Matt?" Lap Pu's voice purred softly from behind her.

CHAPTER 24

"Drop the gun. Now," Pu ordered.

Jet did as he instructed.

"Now turn around."

Pu was holding a small pistol – it looked like a Walther PPK.

"Take the night vision off."

She slowly reached up, flipped the goggles out of her field of vision, then lifted them off her head.

Pu's eyes widened. "Well, well. If it isn't a pretty face from my past."

"What the hell's going on here, Pu?" Matt demanded.

His eyes swiveled to Matt. "I honestly have no idea."

"Where are the diamonds?" Jet repeated, her tone even.

"Why, my dear, around his neck, of course," Pu said. She looked over her shoulder to where Matt stood and saw a small leather pouch dangling from a leather lash circling his neck. "At least some of them are. Isn't that right, Matt?"

"Pu, cut the shit. Get the key from her and un-cuff me. You. Whatever your name is. Give me the key," Matt said.

"Ah, not so fast," Pu warned.

"Pu. What the hell are you doing?" Matt asked, his voice somewhat diminished.

"Thinking. I was wondering how much I see helping you sell them, versus what's around your neck. That's all." Pu's English seemed to improve markedly as his greedy eyes considered the predicament.

"You're kidding me, right? After all we've been through? You would screw me over this?"

"No hard feelings. What you got in there, anyway? Twenty of them? Fifty?" Pu asked.

"None of your business."

"Oh, I think so, my friend. Very much so. You answer now."

A blinding flash of lightning seared across the sky, and the trees shivered from the boom of thunder. Pu flinched involuntarily, and for a brief second, took his eyes off Jet.

That was all she needed.

The throwing knife flew at him in a blur, stabbing through his esophagus with a wet *thwack*. His pupils dilated as he gasped a protest, groped for the knife handle, and pulled it free. Blood spurted from the gash as he dropped the gun. Jet leveled a roundhouse kick and knocked him to the ground, his palsied fingers still clutching the knife, staring at it in fascinated awe, holding his free hand to his neck in an effort to stop the life from streaming out of him.

"That's for all the children you've ruined," she hissed, then kicked him in the groin. "And that's for me, you piece of shit."

He rolled into a fetal position and convulsed, once, twice, and then shuddered and lay still.

She leaned over, picked up her Beretta, and trained it on Matt again.

"I'm going to ask one more time, nicely, and then I'll start shooting pieces off you. Where are the diamonds?"

He hesitated. "I have some in the bag around my neck. Five million worth. The rest are in a safe place."

"Not good enough. Where are they?"

"In a bank vault in Bangkok."

She nodded. "Then it sounds like we're going to Bangkok. Walking, for the most part. Hope you're in better shape than you look."

Jet stepped closer to him and pulled the leather thong from around his neck, weighing the heft of the diamonds in the pouch before sliding it over her own head. Matt watched her with a stony countenance, his five-day growth of beard dripping beads of water.

"Then it's really just you? Nobody else?"

"I'd say that was enough, wouldn't you?" She picked up the night vision goggles and put them on again, then walked over to the P90 and retrieved it, pausing briefly before also grabbing the bow and arrows. She slid them over her shoulders and adjusted her backpack and then turned to face him.

"Come on. Let's get going."

"You realize that trying to walk out of here in the dead of night in a rainstorm is going to be pretty close to impossible, right? These hills are teeming with drug smugglers who would kill you just as soon as look at you. I didn't have all this protection for no reason."

"Did you a lot of good, didn't it? Come on. Move it."

He sighed. "You want me in front or in back? I can't see anything, so it might be better if I followed you."

"That works for me. But a word of advice. I just killed twenty of your men and didn't break a sweat. If you try anything, and I do mean anything, I'll cut your ears off and then work my way south. Nothing that will kill you or keep you from walking, but you'll wish you were dead. Is that clear?"

"I understand. I try anything, you filet me."

"Good. I'd say there's the basis of a relationship here."

Without another word, she set off into the jungle, Matt trailing her by three yards.

As they moved up the mountain trail, the rain slowed to a drizzle and then eventually stopped altogether. Soon they hit a rhythm, his boots trudging behind her, occasionally stumbling over a root or a rock. She figured that they could make it twelve to fifteen miles by dawn if they kept up a decent pace, although parts of the terrain would slow them, and they needed to be on guard for unfriendlies sharing the jungle paths.

Matt tried engaging her several times, but she shushed him, preferring to keep her ears tuned for threats rather than idle banter. She hadn't captured him because she wanted a new friend. He was a dead man, and as soon as she had all the diamonds, she'd formalize it with a bullet.

When the first light peeped through the tree tops, they stopped to rest near a creek. She performed a brief reconnaissance of the surrounding area to ensure they were alone, then sat down cross-legged by the water and pulled two breakfast bars from her backpack.

"You hungry?" she asked, after wolfing hers down.

"And thirsty. I could use some water."

"Is the water in the stream safe to drink?"

"Depends on how brave you're feeling. I boil it. Lot of parasites around here. I don't fancy having my organs burrowed through or used as a nest…"

She rooted around in her pack and retrieved two empty liter water bottles, then dropped a tablet in each before filling them from the stream. It took a few minutes for the pills to dissolve, and when she shook the bottles, the water looked milky. She took a sniff and chugged hers before moving to where Matt was leaning against a tree trunk.

"Which do you want first? The bar or the water?" she asked.

"Bar."

She unwrapped it and held it up, fixing him with a cautious glare. "You try to bite me, I'll rupture one of your eardrums just for fun, and you'll spend the next week in constant pain."

"I wasn't going to bite you. Unless you wanted me to." He tried a smile. She noted that he had a certain craggy charm and wasn't a bad-looking man, overall, with his lean frame and chiseled features. Pity she'd be executing him soon to get her daughter back.

"I'm glad to see you're keeping your spirits up," she said and stuffed the first third of the bar into his mouth. He took a bite and chewed it methodically, eyes never leaving her face.

"You're not agency, are you?" he asked between mouthfuls.

"Doesn't matter, does it?"

"How did they rope you into this? What did they tell you?"

"Shut up and eat."

He finished the bar and then nodded towards the water. "How was it?"

"Like cat piss. In a good way."

"Can't say as I've ever had the pleasure."

"Then you're in for a treat."

She held the bottle to his mouth, and he drank greedily from it, finishing it within thirty seconds.

"Boy, you weren't kidding."

"I don't kid."

"How many more tablets do you have? Enough to last us three more days?"

"It won't take that long to make it back to Thailand."

"Don't bet on it. The stretch from here to the border is rough going if you don't have a horse. I've done it enough times to know. Even in the best of circumstances, it sucks. And with the rains, it's not close to being good."

"I have enough."

He grunted. "And what about when I have to use the bathroom?"

"I guess I'll get a show."

"Did my ex put you up to this?"

She said nothing.

"Seriously. How do I attend to my, erm, necessities, with my hands shackled behind my back?"

"Very carefully."

"The reason I ask is because it's going to be that time soon."

She sighed, annoyed, and then stood as she felt around in her pocket for a key.

"I'll lock your hands in front of you for now. But again, one wrong move…"

"And you'll skin me like an eel. I got it."

She helped him to his feet and unlocked one wrist, then stepped back, her pistol leveled at his head.

"Stay facing the tree. Move your hands to your front, slowly, and lock the cuff."

She could see him tense, almost imperceptibly, and she prepared for an assault, chambering a round in the Beretta with a percussive snick. His shoulders relaxed when he registered the distinctive sound, and he obligingly moved his hands in front of him and cuffed himself.

"Very good. Now that wasn't so hard, was it?" she asked.

"I can't believe you didn't have one in the chamber."

"That was for your benefit." She glanced down to where a shiny 9mm bullet lay on the matted grass.

"I kind of figured."

"I'm going to toss you some nylon cord. I want you to wrap it around each ankle, twice, and secure it so you have enough room to shuffle, but not enough to get into trouble." She reached into her backpack with her free hand and pulled out a fifty-foot length of line and tossed the bundle to him, then watched as he did as she'd instructed. Once he was finished, she nodded.

"Try to avoid hitting the rope when you go."

"I see you've done this before."

"Don't move more than twenty feet away. Knock yourself out. Then come back, and we'll reverse the whole process."

He grinned. "Bit cumbersome, isn't it?"

"Life is filled with challenges. Maybe I'll make you dance for me next."

He lumbered over to a patch of plants and busied himself with his business as she picked up the bullet and replaced it in the Beretta's magazine. When he returned, she cuffed his hands behind him again, then sat down by the stream.

"We'll rest for a little while, and then start in again. I'd advise you to get some shut-eye if you can. We won't be stopping again until nightfall."

"We won't be able to keep that pace up. I'm just warning you."

"Thanks for the well-intentioned advice."

They drowsed in the heat, and then after an hour, Jet popped up, appearing as refreshed as if she'd enjoyed a full night's rest. She nudged Matt awake with her boot.

"Let's get moving. You take the lead now that it's daylight."

She powered on her GPS and got a bearing, then put it back into her backpack, along with the two water bottles she'd refilled.

As much as she hated to admit it, Matt was probably right about their progress.

It would be almost impossible to keep up a decent pace all day.

But they had to try.

As he shuffled down the trail, Jet shifted the P90 into fire-ready position and followed him, letting him get five yards ahead so he couldn't easily try anything now that he could see. She wondered what would cause a man who seemed relatively decent to choose a life with sex slavers and heroin dealers, and then banished the thought. It wasn't her problem. And his whole demeanor could be an act. She'd seen firsthand what Pu's world was like, and any friend of his was unworthy of her sympathy. Not that she had any.

As to his stealing the diamonds, she had no opinion on that. It was between him and the CIA. Although a part of her bore him resentment – if he hadn't stolen them, she wouldn't have had her daughter kidnapped and be trudging through this miserable backwater.

He stumbled and almost face-planted into the trail, but caught himself at the last moment and continued forward.

The hard part of the mission was done. She had him. Now all she needed to do was get him to the bank so they could get the diamonds, and she was home free.

Although a niggling part of her didn't believe for a second it would be that simple.

Nothing ever was.

CHAPTER 25

They stopped at five o'clock, this time at the banks of a larger stream, swollen to almost river-size by the rain, which had started again a few hours earlier. They were both soaked completely through, but at least it was warm – the temperature felt like a steady ninety degrees throughout the day, with all the attendant mugginess high humidity brought.

The mosquitoes swarmed as the evening wore on, and they paused to spray themselves again before continuing their forced march. She'd never seen anything like the bugs, not even in Belize – known as the mosquito coast for good reason. But compared to Myanmar, Belize was Toronto; the jungle around them was literally swarming with every variety of bloodsucking parasite known to man, as Matt had been quick to point out during one of their hushed discussions.

They hadn't come across another living soul all day, but Matt seemed preoccupied with listening for others in the jungle, giving her the distinct feeling that he hadn't been joking about the drug syndicates and human traffickers being their biggest obstacle to making it out alive.

She repeated the ritual with the breakfast bars and the water, then they sat in the shadow of a rock overhang, which provided slim shelter from the downpour, but more than the trees did. They listened together to the steady drumming of rain on the leaves, a hail of precipitation that seemed to be never-ending.

"You never told me where they got you from," he began, eyeing her as she chugged more water.

"No, I didn't."

"You're not CIA, I know that. What are you then? Freelance?"

"In a manner of speaking," she answered, uninterested in pursuing it.

"What did they offer you to do this?"

"None of your business."

"Whatever it is, I can double it."

She ignored him, preferring to strip her Beretta and clean it during their break.

"You know about the diamonds. What did they tell you?"

"Guess."

"Ha. Let's see. If I was them, I'd tell a story about how I'm the bad guy, and they're out to set an example. Am I close?"

"You tell me."

"Who recruited you?"

"Again, none of your business. I don't want to discuss it."

"Was it Scarface, the great man himself? Or did he use an intermediary? He's a coward at heart, so I'll bet he used a cutout. Unless he's desperate by now. If so, you met him. Creepy bastard, isn't he?"

She stared at him with dead eyes.

"So what was the story? How did he explain away two hundred million in diamonds being handled by the CIA in Thailand? That must have been quite a yarn."

He smiled at her, and she noticed that his eye color shifted from brown to green in the light. Little flecks of gold in the irises created the illusion of them glinting, sparkling.

She relented. "Two hundred? They told me fifty. You stole the diamonds from the CIA, which was supporting insurgency in Myanmar. A formerly trustworthy career officer gone rogue out of greed. Sad story."

"Not bad. Of course, nothing near the truth, but hey, why let that stop anyone? Why tell you anything even resembling it? Fifty, two hundred, whatever. The only problem being that it isn't true."

"Sure it isn't."

"You actually believe that tripe? Then I've got a bridge to sell you. How about this — tell me which sounds more realistic. That the CIA was funding Myanmar insurgents with diamonds, for unknown reasons. Or that a faction of entrepreneurial CIA scumbags decided to get into the drug business over forty years ago, and the diamonds were just another payment to heroin traffickers in the Golden Triangle."

She didn't show any emotion, but she didn't like what she was hearing.

"During the Vietnam war, some of the power players in the CIA figured out that they had the means and the wherewithal to become the world's largest drug trafficking entity. Back then, drugs in the United States were illegal, but not a huge problem. Because there wasn't any consistent supply. These guys decided to solve that problem by opening up a shipping operation from Vietnam – heroin from the Triangle, in return for guns and cash. The traffickers in the Triangle could sell the guns to the Viet Cong, so it was a great scheme. Of course, the only ethical hiccup was that American soldiers were being killed with weapons the CIA was supplying, but hey, can't have everything. That's why the heroin supply in the United States boomed once Vietnam was under way. And they didn't stop at getting an entire generation of hippies addicted. They also made sure that it was the drug of choice for many of the GIs who were fighting in a conflict they wouldn't ever be allowed to win. It was perfect, and this little club in the CIA made a fortune.

"The pipeline was a simple one. Cash and weapons on army transport planes to Southeast Asia, then heroin on the return journey, concealed in the coffins of dead GIs. The CIA hooked up with the Italian mob for distribution in the States, and the rest is history. There were a few competitors that got involved as it went along – ex-GIs who knew what was going on because they'd been in on it while stationed in Vietnam, and who decided to set up their own railroads using the same technique, but the CIA squashed those once they got large enough to make headlines. It was all good business – they had other bad guys to point fingers at, and meanwhile the top echelon was getting rich.

"Occasionally a shipment would get intercepted as the traffic grew, but they could always blame it on one of these fall guys or claim it was an off-the-books op or a sting. They also got involved in the traffic to Europe – their problem was that once they were taking literally a hundred percent of the Triangle's production, they needed addicts to sop up the supply. A classic supply/demand issue."

"Are you trying to tell me that some faction of the CIA has been running heroin for forty years? Please. Try something more believable," she sneered.

"More than forty, and not just heroin. Of course, as time marched on, the old hands retired or died, and then new blood took over. We are talking about billions of dollars per year, here. You could work for the CIA, and if you were part of the clique, retire a multi-millionaire, easily, all tax free. It was quite a racket."

"And where do you come in?"

"I found out about it. I wasn't one of the in-crowd. They kept everything very hush-hush, all need-to-know, but I figured it out when I was making regular runs into Myanmar and Laos with bags of diamonds and handing them to obvious drug lords. They fed me the same insurgents bullshit, but I soon discovered that there was no insurgency of any meaningful kind in Myanmar. Not over half a billion a year's worth, anyway. And the CIA screwed up – I became trusted by the drug lords over time, and they began to rely on me to create a market for the diamonds – to create liquidity for them in Thailand. Of course, many of the diamonds made it to Europe for conversion, but a fair number stayed in the Far East."

"I thought this was all recent."

"Another lie. It's been going on for decades."

"So you were bringing them the diamonds. A courier."

"Much more than that. I became their conduit. They would have me hold onto ten million's worth of diamonds and convert them into dollars. That's where Pu came in. I'd developed him as a snitch over ten years ago, and he had all the contacts to make the diamonds disappear – at a slight discount, of course." He shifted uncomfortably and continued. "I wanted to know what I was really involved in. Once I saw the lie and figured out that something was going on that had nothing to do with legitimate company business, I started nosing around, and the more I dug, the uglier it got. These guys don't just take the supply from here. They also have the market cornered for heroin from Afghanistan. Which currently produces two times the world total demand for heroin. So they have a price problem. They either need a much larger market of addicts – which they're working hard to create in Europe and Russia – or they need to have total control over the supply, so they can maintain margins.

"Anyway, when I figured out that I'd devoted the last decade of my life to operating the largest illegal drug operation on the planet, I had what you might call a crisis of confidence. It wasn't what I had signed up for…let's just say it wasn't how I saw myself."

She nodded, a twist of anxiety budding in her gut.

"I decided to put a stop to it. Single-handedly. When I had a particularly large diamond run to make – four months' payment – I simply took the money and ran. The drug lords were furious. I told them that the Americans hadn't sent the diamonds because they wanted a twenty-five percent price reduction, which threw the entire scheme into disarray. The drug lords went nuts and immediately went out and started talking to competitive criminal syndicates – most notably, the Russian and Chinese. So now the CIA had a real problem. They'd lost two hundred million in stones, which they'd gotten from trading weapons to Africa in return for the diamonds. Have you ever heard of blood diamonds?"

"Yes."

"Then you know they come from countries nobody is supposed to trade with because they are generally exchanged for guns and bombs and tanks and planes that are used for genocide. The diamonds are typically mined by slave laborers who live in starvation conditions. Starting to see the similarities? You have these slaves on one side who are producing the diamonds, which are traded for arms the CIA sourced using drug-trafficking proceeds, and then the diamonds are exchanged for the drugs that are then sold worldwide, generating more cash with which to buy weapons to trade for diamonds. It's a perfect rinsing machine. But then I stuck my nose in it and spoiled everything. Needless to say, losing two hundred million threw a hitch in the group's cash flow – that was probably a month's worth of profit, but it's not like you can just snap your fingers and easily turn the cash into diamonds – it takes some time to source that many stones. I knew that when I did it. But most importantly, their losing control of the drug supply threatens their whole ugly empire. It could shut them down."

"So your version is that you're on the side of God and right, and you stole the diamonds to shut down an illegal CIA-run trafficking enterprise?"

"Exactly. I may have some moral confusion – what they call 'elasticity' in the biz – but I know that being involved in heroin trafficking is about as despicable as it gets. There's no gray area in there. Once I knew what was going on, I had two choices – I could either continue as before, or I could do something about it."

"And wind up two hundred million richer."

"Yes. As you can see by the lavish lifestyle I crafted for myself in the Myanmar mountains, money is supremely important to me. It's just a bitch finding somewhere to park the Bentley and land the Citation in the middle of the jungle. Especially when you're living in a shack and pooping in a hole."

Jet had grown uneasy as she listened to Matt's version, which sounded far more plausible than Arthur's. But if he was telling the truth, what could she do about it?

As if reading her mind, Matt started in again. "What did they pay you to do this?"

"Pay me? You think I'm doing this for money?" she spat, and then she told him the whole thing. All of it. Her child, the Mossad, Arthur's ultimatum.

Matt studied her face as she recounted the story, saying nothing until she was done. He looked off into the distance, his focus a million miles away, then fixed her with an intense gaze.

"You know you're never going to get your daughter back. There's no way he'll let you live."

She nodded. "I'm starting to get that feeling."

"He's one of the heads of a multi-generational drug trafficking ring. This is not a man who will think twice about having you executed the second he has the diamonds."

"If you're not lying."

He shook his head and snorted. "Hey, I know: how about we wait until you see that there are two hundred million dollars in diamonds in my safe deposit box, not fifty. Will that go far in convincing you?"

"What are you doing with a monster like Pu?"

"He was a means to an end. And you saw how much love there ultimately was between us. He was just a few seconds away from plugging me. Come on. Think this through. You know I'm telling you the truth. I couldn't invent this shit."

She stood and moved out of the shelter of the rocks, the rain having eased over the last few minutes, and paced in front of him.

"I don't see a lot of options here."

"Funny you should say that. Because I see nothing but possibilities. But only if we work together."

"Work together?"

"Let me tell you what I'm thinking…"

CHAPTER 26

Jet didn't trust Matt enough to take the cuffs off, but she had agreed to think over his proposition, which was an interesting one. Part of what had been gnawing at her was what she would do once the mission was successful. That had been rolling around in her head for days – she didn't have any confidence that Arthur would return Hannah to her, no matter what she did, and Matt's assertion that he would have her killed, or at least do his best to try, rang true.

She hadn't come up with a satisfactory plan for dealing with Arthur, and she didn't know whether Edgar was part of the drug ring, or was just following orders and believed the same bullshit she had been fed. She didn't get the feeling from him that he was bent, but then again, he could have just been a good liar. There was no shortage of those in the agency.

Perhaps most troubling to her was that David had relied on Arthur for dealing with Hannah. She wanted to believe that he'd had no idea about Arthur's extracurricular activities, but she couldn't be sure. David's memory was becoming increasingly tarnished the more she knew. She suspected that wouldn't end any time soon.

The gray of dusk transitioned into the black of night, and the rain eased to infrequent cloudbursts. But the trails were still treacherous, and even with the night vision goggles, she had a difficult time spotting all the hazards.

They rounded a bend, and she stopped dead, her senses prickling. She'd heard something up ahead. Matt almost walked into her in the dark, but he sensed her alarm and also froze.

Voices floated through the jungle, ephemeral and directionless – one of the sensory tricks that the creeping night fog played on their perception.

She tried to see any movement up ahead, but nothing registered, even as she slid the P90 strap down her shoulder and gripped it, ready for battle.

When the shooting started, it narrowly missed them, shredding through the leaves, the bullets zipping past with their distinctive sough of death. Matt dropped into the mud and whispered to her as she fired three bursts into the jungle.

"The key. Un-cuff me, and get me a gun. Please."

The moment of truth had arrived. She saw a skulking figure a hundred yards away dodging towards them in a crouch and, sighting carefully, blew his head off. The shooting stopped for a few seconds, and she groped in her pocket for the key.

"Can you crawl a few feet closer?" she whispered.

He did, and without taking her eyes off the trail, she felt for his wrists and unlocked one of the cuffs, placing the key in his newly-freed hand.

Matt wasted no time unlocking the other cuff, then tapped her arm.

"Gun?"

She un-holstered the Beretta and handed it to him, then fired another burst at a fleeting movement near the edge of a thicket. "Take the silencer off for better range. You've got sixteen shots. Already one in the hole."

"You wouldn't happen to have another night vision scope, would you?"

"Sorry. And I'm not giving this one up."

"Fair enough."

"Don't use up all the bullets. I've only got one more magazine, and we're a long way from the border."

"Maybe we can find a nice AK-47."

She thought about it for a second and then smiled to herself. "How about you give me the pistol back and I trade you for the P90? Then lay down some cover fire so I can flank them."

"Okay, but I can't really see anything."

"That's the point. Neither can they. I doubt they have night vision gear, although you would know better than I would."

"No chance. There's no way to recharge the batteries out here. That's why I didn't have any. Even with the solar to run the computer and charge the sat phone, it couldn't sufficiently pow–"

He was interrupted by more shooting. They were drawing a bead on his voice, soft as it was.

She fired another burst down the trail, then slid him the P90, along with the last two magazines. Matt took them then peered at the gun before handing her the silenced Beretta. More shots rang out, and he instinctively ducked, then rolled to the side of the trail where a thick tree trunk provided better cover. He wiped the perspiration from his eyes and squinted into the gloom, hoping to make something out.

"I'm guessing I should wish you good hunting…" he whispered to Jet, but when he turned to her, she was gone.

❧❦

The smugglers were agitated. Whoever the intruders were, they were putting up more of a fight than anticipated. And they had some sort of stealth weapon. There was no muzzle flash for them to shoot at, and it made a snapping crack instead of the much louder explosion of a rifle, like their Kalashnikovs. But whatever it was, it was just as deadly, as three of them had already discovered.

The law of this jungle was shoot first and ask questions later. The Myanmar army steered well clear of the region, and much of the hill country was a no man's land under drug-runner control. For decades, the infamous warlord and drug trafficker Khun Sa had ruled with an iron fist, and even after his death, the old habits died hard as his territory was divided up by squabbling rivals who roamed the hills armed to the teeth.

This group was a ten-man enforcement squad that one of the larger drug production networks used to keep the locals in line, attacking anything and everything they came across to discourage insurgents from cutting into their turf. In a country where poverty was rampant, it was always a temptation for enterprising upstarts to try their hand at opening a channel to Thailand for their opium instead of selling it at a low price to the cartels. Bodies were routinely found in the jungle as these factions battled it out – a necessary part of the trade and one of the risks that kept most out of it.

The wiry Shan tribesman's eyes darted to where his fallen men had been shot. Nothing like this had ever happened before. He, Kyaw, was the fist of vengeance for fifty miles. That three of his men had been cut down in seconds was intolerable.

The looming clouds and fog made a difficult situation worse, the moon's glow cut to near nothing by the overcast. Even his practiced eyes couldn't make out anything down the trail, and the muffled murmur of voices had fallen silent.

He whispered to two of his men to move up the trail. They rose from their positions and edged towards the unknown enemy, their sandaled feet silent on the wet grass.

The first arrow took the lead gunman by surprise as it penetrated his stomach. He screamed, a tortured yowl, trailing off into a keening as he clutched the protruding shaft with shaking hands, his rifle forgotten on the bloody grass in front of him.

His partner fired into the brush, where he estimated the projectile had come from, and was mid-burst when the next arrow tore his throat out, causing him to flip around and drop into the muddy trail face-first.

Kyaw's men fired wildly, no obvious target in sight, but determined to pepper the jungle with deadly lead. Kyaw gestured at them to stop after a half minute, in an effort to conserve ammunition.

The weapon down the trail popped and stuttered, cutting down two of the gunmen, stitching them with smoking wounds. Kyaw gritted his teeth. This was a bloodbath, and he had now lost most of his force to a ghostlike enemy that prowled the night in silence, delivering death at its whim. He wasn't a superstitious man – far from it, he'd killed so many that he'd long ago lost count. But this was unlike anything he'd experienced, and for the first time in decades, he knew fear.

The fighter next to him was turning to whisper something when the arrow skewered his skull. He fell silently against Kyaw, the razor tip of the arrow imbedded in his brain. Kyaw had seen enough. He gestured to his remaining man to follow, and ran along the edge of the path back in the direction he'd come.

When the arrow skewered him through the back of his neck, he collapsed, his body lifeless before he dropped, his spinal cord severed by the arrowhead. The lone remaining gunman emptied his magazine at the dark jungle and was reloading when his life was snuffed out by the nearby pop of a single silenced pistol.

Jet surveyed the carnage and waited for any more assailants to show themselves. After a few minutes of silence, she shifted from her position in a tree forty yards away and dropped to the ground, leaving her now empty quiver at the base of the trunk, along with the bow. Perhaps it would be of some use to an impoverished Shan hill person who was willing to reclaim the arrows and find a few that were serviceable. She had neither the time nor the desire to do so.

She ran to the dead men and emptied their pockets of spare magazines, then selected two of the newest rifles and made her way back to where Matt was hopefully still waiting.

അൗ

"Did you miss me?"

Matt started at the sound of her whispered voice and exhaled noisily before turning to where she stood with two AK-47s.

"What took you so long?"

"There were more of them than I thought."

She could see his jaw clench, the muscles in his face tensing, and then he relaxed.

"You were hoping for some new weapons?" she said. "These are slightly used, but I think they'll do the trick."

She threw one to him, forcing him to drop the P90 to catch it.

"Nice. What is this, about a thirty-year-old AK?" he asked, hefting it and then sighting down the barrel into the distance.

"A classic." She tossed two magazines at his feet. "Nice shooting, by the way. For a guy who can't see anything, you took two out."

"I didn't want to hit you, but I figured you wouldn't be between me and the muzzle flashes."

"Good guess. Now, hand me the P90, and let's get going. I don't want to have to take on any others who might have been drawn by the gunfire. They might not have been the only bad guys roaming around here tonight."

Matt stood and handed her the little weapon. "That's a neat gun. I like the dual-stage trigger, although it could use a three-round burst mode. It felt like I was getting off five rounds with each pull."

"You get used to it. Holds fifty rounds, so if you're careful, you can get off fifteen pops before you're out of ammo. An acquired taste. I prefer the MTAR." She took it from him and checked the magazine quickly. "Feels like it's still at least a quarter full."

"You trust me with a gun now?" he asked, only partially joking.

"Let's just say that I think you're probably better served being able to protect yourself out here. Besides, as you've probably guessed, I can take care of myself."

"I'll say."

They began trudging along the trail, Jet in the lead again, alert and ready for anything the jungle cared to throw at them.

CHAPTER 27

"You're going to have to kill him." Matt had taken the lead at first light, dawn having broken an hour earlier. "Got to cut the head off the snake or it will always be trying to bite you."

"I know."

"But we need a plan to get your daughter back. I can predict he'll screw you. That's what he does. The challenge is to allow him to think he's doing so, and in the process figure out what he did with her. I may be able to help with that. In fact, I'm sure of it. It'll take some time and money, but fortunately I have plenty of the latter. It's the time element that will be the problem."

"What are you thinking?"

"He's predictable in some ways. And most importantly, he believes that he's insulated from most things you or I might be concerned with. But I have my own assets, and one in particular can probably do enough research to catch anyplace he's been sloppy. Whenever you catch a spy, it's because they screwed up. Arthur isn't infallible. He's very smart, but remember that this is an under-the-table deal he has going, so he can't use company resources to do things like find a home for Hannah. Which means that there will be a trail of some sort. We just need to find it and follow it before he realizes we're onto him."

"That's easier said than done."

"I didn't say it would be easy. I said it would be expensive and time-consuming. But frankly, I can't think of a better way to use some of his own money. I've been trying to figure out how to bring him down, and this may present an opportunity. What I'm proposing is that you take him out, along with anyone else we can identify as ringleaders in this scheme, so you, and I, are safe. In exchange for that, I'll spend whatever it takes to find your daughter. This is actually sort of the same deal he made with you, only in reverse. And I didn't have to kidnap anyone to get you to go along."

"Let's say I agree, and we join forces. What's the next step?"

"You have five million dollars' worth of diamonds hanging around your neck. The first thing I'd suggest is getting to Bangkok and converting some of that into cash. Once we have cash, we have options. I know a few of the contacts Pu had, and I think I can arrange for you to be able to convert at least a couple million' worth pretty quickly. Then you have to get some new ID and go to Europe to convert some more – maybe ten million. At that point, you've got a war chest. In the meantime, I'll put my back into discovering whatever can be found. Worst case, I've got a pretty simple alternative that can get you close enough to be able to get your daughter back and disappear – after you kill Arthur, of course."

"Let's hear plan B, since plan A sounds like you haven't come up with it yet."

"I think you'll appreciate the irony in plan B."

"Try me."

They went back and forth, arguing the possibilities in muted tones, still wary of being ambushed by the region's unsavory elements, and as the day wore on, the outline of a strategy with a realistic chance of success took form.

The going had become harder, even with a minimum of rain, and as predicted, they didn't make the kind of time she'd hoped for. Night fell, and they were still in the hills, but within ten miles of the border. They took a two-hour break and then pushed on, Jet driven as if by demons, keeping up the pace even though they were both close to exhaustion.

At four in the morning, they crossed into Thailand and discarded all of the weapons except for the pistol. She stowed it in her backpack and then scraped a hole in the dirt and buried the electronics and the sat phone, on the off-chance that they had some sort of tracking technology in them.

They made their way down the hill into Mae Sai and were in town by dawn. Motorcycles and trucks were already prowling the roads, and after grabbing food at a roadside stand that catered to early-rising laborers and farmers, they found a small guest house where they could clean up and rest.

After they had both showered and rinsed their clothes free of the accumulated sweat and grime, they gratefully fell onto the single hard bed and were asleep within seconds.

ᘐ᙮ᗈ

The bus to Bangkok was a nightmare of unwashed bodies, poor ventilation and a suspension system that had given up several decades earlier. Jet and Matt tried to make the best of it, but by the time they arrived in Chiang Rai, an hour after departing Mae Sai, both had seen enough, and they got off at the bus station and went in search of a car. After some haggling, they convinced a restaurant owner to have his son drive them to Bangkok, and soon they were on their way in the impossible comfort of air-conditioning.

Once in Bangkok, they found a hotel that was modest but safe and checked into separate rooms. Clothes shopping was the first agenda item they quickly dispensed with, along with purchasing several disposable cell phones. Matt wanted to make some calls and find buyers for the diamonds, as well as reach out to his contacts for identity papers. They'd both agreed that it would be unwise to attempt traveling on her passport. Arthur would surely be alerted the moment she crossed a border. Instead, Matt wanted to see how much a genuine Thai passport would cost – one of the nice things about Thailand was that virtually anything could be had for a price.

When they met downstairs for dinner, Jet was surprised at how handsome Matt was once he'd shaved and gotten a haircut – and it looked like he'd had his hair lightened. His deep tan offset his white linen shirt, and she decided that he looked a little like a gracefully-aging surfer.

During their hike, he'd made it clear that he was willing to make available to her as many millions as she needed to get her daughter back and execute those responsible. They'd agreed that fifteen million – the five in diamonds she still had around her neck, and another ten from his bank stash – would be a better than acceptable start, but he'd shown no interest in the money other than as a means to an end.

Once they had ordered dinner and drinks, he having a cold beer and she her customary bottled mineral water, he appraised her with a knowing look.

"What else is going on behind those eyes?"

"What do you mean?"

"I mean, even though I've only known you for a short time, I can tell you're calculating ten steps ahead. But you seem preoccupied."

He'd read her accurately.

"I have another problem. I mean, it's not my problem, but I'm making it mine. Your buddy, Pu, among his many flaws, was a child slave trader, and I want to rescue one of his captives and get her out of a terrible situation. She's not even eleven yet, and she deserves something better than what she's been thrust into. It's heartbreaking."

He nodded. "The world's an ugly place, and Pu was part of the worst of it. Tell me what you know about her."

Jet recounted the story and was just finishing when the food arrived.

"Part of me says it's not your problem and will unnecessarily complicate things, but another part understands and agrees with you. But she won't be safe in Bangkok – Pu's network will still flourish, with him or without him. Sure, there will be some power struggles and a few bodies found floating in the river, but that enterprise will continue or be replaced by an equivalently horrible one."

"I know. I'm thinking of ways to get her out of that mess. If I can buy her..."

"They may not want to sell, and even if they do, you'll be on the radar again. I have every faith that Edgar has eyes and ears on the street. He may be new here, but the basic tradecraft never changes. You show up waving money around and he'll know you're back in the world within minutes."

"That's what I figured. So I'm thinking I'll do something a little different. But once she's free, I need somewhere safe to take her."

"That's not going to be easy. You'll run the risk of her being abused or sold back into the trade anywhere she winds up. People suck, and they'll do anything for money. And no matter what promises are made, the moment you're out of sight all bets are off."

"I don't want to see her go from one nightmare into another."

They both picked at their entrées, lost in thought.

"What are you going to do once we deal with the diamond situation?" Jet asked.

"Go back into the jungle. My situation hasn't changed until Arthur and his crew are eliminated. I'll go back, find some Shan that want to make more in a year than they would in a decade and arm them to the teeth. Until you showed up, that seemed to be the safest bet..."

His eyes flashed in the overhead lighting from the two chandeliers and for a moment seemed to blaze.

"How can you live like that?" she asked.

"I actually like it out there. After a lifetime of subterfuge and treachery and big cities, there's something peaceful about it – something simple. You wake up every day, hunt or barter for your food, and live in harmony with the land. What? Don't look at me like that."

"Harmony with the land? Are you Henry David Thoreau now? Come on."

He put down his fork and stared into space. She noted the way the corners of his eyes crinkled with the beginnings of crow's feet and thought that they suited him.

"It's true. I like it. I feel calmer, more at peace. I mean, I don't want to live like that forever, but I can do a year or two, no problem. And it beats getting killed in my sleep or crossing the street. The fact is that Arthur can get to me anywhere but there. And with no Pu doing diamond runs, there's no danger of anyone leading a hit team back to me. No, disappearing into the jungle isn't perfect, but it's the best I've come up with, and it's worked so far. I move around a lot – I have four other camps in Myanmar and Laos. I'll just ditch the one you erased and return to one of the others, and hire an entourage."

She considered his words as she ate. He had a point.

When the waiter came to take their plates, she reached to take his hand.

"Matt, my new friend. I have another incredibly big favor to ask…"

CHAPTER 28

"I need some diamonds," Matt said, standing at her door.

"You've come to the right place," Jet responded, waving him into her room. "I have them in the safe."

"I found a taker for two million' worth. He'll make a transfer to one of my companies. I'll get a card when I'm at the bank tomorrow and give it to you. That will be your mad money."

She padded to the room safe, then brought the leather bag to the table.

"How will you know how many are two million dollars' worth?"

"I'll guesstimate. I've gotten pretty good at this over the years."

He dumped out a small pile and quickly sorted a little less than half the stones, then pulled out a plastic bag from his pocket and scooped them in. He returned the rest to the leather sack and handed it to her.

"Call that your emergency fund. After I do this deal tomorrow morning, I'll head to the bank. It's a different one than where I keep the stones. Don't want all my eggs in one basket."

"It seems sort of crazy to have millions in diamonds lying around a hotel room, doesn't it?"

"There would be far more risk if we asked the management to lock them in the hotel safe. Besides, if anyone can get past you, I'd say they earned them."

She smiled, then returned to the safe and locked the diamonds away. "What are we going to do about the ten million in diamonds? That's not exactly low profile, and I'll need to get to Europe…"

"I struck a deal with a guy who knows a guy. By the end of the day tomorrow, you'll have a shiny new passport. Legitimate. A diplomatic passport, to boot. Only three hundred grand."

"Three hun–"

"I'm not price sensitive. With a diplomatic passport, you won't have to answer a lot of niggling questions at customs, so whether you have ten million or a hundred million in stones with you, you'll glide right through. You'll need to get a photo taken tonight, which won't be a problem. There are a million shops open, even at ten p.m.. Bangkok is a night city. You want to go take a walk?" he asked.

"Sure. Let me get my gun."

She had bought a purse large enough to accommodate the Beretta with the silencer as well as other odds and ends. She shouldered it and turned to Matt, who was pulling on a baseball cap.

"Lead on."

She was still getting used to the casual way that he tossed around figures like a million dollars, and it struck her how completely arbitrary money was. He had a virtually bottomless well of cash, so all the typical financial constraints were meaningless to them.

"How many millions do you have left?"

"About two hundred million," he said nonchalantly.

"You haven't spent any of it?"

"On what? I had Pu liquidate a few hundred grands' worth each time he came out to see me, but that wasn't a lot. I had to buy guns and ammo, and pay everyone for protection – but even so, it didn't come to a hundred grand. The truth is, I don't have anything to spend money on out in the jungle other than weapons and slipping cash to the nearby drug lords to leave me in peace. So technically, I suppose the correct answer is a hundred ninety-nine million and change. But deduct the five million worth I had around my neck, and we can call it a hundred ninety-four."

"That's just such a huge amount of money."

"It is. But it's blood money. Not that I have a problem with that. But I didn't do this to get rich. I did it to shut these pricks down."

"So even if we have to do plan B, you'll still have..."

"...a lot of diamonds," Matt finished for her.

They exited the hotel and walked slowly down the sidewalk towards the blinking neon forest a few blocks away, where every kind of shop clamored for customers with thousand-watt signs.

"It's quite a spectacle, isn't it?"

"Have you ever been to Tokyo?" he asked.

"No. It's one of the places I've meant to go. Just never was a right time."

"You've never seen anything like it. Blinding. It's like nothing else on the planet."

They rounded the corner and found themselves facing a seemingly endless pedestrian thoroughfare lined with shops and bars. Groups of young Thai men roamed in packs, eyeing the giggling swarms of teenage girls while the inevitable bar girls called to passersby, inviting them to come in and sample their charms.

"Not getting too personal, I hope, but what are you going to do once all this is over?" she asked. "I mean, once you're no longer in danger."

"I haven't really thought about it. I like Thailand. I've been here too long to feel comfortable anywhere else, I suppose. For all its idiosyncrasies and frustrations, it's home for me. I don't know. If I had my choice, I suppose I'd go to one of the islands and live on the beach. But there's no point torturing myself with dreams of tomorrow. It just makes it harder to be happy today."

"Very existentialistic."

"It's the Buddhist thing rubbing off on me. You stay here long enough and eventually everything seems illusory."

"Why one of the islands?"

"Different pace. You still get the civilization feel if you want it, but it's much more laid-back. None of the bustle of the big city. Places like Ko Samui are magical. I gather you've never been."

"No. But I liked living in Trinidad. Islands can be nice. Nice and boring."

He laughed, genuine merriment evident in his eyes. "I suppose you've had enough excitement to last a lifetime."

"You could say that."

"There are worse places to disappear forever. You should check out Ko Samui. You'd love it. Breathtakingly beautiful, well-developed, yet still rural enough to have appeal. Time slows when you're there. It's almost as if it's enchanted."

"You work for their tourism bureau? You make it sound like heaven."

"For me, it's the closest thing going."

He pointed to a photo shop, and they went inside. The old *mama-san* was all efficiency, and they had their photos within ten minutes.

"You're also getting diplomatic?" she asked.

"Why not? Such a deal. Two for five hundred. Couldn't let that slip by me."

"That should make it easier to move around, don't you think?"

"Not really. I have about ten passports from my old life stored in with the diamonds. But diplomatic immunity has a lot of appeal, and when it's safe to go back in the water, I'll probably use that for the long term."

They strolled along, no particular destination in mind, surrendering themselves to Bangkok's nocturnal ambiance.

"You think you'll be done with everything that needs to happen by the end of the day tomorrow?" she asked.

"I hope so. I don't want to spend one more second in Bangkok than I need to. I'm not exactly a household name here, but the longer I'm in town, the greater the chance that someone from my past spots me."

"Then isn't it a bad idea to be strolling along here?"

"I'm pretty sure that with the dye job and the shave and the cap my own mother would have a hard time recognizing me. Tonight isn't my worry. It's the banks." He looked at his watch. "Which means it's probably a good idea to get back to our lavish digs. It's going to be a marathon tomorrow."

"I'll say. More for you than for me, but still, I need to catch up on sleep after the last week."

They looped around and ambled back to the hotel, taking their time: a couple out on a stroll, taking in the sights of Bangkok at night, not a care in the world.

CHAPTER 29

The Top Cat had closed at three a.m., and by four, the only ones left after the cleaning crew had departed were the *mama-san* and the two guards employed to keep intruders out. Most of the girls lived elsewhere, but the children stayed in the club with the *mama-san*, who had a small apartment on the second floor. The guards were armed with pistols, which they kept concealed in shoulder holsters – a constant for most of the clubs, due to their organized crime affiliations and the large amounts of cash they took in on any given evening, usually stored overnight in floor safes.

The surrounding streets were dark, and the crowds had gone home, the weeknight's diversions abandoned in favor of a few scant hours of rest before the work day began. An occasional tuk tuk or motor scooter buzzed down the street as a tan-colored mongrel with protruding ribs nosed through the piles of trash stacked on the sidewalk.

Jet watched the area for another ten minutes and then pulled the mask down over her face. She wore black, loose-fitting lightweight parachute fabric cargo pants and a matching top she'd bought that morning. Her backpack was strapped snugly in place, and she adjusted it one final time before darting to the alley mouth in a blur of motion.

Her left foot bounced against the building's wall and propelled her upwards using the momentum of the run. Both hands gripped the rim of the flat roof, and she pulled herself up and over, then moved to where the security camera was fixed and cut the cable with a flick of her knife. The *mama-san*'s apartment lay at the back of the building, creating a small second floor. She edged silently to its security-barred window. Listening intently, she confirmed that the woman was asleep, then padded to the ventilation ducts and went to work.

The interior of the club was dark except for a single light at the front, where the two guards sat playing cards. Jet heard one of them cough and fan the smoke curling from his partner's cigarette away before resuming his play. She lowered the overhead vent grid and dropped to the ground, her black Nike cross-training shoes making no noise on the polished concrete floor. The men didn't look up. If they had, they would have seen her creep to the rear hallway and disappear up the stairs to the *mama-san*'s room and the sleeping area for the children.

At the top of the stairs, she was confronted with two doors – one of which had a sliding bolt locked in place from the outside. That would be the children. She took three silent steps towards the other door, and her gloved hand softly turned the knob, wary of making any sound.

Light from outside filtered through the sheer curtains that framed the window, and Jet could just make out the *mama-san*'s sleeping form. Her eyes roved over the squalid quarters, stopping when they fell on a pair of ceremonial swords in scabbards affixed to a plaque on the far wall.

❧❦

The guards looked up from their card table, startled by a rattle at the back of the club. Probably a cat trying to get to the garbage. The younger of the two made a lewd comment, and both men laughed, and then the rattle disrupted their game again.

"Go look to see what's happening, Alak. Could be trouble," the older man ordered. The younger threw down his cards with an exasperated exhalation of smoke. "When have we ever had trouble? Come on. Nobody would dare look crooked at this place with the old man's reputation. You're just trying to cheat me out of another hundred baht. I'm onto you."

"Nobody forces you to play. Now go see what that's all about while I take a leak."

Both men rose, the younger taking the lead as they strode down the long hall at the back of the club to the restrooms and entertainment suites.

The older man entered the bathroom and hit the light switch. The overhead fluorescent bulb sputtered to reluctant life. He was unzipping his fly with a sigh of relief when he heard a muffled thud from outside.

"Alak? What the hell are you doing?"

There was no response.

Torn by the pressure on his bladder and his duty, he called for his partner again.

"Alak. Don't screw around. What's going on out there?"

He was growing annoyed when the light flickered off.

He hastily drew his weapon as he neared the door in the complete darkness, feeling along with the toes of his shoes until his gun barrel knocked into the wall. He swore silently and took a deep breath, then pulled the door open.

The hall was equally dark, the only light a sliver of dim illumination from the rear alley exit. He peered along the corridor and could barely make out an inert form on the floor. His startled recognition of the younger man's corpse was accompanied by a whistling as the razor-sharp sword blade swung at his neck, neatly decapitating him before he could raise his pistol. An expression of puzzled surprise froze on his face for eternity as his head tumbled to the floor and then rolled halfway down the hall while his torso collapsed lifelessly at Jet's feet, blood still pumping from the neatly severed stump of his neck.

The air was heavy with the gamey scent of blood as she leaned down and wiped the sword on the guard's suit before returning it to the scabbard strapped across her back. A creak sounded from above, and she spun, returning to the stairs.

Jet waited, willing her breath to a near stop, listening, senses tingling from adrenaline. Another creak and then shuffling footsteps above.

The barrel of the *mama-san*'s gun preceded her as she descended the stairs. Jet waited until she was standing in the hall before leveling a brutal strike at her wrist, forcing her to drop the weapon and grip her arm in agony. The woman looked up at her through tears of pain, and then her features twisted with hate as Jet pulled off her mask and spoke.

"So, you bitch, how does it feel when you're on the receiving end of the hurt?"

"You dead when Pu find out about this," she spat in broken English.

"Pu's dead. I danced in his blood. He cried like an old woman when I killed him."

The *mama-san* screamed in rage and threw herself at Jet, who easily parried her frenzied attempts to claw at her face, then grabbed the woman's head and gave it a brutal twist. Her spine snapped with an audible pop, and she sank to the concrete floor, her life seeping from her lips with a gurgle.

"Rot in hell," Jet muttered and then, gazing around, stepped over the woman and opened the breaker panel before flipping the master back on.

She made short work of dragging the bodies into the nearest room, trying to minimize the gore in the hall, then paused, listening, before moving to the stairs.

The club was silent, except for her footsteps as she ascended the steps and approached the locked door.

The bolt sliding open sounded like a rifle shot. She pulled the door towards her and edged forward, feeling for the light switch as she heard the rustling of bodies on the floor.

The harsh glare of a single incandescent bulb illuminated a scene out of hell. Three children huddled together on the floor in a space the size of a broom closet, a metal bucket their toilet. The stink was overpowering, and Jet retched, fighting back the urge to vomit. She forced herself to smile as the three children's faces stared up at her in apprehension. The boy was a little older than Lawan, with an adult air about his adolescent face, and the other girl was already aging in an ugly way, years of abuse and disease leaving dark rings under her eyes, her features unhealthy looking and starved, but her eyes calculating.

Lawan's face brightened with recognition, and she leapt up and hugged Jet, tears rolling down her face, her body shuddering with sobs. The other children watched uncomprehendingly as Jet stroked Lawan's hair with her left hand and gestured to them with her other.

"Come on."

The two exchanged glances and rose. Jet led Lawan down the stairs, guiding them to the rear exit in the darkened hall, their feet squishing in the blood underfoot. She hesitated for a few seconds, then twisted the deadbolt and threw the back door open. Peering outside, she stepped out into the alley with Lawan, the boy and girl following her. She motioned for them to come with her, but the boy shook his head and then took the girl's hand. Jet nodded and fished in her pocket, retrieving a thick wad of baht. The pair's eyes widened at the money, and then turned to shocked surprise when she peeled a few notes off and handed them the rest. The girl snatched the money away and took off at a full run, the boy trailing her as they escaped their past and bolted into an uncertain future.

She watched them disappear and then turned Lawan's face to hers, crouching down so they were at eye level. They exchanged a long look, Lawan's eyes brimming with tears, and then Jet stood and took her hand, leaving the club's door open to the night predators, and walked with her towards the long shadows at the alley mouth.

ತಿ•ೂ

Lawan stood in the hotel shower for a half hour, washing away the horror with a stream of warm water and a shrinking bar of soap. Jet let her take her time, knowing that she needed to process that she was free, safe from the ugliness that had defined her last week. Hopefully over time, she would put it behind her, as Jet had surmounted the ugliness of her past, although she knew all too well that the scars never fully healed. She wished that she could communicate with the little girl, tell her that it was all going to be okay, that she would never need to go back to the club and that nobody would hurt her any more, but Jet had to be satisfied with whatever her eyes and touch could convey. There would be time in a few hours, when morning came, to hear her story and tell her the news. Matt would help – he'd promised her that he would as part of their bargain, but also because she sensed he was trying to make amends for his associate's sins, even if he hadn't participated in them.

Eventually, the water shut off, and Lawan emerged from the bathroom with a towel draped around her tiny frame. Jet had bought a change of clothes and an oversized T-shirt for her, which she gratefully pulled over her head. Jet balled up the filthy rags she'd been sleeping in and threw them into the trash. Lawan gave her a shy smile.

The neon dawn outside the window flickered at the curtains as they lay together on the bed, Lawan's wet head snuggled against Jet's shoulder as her eyelids fluttered and she drifted to sleep, her breathing soft as a lamb's. Jet stroked her hair absently while staring into the void, and then she, too, shut her eyes and quieted her thoughts, secure in the knowledge that for the moment, at least, they were safe.

CHAPTER 30

"That's not good enough," the voice on the phone raged. "I want to see you. Twenty minutes."

The line went dead, and Arthur stared at the scrambled cell phone with dread.

He had spent years climbing to a point of dominance in the hierarchy of the group that controlled so much of the international drug trade, but he still had to answer to one man. A man who represented powerful interests – interests that were anonymous to all but the most senior in the group – Arthur being the second highest ranking of the CIA group members, and the most active in the day-to-day operations.

He remembered the early days, when he'd been recruited into the scheme by the then number-two man in the agency, who had explained to him why it was necessary for global peace and America's interests to control the worldwide supply of narcotics, and had invited him to become part of the elite within the elite. Arthur had gladly joined and had pursued his new duties with a vengeance, becoming a trusted confidant to the top brass, and then when they had gotten out of the game or moved on to even more elevated offices, to their replacements.

He'd become a wealthy man in the process, capable of any life he chose. But his physical attributes had made him reclusive, and other than a twice-monthly visit with a five-thousand-dollar-a-night escort, he limited his enjoyment of the finer things to rare wine, wristwatches and antiques, season tickets to the ballet and opera, and his palatial townhome in Georgetown.

But some of his responsibility outside of the official duties he performed for the CIA was to ensure that the business he'd inherited and later built into a powerhouse remained viable, and that any complications were resolved in a timely manner. He'd been sorely tested in the mid-Eighties by the Iran-Contra nightmare but had emerged as a star, the group's participation in the arms-for-cocaine scheme covered up with a baffling barrage of complex explanations. He recalled the director of the CIA, his superior not only in the agency but also in the group, joking with him one day that even he couldn't tell what the hell the whole ruckus was about after the press and Congress got done mangling the facts.

That was part of the art that Arthur brought to the table – an ability to hide in plain sight and make even the most obvious indiscretions seem unfathomably convoluted. He'd long ago discovered that the public had no patience for details or complexity, preferring simple sound-bites of easily-digestible spin, so whenever they had a crisis, he engaged what he thought of as his complexity engine, and soon something as simple to grasp as a ton of cocaine stopped in Miami with a CIA asset handling the distribution became a labyrinth of detail and unknowable tangents. Eventually, everyone moved on to something that was easier to grasp, and nobody asked the painful questions he didn't want answered. He'd watched many a hearing where a simple inquiry from a Congressman was answered in a ten-minute rambling dissertation that would put even a speed freak to sleep. It was a skill. One he'd mastered.

He was also chartered with handling the messier aspects of the trade, including coordinating wet jobs disguised as CIA missions, money laundering, and managing the group's supply chain. The trading of weapons for diamonds had been a masterstroke. Every wild-eyed despot in Africa wanted bigger and better weapons, and Arthur could supply whatever they wanted, through middlemen, in exchange for blood diamonds. The drug trade profits went to the middlemen who laundered them through Panama and Miami, then bought weapons from U.S. companies with the newly sanitized money, which then went to Africa in return for diamonds that Arthur exchanged for heroin.

In Afghanistan, the laundering and payment mechanisms were different, but in Asia, diamonds were a drug lord's best friend, and the scheme had worked flawlessly until Hawker had figured it out. If there was a fault in any of it, it was Arthur's failure to have him killed the second he'd started nosing around, rather than trying to brand the trade as a legitimate op. He'd hoped that he could rely on Hawker's strong sense of duty to continue as before, but he'd misjudged the lengths to which he would go to discover the truth – a rare quality, fortunately, in his field staff members, who typically followed orders without question.

Arthur punched the intercom and told his secretary to have his car waiting, and then trudged down the long halls to the main parking lot, where his driver sat ready for his instructions. Arthur slid into the rear seat and told him to head to the mall a few miles away, where he would be taking an early lunch at his favorite Chinese restaurant.

Once inside the sprawl of the mall complex, he ducked into a franchise coffee chain and ordered a frozen blended concoction – one of the guilty pleasures that he could manage with a straw. The place was nearly empty at eleven a.m., so he had the lounge area to himself, Billie Holiday crooning over the loudspeakers as truculent youths with multiple facial piercings and flamboyantly dyed hair wiped down the display cases while sneering at passing shoppers.

Arthur watched a heavyset man in a long overcoat move to the register and gruffly order a cup of drip coffee, then flip a bill at the cashier before dropping his change into the tip box and moving to where Arthur sat.

"Explain to me why we haven't recovered the lost merchandise and put an end to the problem yet," Briggs said by way of greeting, sitting in an overstuffed chair facing Arthur.

"We're waiting for more detail."

"What the hell does that mean? Don't give me doubletalk. Let's start with the tracking device that was supposed to lead your secret weapon straight to him. Where is it?" Briggs demanded.

"It's approximately fifty miles inside Myanmar, in one of the most remote stretches of jungle hills on that continent. Hasn't moved for four days."

"So doesn't that tell you that's where the bastard is?"

"Not necessarily. I repositioned a satellite over the area and have studied every inch, but all I can make out is the overgrown roof of an abandoned temple."

"So he's hiding in the temple. Send in a full team and get it over with."

"It's not that simple. We don't want to just mow him down. We want the merchandise back. It's more delicate than that."

"Bullshit. Go in, kill 'em all, then hang him upside down and work him over with a blowtorch. Do I have to break this down into fine detail for you?"

"Well, there are a number of assumptions in your statement. First, it assumes that he's there. The tracker was on his Bangkok partner's wrist. Just because the partner's there, doesn't mean our boy is. Second, it assumes that the partner didn't figure out somehow that he was being tracked, or alternatively, that he didn't get killed by any of the dozens of factions in the region. Third, it assumes that I could quickly get a heavily armed team fifty miles into Myanmar without being detected. And fourth, it assumes that our boy would be anywhere near the site when they got there." Arthur slurped noisily at his beverage then blotted his mouth with finality.

Briggs sipped his black coffee and frowned.

"You're paid to ensure this kind of thing doesn't happen. And if it does, you clean up the mess. Now we're facing the KGB's grunions negotiating for our heroin, and they're willing to pay twenty percent more than we are. Worse yet, they'll sell it for half the price on the street to turn it over."

"I understand. I'm working on putting together another shipment of rockets and ordnance to our friends in Africa. But it will take time for them to come up with enough rocks to trade. In the meantime, I'd suggest we just figure out how to get a quarter billion in cash into Myanmar." Arthur held up his hand as Briggs began to protest. "I know, it's messy, but we may never see the diamonds back. I'm hoping that we do, and I'm confident that our woman will get them if it's possible, but there are a hundred things that could go wrong. Hawker could get wounded and die before she gets the merchandise. They could have already been transferred elsewhere and converted into cash. She could get killed."

"I thought you were confident."

"I am. She's the best. But it's impossible to guarantee anything with hundred percent certainty. So, I'd say we write this one off while we wait. As far as the money goes, I know it's painful for all concerned. But realistically, it's a drop in the bucket, long term."

"Perhaps, but it's a large drop."

"Quarter billion is nothing. It's barely a few decent tanks. Aren't hammers now about a quarter billion over in your shop?"

"Fair points, but it's caused a lot of headaches, and now we have a much larger problem." Briggs frowned. "Arthur, we've been around the block a few times, and we're not kids anymore. This is a shitstorm we don't need. Have you heard anything from her?"

"Negative. She's gone dark. Which doesn't mean much. She's secretive. And it could easily take three days each direction to get in and out. Could be that she's waiting for the target to appear. Could be that she's planning. I don't know. I'm already thinking about a contingency, but as with all things, it could take a while. What I'm suggesting is that whether or not she's successful, we should prepare for failure on this one, and then if we win, it's a bonus."

"This is the largest loss we've ever sustained. It's not going to be popular."

Arthur swallowed the last of his beverage. "I understand. It affects my cut, too. Look at the bright side. The dollar is only worth ten percent of what it was when we started forty-plus years ago."

"Very funny. I'm sure the others will be equally amused."

"Briggs. Don't bust my chops. I'm on this, doing everything I can. But I think it would be best to go in, seal the deal with the suppliers while we can, and ship them a container of C-notes or whatever else they want. Gold. Swiss Francs. Whatever."

Briggs rose, tossing back his coffee. "I'll pass this on. But I think it's safe to say if you don't fix this, you won't be seeing any Christmas bonus this year. Not that I think you care."

"I always care."

Briggs dropped his cup into the trash and walked out without saying another word. Arthur waited for a few minutes and then stood, his joints painful from his old injuries, and walked towards the mall entrance.

Had he misjudged this Jet woman so badly? He didn't think so, but it had to be considered. Perhaps she hadn't been up to the task. Perhaps this was her unlucky mission. Everyone had one eventually.

His driver spotted him and pulled to the curb. Arthur adjusted his coat against the chill and waited as the man rounded the car and opened his door for him.

He took a last glance at the sky and shivered.

Looked like it might snow again.

CHAPTER 31

Lawan was staring at Jet with trepidation as Matt explained what was going to happen.

"She doesn't look happy," Jet said.

"She says she wants to stay with you," Matt related. "But that she understands that if you have to go away for a while, you have to. She's remarkably clear for a ten-year-old. Although you can tell she's been to hell and back."

"She's very firm that she's almost eleven." Jet smiled at her. "Yes, she's been through hell."

"I told her that she's going to be accompanying me back to the hills to camp out for a while. She doesn't look like she believes a word I'm saying, but she's playing along. I'm thinking I'm going to have to hire a female to watch over her and teach her, well, female stuff while she's in the jungle with me. I can't be responsible for her twenty-four seven. Maybe after a while, I can find a local family that will adopt her, and I'll make them the richest in the village. That seems like a good solution."

"I'm sorry to saddle you with this, but I don't know what else to do."

"I bit off on it, so no problem. I feel sick that Pu was such a lowlife. I mean, you know these things in a descriptive sense, like reading a dossier, but it's an entirely different thing to see it in person."

"Sort of takes the victimless thing out of the equation and just leaves the crime part."

"Speaking of which, I'm sure that the Top Cat incident will cause some major ripples. It's not every day that a ping pong club gets attacked by a ninja."

"Maybe it's about time they did. Might make some of these dirtbags think twice about the business they're in."

"Hard to change an entire society with the barrel of a gun."

"I know. More's the pity."

Lawan watched the exchange between them with calm eyes, and then Jet approached her and put an arm around her.

"Aren't you supposed to be busy with multi-million dollar transactions today?" she asked, glancing at her watch. "The photo session was a winner, by the way. Very convincing. Want to see the shots?"

"Why not? It's not every day you get to see pictures of your own death."

He moved alongside her as she thumbed the little camera she'd bought and showed him a few particularly grisly snaps; the bullet hole in his temple looked extremely realistic.

"Wow. You're a whiz with Photoshop, all right. Think it will fool anyone?"

"Sure. Just don't show up on any reality shows and you're good." She tapped her watch and raised an eyebrow.

"I've got time. The buyers are expecting me at nine o'clock at one of the largest banks in Bangkok. It will only take me fifteen minutes to get there from here."

"Sure you don't want me to run backup for you?"

"Appreciate the offer, but no need. I won't be walking out with cash. It's all handled with a wire transfer. Like I said, I'll have a card for you by this evening. And a present, of course." He smiled, and she again acknowledged that he was a handsome man, especially in the navy blue blazer and khaki trousers he was wearing.

"No chance the buyers or your passport contact would sell you out?"

"To who? It's not like there's a most wanted poster of me up. No, as long as I'm in and out today and headed north by nightfall, I feel pretty good about things. I think this time I'll cross over in Laos. But no matter. I still need to get the passports and rocks, and deal with a few other items." He looked at her with a strange expression, part curiosity and part something else. "I'm also waiting for some feedback from my agency contacts. But that could take a few days."

"You going to buy the sat phone, or should I?"

"I'll do it. I know where to go. But you should get a few burner cell phones and plan on chucking them after a single use. Don't power them on until you need to use them."

"I know the game."

"All right, then." He spoke to Lawan for another minute and then patted her shoulder with warm concern. It was a good sign that she didn't shrink from his touch. Maybe there was hope.

"Well, while you're out and about, we're going to go shopping for some suitable jungle clothes. A girl's got to have some basics. Panties, socks, couple of pairs of shoes, a backpack, ninja sword..." Jet said.

"Just don't spoil her too rotten. She's going to hate coming with me if you do."

"Something tells me that I might not be the only one spoiling her over the next few days." Jet had seen something tender in the way Matt talked to Lawan.

He merely waved as he turned the knob.

"Good luck," Jet called, and then he was out the door.

Lawan regarded her with a serious look. Jet pulled on the front of her blouse and then pointed at the little girl.

"Yes?"

Lawan's eyes lit up with understanding, and for the first time, she grinned.

Maybe there was hope, indeed.

❧

Matt returned at five, carrying two backpacks and an elegant brushed aluminum briefcase. Jet insisted on showing him all of Lawan's purchases, holding them up so he could approve. He was good-natured about it, but obviously impatient, and Jet got the hint and suggested to Lawan that she take a last shower before they left. The young girl nodded and padded to the bathroom. When the water was running, Matt slid the briefcase over to Jet. She went to her backpack, pulled the Beretta out and handed it to him along with the extra magazine.

"I'll trade you. You'll probably need this more than I will."

He slid it into his bag and then motioned at the briefcase with his head.

"Open it."

"I'm almost afraid to. I've never seen ten million in diamonds before."

"Go on."

She unsnapped the latch and lifted the lid. Inside was a new Thai passport and driver's license, four stacks of crisp hundred-dollar bills, and two packages wrapped in brown paper.

"Wow. That's more than I thought it would be based on the amount you said you were carrying around your neck. Which I still have three million of, by the way."

"Keep those. I got another five million' worth at the bank."

"How much cash?"

"Two hundred grand."

She nodded and picked up the passport.

"You're now a member of the Thai diplomatic corps, Elyse Nguyen. Congratulations." He had used the name they'd agreed upon – French first name, Vietnamese family name.

"I have a feeling my style of diplomacy may be a little different than they're used to, but hey."

"That's a safe bet."

She handed him a list scrawled on a piece of hotel stationery. "I need to see if your CIA contact can get me these once I'm in the States."

He studied the items. "How do you know about these neurotoxins? They're top secret."

"The Mossad isn't living in a cave, Matt. You should know there are no secrets."

"I'll see what she can do. You may need to have a specialized lab make them. If she can't get her hands on any, I'm sure she'll be able to get you the chemical recipe."

"Fair enough. Then I'll also need a lab that will moonlight for the right kind of money."

"Consider the request made."

"Can I check out the diamonds?"

"Sure."

She lifted the smaller package first, then carefully peeled back the tape and unwrapped it. Inside was a plastic freezer bag with what looked to her like at least a hundred stones, starting at three carats. She opened the second, larger package and found more like four hundred in that freezer bag, all larger cuts, between four and seven carats.

"That looks like more than ten million, Matt."

"It is. The larger package is fifty million. In case we need to go to plan B."

She stared at him wordlessly, then folded the two packages back up and replaced them in the attaché and lifted out the passport to inspect it.

"I thought we discussed buying fifty million of laboratory manufactured stones."

"You run a big risk that he has them tested and figures it out. After giving it more thought, it isn't worth taking the chance. So you now have sixty-three million dollars of diamonds in your possession."

"It just seems like too much…"

He grinned and feigned outrage. "What, you mean I'm going to have to limp along now on only a hundred thirty-five million until you bring the fifty back? What will I do? How will I survive?"

"You're hell-bent on doing it this way?"

"You want your daughter back. Hopefully, plan A will work out and you'll never have to give him the diamonds, but if for some reason it doesn't, you now have a solid plan B. Not to be casual about it, but we're playing with house money. Whether it's fifty or ten, there's more than I could spend in ten lifetimes sitting in my safe deposit box, so to me it doesn't matter. Believe it or not, I'm not a money guy. It's never been a big priority for me. You don't go into intelligence work to get rich," he said, then added bitterly, "unless you're planning to be in the drug business and sell poison to the world as your sideline. Like our friend."

"I still go to Zurich and do the deal on the ten million?"

"Of course. I already set it up. You'll meet them at their bank – they'll have a private room with verification equipment – and remember that the value of the stones I use is wholesale, not retail, so don't let them mislead you. Retail value would be triple that – I've horse traded these stones enough to know that the values the CIA used were the very bottom of the spectrum." He pointed at the briefcase. "All of their contact info is on a note in your passport." He slid a bank card to her, with a slip of paper wrapped around it. "That's a card with your new name on it that will allow you to access the funds, up to a hundred thousand a day, from anywhere in the world. Between the two I deposited today and the ten you'll get in Switzerland, you should be able to afford whatever you need to get the job done. Whatever you don't use of the fifteen you now have, you keep.

Consider it your fee for eliminating Arthur and his band of cockroaches. I sort of expect the fifty back..."

She nodded. "That's more than generous."

"Again, it's play money. Just get your daughter back safe and erase Arthur and his gang. To me, it's a bargain. I'd pay ten times that to have my life back and shut those bastards down once and for all."

"Do you really think that I'll need that much?"

"You're going up against very powerful, very rich men. They routinely deal in billions. Trust me. Fifteen million total firepower is not overkill. You may find yourself having to buy your way into or out of some difficult situations. Specialized weapons. I have no idea. But I do know that I don't want to hear about how you failed because you didn't have adequate resources. As an example, to avoid any customs unpleasantness, you should charter private jets to get to Europe and then to the U.S. – it's a completely different system from the airport cattle lines when you're a diplomat on your own jet. That alone will run a few hundred grand, easy. And then you have to plan your getaway. That won't be cheap. Not to mention that if you need to bribe anyone in the U.S., it could cost a few million for anything truly risky."

"Fine. I'm not going to argue. I'll bring back the fifty."

"Just get your daughter. We'll figure the rest out once you're done with this adventure. Deal?" He smiled, obviously enjoying playing Santa Claus, and reached his hand to her.

"Deal," she said, and shook it.

They stayed together like that, her hand in his, for an uncomfortable time, and then he rose and leaned across the table and kissed her. She found herself responding, her pulse quickening in her throat and her breath slowing, a rush of adrenaline hitting her at the unexpected contact.

The bathroom door opened, and Lawan stepped out, and they quickly separated, the moment over. She studied them both with no expression, then the hint of a smile played at the corners of her mouth.

Matt finally released her hand, then cleared his throat.

"Just do what you have to do, and come back safe. There will be plenty of time to figure everything else out," he said, his voice thick.

"That's a lot of surprises in a very short period of time."

"Agreed. But seeing as I'm leaving in a few minutes, I wanted to get it out on the table."

Matt turned to Lawan and told her to get her backpack and to put her small hygiene kit in it. He moved to the bed and picked his up, hefting it.

"I got a set of night vision goggles and a sat phone. Number is on the slip with the bank info, but scrambled — start on the left then right outermost numbers and work your way inward to the middle. Then add a zero after the fourth and seventh numbers."

Jet nodded. "How are you planning to get to the border?"

"Nothing quite as fancy as a private jet. I rented a car under one of my throwaway IDs, and I'll ditch it once we get there. But it's better than riding the bus."

"I think we've established that."

When Lawan had finished packing, Jet held out her arms. The little girl ran to her and hugged her, tears running in rivulets down her cheeks. Jet held her for a full minute and then gently pushed her away, got down on one knee, and stared into her eyes. She wiped Lawan's tears away and smoothed her hair, and nodded. Lawan returned the unspoken affirmation, and then they both faced Matt, Jet rising and meeting his gaze unflinchingly. He leaned in to her and kissed her again, this time cradling her face with his hands, then stepped away and motioned for Lawan to join him. She trailed him as they walked to the door. They both turned and waved to Jet before disappearing into the hall, the door closing softly behind them.

CHAPTER 32

Jet sat staring at the briefcase for several minutes and then carefully repacked everything. She checked the time and moved to her backpack to retrieve one of the six cell phones she'd bought that afternoon. After carefully slotting the battery in place, she powered it on and walked back to the desk, then searched in her purse for a card she'd scrawled some numbers on earlier in the day at an internet café.

Half an hour later, she had confirmed her first charter – a Global XRS out of Hong Kong that would fly her to Zurich, non-stop, at fifty thousand feet – close to Mach 1 – for the bargain price of a hundred and seventy grand. For that, the company would also supply catered food and get a visa for her. They explained that it was a deal because they had to fly the plane in from Hong Kong, which was over a thousand miles away, at an internal cost of roughly ten grand an hour.

She confirmed that she'd be ready to go that night, and after some calculations, they told her that she could depart Bangkok by eleven p.m..

Jet spent the rest of the evening in the hotel room, unwilling to go out anywhere and leave the briefcase, or take it with her and risk being robbed – even though it was hard to imagine anyone doing so successfully. She called the plane company back and told the concierge she wanted a late dinner ready upon takeoff, and he assured her that they would happily prepare anything she wanted. She punched the phone off, then lay on the bed and thought about Matt and the strange rush she'd felt when they'd kissed – a rush that confused her, especially so soon after David's death. She'd kissed Rob as part of their cover and had felt nothing, even though he was a handsome man. But Matt, for some reason, had triggered something that warranted more consideration.

Her thoughts shifted to Lawan – a brutalized child who now had a second lease on life. It would be rough on her living in the wilds with Matt, but not nearly as hard as being forced into prostitution while she should still have been playing with teddy bears. Jet swallowed the rage that boiled to the surface whenever she thought about it. There was no point in getting angry. But it brought back so many of her own unpleasant memories, of her foster father when she had been that age…

The trip to the airport was predictably tardy, with traffic still heavy even at night due to the dense layout of Bangkok coupled with a conspicuous lack of urban planning. As she watched the suicidal motorcycle drivers dart past them, Jet wondered what the morose cabbie would have thought if he'd known he was driving sixty-three million dollars and change around. She smiled inwardly. The world was an odd place, made more so now that she was carrying a king's ransom in her briefcase.

The airport experience was lavish, with two armed guards accompanying the executive from the charter company due to the large amount of cash involved, and two stewardesses waiting to attend to her every need. After a few minutes of counting money and shaking hands, she was speeding down the runway, en route to a frigid country almost six thousand miles away.

Zurich customs turned out to be a non-issue, her passport and arrival on a private jet ensuring that the ever-discreet Swiss waved her through without a glance, and once she was finished with the formality, she approached the taxi line. The driver nodded in approval when she told him to take her to the Widder hotel, right in the center of everything and only a long block from the river. She had been in Zurich once before on an assignment. As she watched the streets glide by, she was reminded of how antiseptically clean everything seemed – the streets, the buildings, the cars and people – especially after Bangkok, which was a kind of controlled chaos. Switzerland oozed civilized order.

The drizzly, cold dawn had barely broken, but when she got to the hotel, the staff leapt to attend to her in spite of the early hour. The suite was fifteen hundred dollars a night, with every amenity she could have wanted. She unpacked the briefcase and secured the fifty million dollar package in the room safe, then retired to the bathroom and savored a long hot soak in the bath – her first in months.

The diamond buyers weren't expecting a call until nine a.m. at the earliest, so she went downstairs and imbibed a pot of steaming dark roast coffee in the restaurant as she read the newspaper, which was thoughtfully provided in six different languages by the front desk.

The weather was forecasted to be in the forties all day, so she had a clothing problem – no coat. She'd seen nothing suitable during her shopping in Bangkok, so she'd had to content herself with a navy blue knockoff Ralph Lauren sweater that was far too light for any real cold. She asked the concierge at the front desk about nearby shops, but they apologetically informed her that the stores wouldn't open until ten, at the earliest.

Jet waited in her room, pacing in front of the window, until nine thirty, when she called the buyers. After a brief back and forth, they agreed to meet at one of Zurich's largest private banks at eleven and warned her to allow several hours for the verification process.

She exited onto the boulevard in front of the hotel and followed the concierge's directions, arriving at an upscale women's apparel store that exuded prohibitive pricing. The shopkeeper was just opening, and after browsing the selection while the hawkish woman looked on, she paid three times more than she would have anywhere else in the world for a heavy wool Italian coat. Jet checked her watch as the woman counted out her change and then made for the bank, stopping across the street at a bakery to watch the foot traffic going into the building while she waited for her appointment time.

When she entered, she was directed to a private suite with two armed security guards flanking the door. After exchanging polite introductions with the buyers, she placed the briefcase on the table, flipped the latch, and withdrew the package containing the diamonds. The two men carefully inventoried each stone, noting color, clarity, cut and carats, grading each with the precision of a locally-manufactured watch. The entire process took an hour, at which point the haggling began. Twenty minutes later, she walked out of the bank, nine million seven hundred thousand dollars richer, having made a concession in the interests of getting the deal done. The buyers hadn't batted an eye when the banker stamped the transfer agreement, instantaneously moving the money to her bank a block away – one of the operational accounts she'd set up years earlier, requiring only the account number and a passcode to access from anywhere in the world.

Once in the branch, she confirmed the balance and withdrew a hundred thousand dollars in cash. The bank vice president confirmed the amount and returned ten minutes later with two packages of new hundred dollar bills, which she counted and then slipped into her briefcase.

Logistical necessities concluded, she returned to the hotel and had lunch, and then used one of the hotel computers to locate several jet charter companies. The second one she contacted had a Gulfstream G-550 that could be ready for her within twenty-four hours at a cost of a hundred and ten thousand dollars. She booked it, and the company volunteered that it would be delighted to handle the visa she would require for up to a thirty-day stay. Ordinarily it would require a full business day, but the company had strong relationships with the people at the embassy and could arrange everything, if she would be kind enough to stop in as soon as she could. She got the bank information and committed to doing a transfer within the hour, and then made her way back to her bank and signed the order.

Jet now had over nine and a half million in her account, as well as a card that would allow her to access another two million. Three million in loose stones. And of course, fifty million for Arthur. *Good old Arthur.* There was something primal inside of her that couldn't wait for their reunion.

The following day, after a two-hour workout at the hotel gym and a one-hour run, she packed and prepared to meet her plane after lunch. Takeoff was smooth, and she settled into the jet's plush swivel chair as the plane whispered into the sky, ready for seven hours of travel before she landed in Washington in the late afternoon, local time.

CHAPTER 33

The difference between Washington and Zurich was striking, although the weather was largely the same – cold, with snow threatening. Customs was straightforward with no search of her bags, the diplomatic passport working its little miracle again in a town where the officers were accustomed to diplomats arriving by private jet at all hours of the day or night. The experience at the cab line was completely different, though, having to stand in line in the wind chill for ten minutes, and when she told the driver to take her to the Four Seasons, he practically sneered at her.

The hotel was gorgeous, the service impeccable, and the room nosebleed expensive, but she'd decided that it was better to hide right out in the open than skulking around in motels – especially with the payload she was carrying.

Once she was settled, she went downstairs to the business center and booked a rental car online, and then took a cab to the rental yard to collect the keys to her new Ford Focus. First stop was Walmart, where she chose four disposable phones, and then a superstore where she selected a laptop computer, paying cash. She went to an internet café and activated all four of the phones and then placed a call on the first to Matt's satellite phone, which just rang unanswered.

They'd agreed that she should try him every three hours at thirty minutes past, Pacific Time, so she resolved to call later.

She'd thought about both Matt and Lawan a lot on the flight over, forging their way through the jungle while she was flying on a lavish private jet, and had sent a silent prayer that they would get to their destination safely.

A web search showed a list of gun shows taking place over the next few days in nearby Virginia, and a cursory perusal of the laws told her that she could buy whatever she needed, within reason, without a permit or any kind of background check. That would save her the trouble of having to source weapons on the street. There was one at the fairgrounds the following day in Richmond, Virginia, a hundred miles south. She calculated it would take two hours to drive there – perfect – far enough away so that she'd never be remembered if any questions were ever asked.

Evening came without her reaching Matt. She called his phone every three hours at the appointed time, but he never picked up, and by ten, she decided to call it a night and resume her efforts in the morning.

❧

"I've only fired it maybe twenty times," the heavyset man assured Jet, beaming a boozy smile, beer on his breath. "A nice ladies gun." He pronounced ladies: ladeeeeees.

Jet hefted the Beretta and then regarded the owner; an orange T-shirt with a silhouette of a man shooting a pistol strained in vain to contain his substantial belly.

The gun appeared brand new, and experience had taught her that Berettas could take a substantial amount of abuse and still perform. She cocked the slide and peered down the barrel. It had a thin film of oil and looked unused.

"Kind of pricey for a used one, don't you think?"

"Not hardly. That gun's a winner. One of the most popular in the world."

"Really."

"I wouldn't lie to you. But, tell you what. Seeing as you're interested and you seem to know your way around a weapon, I'll knock twenty-five bucks off, assuming it's cash."

She considered the proposition.

"I had my heart set on getting a spare magazine or two as well. You know anyone selling those?"

"Seem to recall old Clovis over on the end of this row had a few. He's a character, but he knows his stuff. Might want to look there."

"All right. I'll take it. Where can I get some ammo for it?"

"'Bout a million sporting goods places in town. Should be able to get a box of shells."

"Shame you don't have any. That would be a lot more convenient." Jet winked as she pulled a small wad of hundreds out of her pocket. The seller almost salivated when he saw the money and rubbed the stubble on his face with a grimy hand.

"Didn't say I don't have any shells, did I? Got a carton out in my truck."

"Want to meet me out there in fifteen minutes? In the meantime, I'll go see if I can find another magazine."

"Sure thing, little lady. I'll see if one of these trailer trash will watch my gear for a few minutes. Hey, Marty!" he bellowed, and an old man wearing a battered Hooters baseball cap looked over at him. "Gotta hit the can in a few. You watch my stuff?"

"Lemme know when. Won't be hardly any stealing going on while you're gone."

Both men had a good laugh, and then she handed him the money.

"I'm supposed to check your driver's license, but for another fifty I could sorta skip that part."

"You drive a hard bargain. How about fifty including the bullets?"

"You got it."

"I'll give you the money when you give me the shells."

"Seems the right way to do it," he agreed. "I'll meet up with you out by the bathrooms in fifteen, okay?"

"I'll be looking for you."

Clovis had one extra magazine as well as a shoulder holster for the Beretta, and a quick turn around the booths located one more – more than sufficient for her purposes. She slipped everything into her purse and then went out to meet her new admirer.

He was waiting by the bathrooms, as promised, and she proffered a smile as she approached him. He had a plastic bag with a box in it in one hand and a beer in the other. She took the bag from him and peered inside, then slipped him the fifty and moved off, his eyes burning holes through the back of her jeans as she walked to her car. She fished her cell out of her pocket as she unlocked the door and dialed Matt's number again, and was surprised when he picked up. He sounded exhausted and got straight to the point.

"My contact couldn't find anything obvious on likely sites for your daughter, but was able to discover Arthur's home address. You got a pen?"

"I'll remember it."

He rattled off the address, and she repeated it back to him.

"If my contact doesn't find out anything more in the next twenty-four hours, you should plan to do this the hard way. And she's working on the other two who run the show with him. Hopefully, she'll have those soon as well. Oh, and before I forget, she was able to arrange to get you the chemical breakdown of the drugs you asked for. She'll leave it at a dead drop we arranged." He recited the location and details of the drop.

"Okay. Got it. I'll swing by now. I'll call you again at this time tomorrow, okay?"

"Fine. We made it to one of my camps okay. No drama. Lawan says she misses you. I'm hiring a woman to help out with her and recruiting some new guards from the local warlord. Everything fine on your end?"

"Never better."

"Good luck with the drug manufacturing."

"Thanks. Talk tomorrow." The line went dead.

Now she knew where Arthur lived.

Which was probably his worst nightmare come true. If not, it soon would be.

Her next stop was at a hardware store, where she bought a vise, a padlock and some welding gear, and then a machine shop supply store where she paid cash for several pieces of specialized machinery and sundry odds and ends that she loaded into the trunk, along with a collapsible work bench. When she was within an hour of Washington, she pulled over at a monthly storage facility and rented their biggest stall for six months, and then unloaded her gear into the unit and locked it. She would be back tomorrow to start her project – it would take a day, two on the outside.

Jet drove to the drop – an office supply superstore – and retrieved the single page document that had been left for Elyse. On it were two strings of chemical sequences only a chemist would be able to make sense out of, and a name and address. Twenty minutes later, she was sitting with the director of R&D for the company – a pharmaceutical manufacturer. She passed the slip of paper to him and waited for a price.

He seemed agitated, but after a number of admonitions about how difficult it would be to synthesize the drug, he named a number. Six figures.

She agreed to it without hesitation, and he assured her that he could have it ready within two days. They shook hands, and when she promised to have him half the money within the hour, his demeanor relaxed. He would probably blend the cocktail himself that night, she figured, and wake up tomorrow a hundred grand richer.

She hummed along with the radio as she drove back to the city, tapping her fingers with the beat, and realized that her spirits were better than they had been for some time. She was finally doing something, preparing for the encounter that would get her daughter back and rid the world of a dangerous parasite.

Now it was just a matter of time.

CHAPTER 34

Jet lifted the welding mask from her head and studied the result of her efforts with approval, then loosed the vise and moved to the grinder to create a smooth seam. The internal baffles had been the most difficult part, but she'd studied the physics and understood the concept of attenuation, and had dismantled enough similar devices to understand how they worked.

Once she was finished, she screwed the tube onto the barrel of the Beretta and checked it for fit. Satisfied, she turned and fired a shot at a pile of sandbags she'd placed in a corner of the workspace. The pop was loud, but no worse than any of the professionally-crafted silencers she'd used. It would do.

She had already reloaded the fifty shells so that they would be subsonic with the silencer, further reducing the sound, and she fired one more round to make sure. It would take a little adjustment for a miniscule drop in the bullet's trajectory at greater range, but for her purposes, it was more than suitable.

After dusting the silencer with a coat of flat black primer, she checked the time and picked up her cell phone. Matt answered on the first ring.

"Bad news is nothing more on Hannah. Good news is my contact's gotten the address of two of the other top dogs. The operational side of this is Arthur and his counterpart at the DOD, and the associate director of the CIA. If you eliminate Arthur, his DOD buddy and the associate director, you've hopelessly crippled their operation. By the time the underlings are able to regroup, the natural competitive pressure in the market will have flattened them, and the Russians or whoever else will have taken over the supply side. We can't eliminate the drug trade, but we can make it so the CIA is no longer the largest trafficker."

"Give me the info. I'll add them to my shopping list."

"The DOD man's name is Briggs." Matt gave her the details. "And here's the director's information."

She scribbled a note on the back of a reloading materials brochure.

"Okay. Got it. How are you holding up?"

"Good. I've now got thirty men from one of the largest opium warlords in the Shan. All seasoned fighters, or at least so he claims. They look tougher than the last bunch, so that's a positive. Lawan is doing well, settling in. I hired two women, one to cook and keep the camp presentable and the other to tutor her. Although I don't think she's had more than an eighth grade education herself. But it's better than nothing."

"I take it you're able to recharge your phone."

"The miracle of solar power. Even in the jungle."

"All right. I'm about ready to move."

"Wait another day or two. Let's give my contact more time to see if she can dig up anything more. She's working on blueprints and security diagrams for all three of the targets' houses. That will come in handy, I'd imagine."

"It will. You think I'll have it within forty-eight hours?"

"Absolutely. She was confident. And another couple of days shouldn't change anything."

"It's another two days without my daughter."

"I know." He paused. "Have you decided how you're going to do this with Arthur?"

"A hybrid of plan A and B. I'll try B first. Although I suspect you're correct – there's no way he's going to give me Hannah back and let me go."

"No, now that you know the whole story, you can see why he won't."

"Which is why I'll lead with B and then be prepared to shift to a modified A. On the others, it will just be straight sanctions. All on the same night so nobody has time to figure out what's happening."

"All right. Figure on making your move forty-eight hours from now. Call me tomorrow, same protocol."

"Will do."

Waiting was like Chinese water torture, but the stakes were high, and Matt was a seasoned field agent and operational planner. If he felt her chances were best waiting, then difficult as it was for her, she would wait.

Jet moved to the sandbags, taped a piece of paper to the front one, and walked to the far end of the twenty foot space. She fired three shots in rapid succession at the black circle she had drawn on it. The grouping was within a half inch. Admittedly at twenty feet it wasn't much of a test, but she could extrapolate. The weapon would do the job.

She spent the next two hours cleaning up every trace in the stall and moving the equipment back to her trunk. She'd get rid of it on the way back to Washington, eliminating all evidence of her preparations.

By the time she was finished dropping the gear at the dump, it was late afternoon, and she mentally ticked off another checklist item completed. The car clock reminded her that the day was winding down, so she needed to get busy on her next task.

It was time to buy some vehicles.

❧❧

Muzzle flashes illuminated the night as the tribesmen's Kalashnikovs chattered from defensive positions around the camp. The answering fire from the jungle was smaller caliber, three round bursts, cutting away at the camp defenders with precision. Matt darted to a cluster of rocks, pistol in hand, and retrieved one of the fallen guards' rifles, then flipped Jet's night vision goggles in place and scanned the jungle.

He saw the flares of three gunmen a hundred and fifty yards away. They were using flash suppressors, but in the verdant luminescence of the goggles they lit up like starbursts. Matt switched the AK-47 to full auto and fired a sustained burst at the first and second positions, the hot 7.62mm shell casings flying around him. When the gun was empty, he ejected the exhausted magazine and pawed another free from the dead guard and slammed it home, then peered around the rocks.

The shooting from the two gunmen he'd spotted had ceased, but there was still another out there firing at his position – no doubt also equipped with night vision gear. He leaned towards one of the pair of guards cowering behind the rocks and barked a terse command. The closest one nodded. He shouted a rough bearing to the men, and on his signal, they began laying down covering fire while he dodged to another outcropping.

Bullets pounded into the ground around his heels, and then he was behind the boulders, the tribesmen still shooting. Judging by the incoming fire, there were two more left. At least.

He popped up and fired half the magazine at the position of the last gunman he'd seen, and the shooting from that position stopped.

A chunk of rock flew off near his head and grazed his cheek. He wiped away a trickle of blood as he tried to gauge where the final shooter was concealed. At the edge of his field of vision, he saw another bloom of bright light, his ears confirming that the shooter was to his left. He took two deep breaths and then emptied the rest of the magazine at the hidden man, strafing the area with measured precision.

No further gunfire answered him.

He waited, thirty seconds, and when there was no more gunfire, he called to the leader of his security team, "Go get flashlights from my hut. I have three by the door. Don't touch the bodies. I want to see them as they fell."

The leader nodded and was back in a blink with the lights. Matt watched as his men crept into the brush searching for the attackers' corpses. A shout from one of them confirmed a find, and then another a few yards away.

He looked around, mentally counting the number of his guards that had been killed, and spotted eleven bodies in the near vicinity. It was a bloodbath, and two more men groaned where they had fallen, wounded, not long for this world.

Matt stood, still wary, and made his way to the edge of the clearing where the flashlight beams burned bright in the gloom. One of the attackers was still breathing, gasping for breath, and Matt looked down at his Caucasian features and battle-hardened face without pity.

"Who sent you?" he demanded, but the man's expression froze as he shuddered and then lay still. Matt was walking over to the second body when a woman's scream pierced the night. He spun and ran back to the camp as the cook came running out of her hut, hands stained with blood, screaming into the night sky.

&divider;

"Runs like a champ." The young man patted the hood of the black Chevrolet Tahoe with seeming affection.

The bright morning sunlight exposed where the rust damage on the quarter panels had been sloppily repaired. She'd spent the evening scouring the classifieds and the internet for vehicles and had set off early to get the chore over with.

"You mind if we take it to a mechanic for a quick once-over?"

"I've got a lot of people who want to buy this baby. I don't have time to take it somewhere so a mechanic can nitpick it."

"That's a shame. Good luck selling it." Jet returned to her rental car and pulled away, frustrated that this was proving so difficult. She'd looked at three possible candidates, and all were garbage. Not that she particularly cared, but she couldn't afford a vehicle to break down in the middle of an operation. She moved to the next on her list, five miles away.

The black Ford Explorer was owned by an older couple who seemed genuine and had no reservations with her taking it to a mechanic. After an hour inspecting all the basics and running a compression check, the mechanic she'd lined up gave her the thumbs-up, and she paid the couple in cash. She arranged to have the husband follow her to the rental yard so she could return her car, and paid for a taxi to take him home.

Her first hurdle had been surmounted, and she knew that the DMV system wouldn't list the Ford as sold for days, by which point she'd be long gone.

She thought the next vehicle would be harder to acquire, but was pleasantly surprised when the first one she looked at proved to be exactly what she was looking for – a 2010 Coachmen Freelander RV with only eighteen thousand miles on it, owned by an old man who could hardly walk. The wife told her their sad story – about the dream trip they'd taken around the country before the husband endured his final battle with non-Hodgkin's lymphoma – and tearfully told her that they'd be willing to take a beating on it because they could use the money.

Jet paid them full price and asked if she could leave the vehicle sitting in their driveway until she could come and get it. They were overjoyed to do so, eyeing the stack of hundred dollar bills as though they'd just won the lottery.

As she pulled away, she tried calling Matt, but he didn't answer, and she resolved to try him again in three hours, as agreed.

After a late lunch, she drove through both Briggs' and Arthur's neighborhoods, familiarizing herself with the layouts. Briggs lived outside the city limits in Arlington, Virginia, in an estate home near the river at the end of a cul-de-sac that backed onto the George Washington Memorial Parkway. She had studied the satellite images and confirmed her impression on the drive by. Relatively rural suburb for the well-heeled. Nice, but in keeping with a man who wasn't living beyond his means.

Arthur's townhouse was a different story. In the heart of Georgetown, a densely-populated, affluent section of Washington near the university, it would present some challenges. It was an older building that had been remodeled, she could see, and looked expensive. A security camera peeked from under the edge of the roof, another by the front door. It looked like the home had been built in the 1800s, but was immaculate. Easily worth ten million dollars these days. Unexpectedly opulent digs for a CIA career man.

She would need to look at the blueprints and the schematics, but it looked do-able for someone of her skills. Briggs' house was child's play.

Her final stop was a lavish nine-thousand-square-foot mansion near CIA headquarters, adjacent to Pimmit Bend Park – a faux Tudor home at the end of a long private drive. That one would require some additional research, but she was confident.

Matt's sat phone continuously rang without response, and she spent the remainder of the day growing increasingly concerned. He didn't strike her as the type to go dark for no reason, but there was nothing she could do but wait. Jet checked the blind e-mail account he'd had his contact send the blueprints to, and saw three large files sent from an anonymous remailer. She downloaded them to her laptop, opened them, and studied the floor plans and electrical diagrams with interest. As she had suspected, there were a number of weak areas, and she made mental notes as she pictured the layouts in three dimensions.

She tried the sat phone one last time after dinner but still got no response, and as she lay her head on the down pillow for the evening she had a sense of dread in the pit of her stomach.

Something was wrong.

She knew it.

CHAPTER 35

The following morning, Matt answered on the third ring.

"Where have you been? Is everything okay?" Jet demanded.

"No. There was an attack yesterday. We took heavy casualties."

"Are you okay?"

"For now."

His voice sounded odd. Tight.

"What happened?"

"Best I can tell the drug lord who provided the men sold me out. That's the only possibility. They knew where the camp was."

"Tribesmen?"

"Negative. American, by the looks of them. Four. All dead."

Her thoughts raced at the implications. "All they understand is retribution. You know that. The drug lord has to go."

"I know. I'm making plans to take him out tonight, before word gets back to him. But…I don't know how to tell you this…"

"What? Tell me what?" she asked, her heart sinking.

"It's Lawan. She was hit by a stray bullet. She didn't make it. She's dead."

Jet couldn't breathe. It felt like someone was standing on her chest, and Matt's voice seemed to come from the end of a long tunnel. Then the sensation passed, and she gulped air. Her hand shook almost imperceptibly as she brushed away the beginnings of a tear.

"Those bastards. Saved from a nightmare only to be killed by…this had to be Arthur's doing." She fought back the rage, replacing it with a glacial calm. "Did she suffer?"

"No. I don't think so." The lie trembled over the line.

"Bury her and say a few words for me, will you, Matt? She deserves at least that."

"I will. I'm sorry."

"Just make sure you take care of yourself. You've used up all nine of your lives." She paused. "What are you going to do?"

"Kill the warlord and then move the camp to one of my other sites."

"All right. This cinches it. I'm going to go in tonight. This will be over soon."

"Believe me. There's nothing I want more. But I'll believe it when I hear you confirm it, not before."

An uncomfortable stillness hung between them.

"I'm going to get going. Good luck," Matt said.

"Luck will have nothing to do with it," Jet responded, then stabbed the cell off.

She brushed her arm against her eyes, blotting tears, and then overcome by fury again, hurled the phone at the wall. It exploded into fragments. Jet buried her head into the pillow and sobbed for Lawan, whose life was over before it began, her brutally short interlude marked by tragedy and abuse. Shuddering rocked her as she screamed her anger and frustration into the bed, and then she quieted, her body growing still as the emotional storm blew over.

She looked up at the mirror on the far wall, face distorted and eyes red, and vowed silently to avenge Lawan, even though it wouldn't make anything better or bring her back. It didn't matter.

They would pay.

&>~&

Jet's tires whirred beneath her as the anthracite mountain bike carved through the moist soil and dirty gray patches of snow that clung to the ground between the tall trees. Her breath steamed out of her mouth as she panted, having ridden two miles from where she'd left the Explorer. The moon peered through the patchwork of heavy clouds, pregnant with snow, as she glided like a silent wraith through the woods.

When she was a hundred yards from the house, she leaned the bike against a tree and adjusted her backpack, then trotted towards the hedges that ringed the palatial rear yard.

The lights were on in the ground-floor living room of Briggs' house, and she watched as he reposed in a green silk bathrobe, reading the paper, a bottle of expensive cognac on the table beside him. Upstairs, she could see a woman in her fifties sitting at a makeup table brushing her hair, her face a mask of unhappy resignation as she considered her reflection, a glass of wine near her right hand.

A dog barked several homes down the row, and she waited until the animal settled down before edging to the rear dining room door, next to the room where her target sat scratching himself. She reached into her backpack and pulled out plastic bags, which she quickly slipped over her feet, holding them in place with a rubber band on each ankle, then donned a pair of latex gloves. The lock took twenty seconds to open, and then she was creeping into the house, the soft soles of her Doc Martens boots inside the plastic sheaves soundless on the hardwood floor.

Briggs must have sensed her presence a few moments before she looped the wire over his head. He was in the process of turning when she wrenched it tight, the wire biting into his skin as he writhed in an attempt to get free. A line of blood trickled from the gash it had sliced, and then a geyser sprayed forth as the garrote severed his carotid artery.

"Honey? What's going on down there?"

The woman's voice sounded worried, but obviously not enough to descend the stairs. Briggs's blood sprayed the painting that hung lavishly on the wall in front of him; a stern nobleman rendered in ancient oil – now with crimson splatter marring the surface.

Briggs stiffened and then went limp.

"Honey? Answer me." Annoyed now, the words slightly slurred.

Jet dipped her finger into Briggs' blood and scrawled Lawan's name across his forehead, then pulled the wire free and glided quietly back to the dining room door, leaving blood-smeared footprints on the polished hardwood as she went. Once outside, she retrieved a liter water bottle filled with gasoline from her backpack and unscrewed the top, then stuffed a rag into the neck and lit it with a disposable lighter, leaning it next to the home's wood siding before vanishing into the dark.

A minute later, Jet heard the woman's scream even through the closed windows, a muffled high-pitched bleat of shock and horror. She slid the bloody shoe bags off her boots and packed them into a third bag along with the gloves and the garrote, and then bolted for her bike as flames licked at the outside of the house, the gasoline having erupted a few seconds before, igniting the shingles in a fiery blaze.

By the time the police arrived, there was no trace of her, a phantom come to exact a terrible retribution before disappearing into the night.

She looked at her watch as she pedaled hard through the woods. She would be at the second target's home within ten minutes. Jet turned onto the pavement a quarter mile away and pointed the handlebars east.

૏∙ૐ

The assistant director of the CIA stirred and turned onto his side, his small frame dwarfed by the ornately-wrought headboard of the king-sized bed. An antique that had been chosen by his third wife, he'd battled her for the bed during a bitter divorce and won in the end. It wasn't so much that it was important to him as it meant a lot to her. She loved the damned thing. Not that she ever seemed to enjoy being in it with him.

Something caused him to start, and he slowly came awake, opening his eyes to see the shadowy outline of a figure standing at the foot of the bed. A figure dressed entirely in black. He tried hard to focus without his glasses and saw that it was a woman. A beautiful woman.

Pointing a gun at him.

He sat up.

"I…I have some money in my wallet, and my watch is a Piaget," he stammered.

"That figures. Piagets are crappy watches for rich morons with no taste."

"It's…worth a lot of money. Take it. And I have a few thousand dollars here."

"That's good to know."

Confused by her tone, he reached for the bedside lamp.

"Move one more inch and I blow your head off."

He froze, then slowly resumed his sitting position.

"What do you want?"

"I'm here with a message."

"A message?"

"Yes. It's a short one. Either you die by the gun tonight, or you die by the needle. Your choice."

He swallowed with difficulty, his throat suddenly dry.

"What the hell are you talking about?"

"I'm here to kill you. But I'll give you a choice. Do you want a bullet, or a shot of the heroin you're responsible for selling to millions of kids all over the world?"

"Look, lady, you've got this all wrong…" The pistol didn't waver. "Do you have any idea who I am? You're making the biggest mistake of your life," he snarled.

She ignored him.

"What's it going to be? Bullet or needle? I don't have all night."

He lunged for the bedside table, and she shot him in the leg, shattering his kneecap. His scream was cut off by another round directly between his eyes. The back of his head blew onto the coveted headboard. She stepped to the bedroom door and flipped the lock closed, then moved to the window and slid it open. His scream would bring his two bodyguards and his maid within seconds, but by the time they got in, Jet would have vanished.

With a final look at the dead man on the bed, she climbed through the window and lowered herself until her feet were ten feet above the grass, then dropped softly, rolled backwards, and took off at a full run to where she'd left her bike in the dense cover of the park.

Five minutes later, she was in the Explorer, driving the speed limit on her way to Washington.

ॐ∂≈ॐ

"Yes?"

Silence greeted Arthur's interrogative. He held the handset out and stared at it, then clenched it to his ear again.

"Who is this?" The line was unlisted. *Perhaps a wrong number?*

"Wake up, Arthur," Jet finally said.

"Who…where are you? I haven't heard from you for a week," Arthur demanded into the phone.

A sound rattled from downstairs, and then the line went dead.

Arthur rose from his bed and wrapped a robe around his pajamas, then slid his nightstand open and removed a small pistol – a Ruger LCP 380. He lifted the handset again to call for help, but there was no dial tone. And he'd left his cell phone downstairs to charge overnight, as was his custom.

Mitzi, his pug, whined and stretched, peering up at him in confusion. Was it time to wake up and go for a walk?

He crept cautiously down the steps and turned the corner at the base, entering the living room, where Jet sat in the dark in one of his colonial-era chairs, a briefcase in her lap, one foot swinging lazy circles. He flipped on the light and regarded her, the pistol trained on her head. Mitzi yelped happily and ran to her. Jet reached down and scratched her furry little head. Mitzi pushed her face into Jet's hand and then lay by her side with a plop.

"You won't need the peashooter," she said with a smile.

Arthur looked worse than she remembered, the mottled skin puckered around his neck, which had thankfully been covered by his shirt and tie before.

"Perhaps. But this is highly irregular." He appeared to consider the situation and then dropped the pistol into his robe pocket – but kept his hand in it, she noted.

"I suppose. So is having your baby kidnapped and being blackmailed. I guess we live in an irregular world…"

"Why didn't you call me?"

"I lost the number."

He studied her calm face, and then took a seat across from her with a sigh.

"And?"

She lifted the briefcase and put it on the coffee table between them, and then lifted the lid, turning it towards him.

The freezer bag of diamonds twinkled in the ornate chandelier's glow.

"There are your diamonds. Next to them, you'll find snapshots of Hawker. He's been neutralized. Now, where's my daughter?"

Arthur leaned forward and picked up the photos, taking his time to scrutinize them suspiciously before dropping them into the briefcase and lifting the diamonds out.

"What is this? Some kind of joke?"

"What do you mean? Those are your diamonds. Now it's time to end this charade. I've done as you asked. Time for your end of the deal. Where's my daughter?"

"That's only…maybe a quarter of them. Do you take me for a fool?"

"That's what he had. I looked online and calculated the number and carats. It's over fifty million, wholesale. It's all there. Now, where's Hannah?"

He stood and pulled the pistol from his pocket. "This is all he had?"

"That's what I said, isn't it? Now put the gun down, tell me where my daughter is, and get ready to hand me a million dollars."

"Not so fast. I need to verify they're real."

He hadn't dropped the gun.

"Fine. They are. That's what he had. You can pay me once you check them. But for the last time, tell me where my daughter is."

His skin tightened as he grimaced, and she realized he was smiling. He raised the Ruger and pulled the trigger.

Nothing happened.

His eyes widened as he tried to chamber a round, but the gun was empty.

"Now that definitely wasn't the deal," she said, pulling her silenced Beretta from behind her and leveling it at him. "I didn't think you'd honor your part of the bargain, but I figured I'd at least give you the chance. More than you gave me."

Arthur flung the Ruger at her and sprang for the hall. The impact of Jet's feet slamming into his side sent him reeling into the wall with a crash. He dropped to the floor, groaning.

Jet got up, brushed herself off and then walked to the table and closed the briefcase, locking the latch with a soft snap. She eyed Arthur's quivering form and approached him.

"Now we'll do this the hard way. I actually hope you don't tell me where Hannah is until I've had a real opportunity to convince you. I'm usually ambivalent about torture, but in your case, I'm looking forward to it. I suppose all that expensive surgery on your face will get destroyed by the acid, but before it does, you'll wish for death a hundred times over." She kicked him, hard, in the stomach. "I even went shopping for items to use. You know, I once kept a subject alive for six hours before his heart gave out? I mean, he was unrecognizable as anything human by then, but still. It's an art, really. I'm sure you'll appreciate it. By the time I'm done, you'll have not only told me where Hannah is, but you'll have told me anything and everything you can think of just to get me to stop."

She moved to the dining room and lifted a shopping bag from behind a chest, then brought it to the living room and set it near the coffee table before putting on a pair of gloves.

"You have no idea what you've gotten into. You'll be dead by morning," Arthur snapped.

"Oh, you mean the drug ring? Is that what you're talking about? Guess what. I know it all. I know about the heroin you've been importing from the Golden Triangle. I know about the heroin from Afghanistan you're shipping using military transports as well. I know about the cocaine and meth from the Mexican cartels. The ecstasy. I know everything."

Arthur's eyes took on a veneer of worry for the first time.

"How…"

"Seems like Hawker had the goods on all of you. Briggs. You. Everyone in the ring. Documented."

"You'll never prove it. You can't prove anything."

"You mean nobody will believe that the Central Intelligence Agency is the biggest drug trafficking organization in the world? You sure about that? Sure a paper or TV station or three wouldn't be interested? Maybe Congress?"

"You have no idea how high this goes."

"Right. Higher than the associate director? And the director?"

"It's bigger than you can imagine."

"Arthur. Look at me. I know everything," she said quietly.

"Then you know you don't have a chance."

"I know that if you get between a female lion and her cub, you can expect no mercy. Which brings me to the part of the show where I start peeling your skin off and feed it to Mitzi. That's gotta hurt."

The timid little dog gazed up at her from where it was hiding behind an armoire, alert at the mention of her name. Jet withdrew a cattle prod from the bag.

"I modified this so it's capable of delivering a continuous current. I hear you use them for torture. Nice." She placed it on the table and then held up a syringe. "This will completely incapacitate you so you're incapable of movement, but can feel everything. Curare – crude yet effective, wouldn't you agree?" She placed it on the table next to the prod and produced another hypodermic. "And this is a little favorite that heightens the synaptic response so sensations are magnified exponentially. I've been told that it can make a paper cut feel like you're being disemboweled. My thinking is I start on your eyes. You won't need them any longer. Then I move to your genitals. Not that you probably get much use out of those, either. Then, when you think it can't get any worse, I'll use this." She extracted a bottle and placed it carefully next to the syringes. "Acid." She fished the final item from the bag and held it up – a soldering iron. "I watched David cook a Mossad traitor with one of these. Just the smell is enough to make you gag. I can't even imagine how it will feel after the injection and acid wash."

She picked up the cattle prod and walked towards him.

"This is your last chance, and then I zap you till you're twitching, inject you, and start on your eyes. Think very, very hard about your answer. Because once I start, there's no going back. You know my history. Make your choice. Honor our agreement or become hamburger."

"You'll never do it. You'll never kill me," he spat. "You won't get your daughter back if you do."

"Why, Arthur. Perhaps I need to work on my communication skills. I have no intention of killing you. I'm going to leave you paralyzed, with no tongue or eyes, in permanent agony for the rest of your hopefully-long life. Nothing – no amount of money, no specialized treatments – will ease the suffering. Think about it. Blind. Pooping yourself. Every nerve amplifying your pain tenfold. The injection is irreversible. The best you can hope for is that I'll take pity and kill you once you've told me where she is. Because you will, Arthur. You will. Nobody ever holds out once this gets underway. You're no different. You of all people should know that. Again, I really, really hope you decide not to cooperate."

Arthur looked panicked, her message finally having hit home.

She waited, but he didn't say anything, preferring to glare at her with raw hatred. Jet shrugged and moved towards him with the cattle prod and pressed it against his face, then engaged the current.

Arthur bucked and jerked for ten seconds, foaming from his nose and mouth, and then she cut the power, his limbs twitching spasmodically from the lingering effects.

"You should start regaining the ability to move in twenty seconds or so. By then I'll have injected you with the nerve agent. Imagine what you're feeling right now, the agony, amplified immeasurably. Have I got your attention?"

She picked up the smaller syringe and pulled the orange cap off, then squirted a little into the air for effect.

"You'll get nothing," he growled, laying his last card on the table.

Jet shrugged and knelt next to him, then drove the needle into his leg, depressing the plunger before pulling it out and tossing it aside.

It took half a minute for the full effect to hit.

"Argghhh,"Arthur screamed, writhing in agony as the full force of pain arrived.

"That's what I thought. Now I'm going to cut your eyes out. You ready?" She flipped out a combat knife and opened it, waving the shiny blade at him.

Arthur croaked, a rasping sound with a wet bubbling at the end.

"What's that?"

"I'll tell you," he rasped, the fight gone out of him, waves of pain racking mercilessly through his body.

"What? You said left eye first?" she asked, her face a blank.

"Please. I'll tell you." He spat out a slug of bloody saliva from where he'd bitten his cheek then convulsed again.

She reached behind her and pulled a pair of handcuffs free, then tossed them on the floor.

"As soon as you can move, put those on. And start talking. Where is she?"

"God. The pain. Help me…"

"I told you. Once you're injected, it's out of my hands. Now where is she? Or the eye goes."

He struggled for breath. "A…private hospital we use. They have a pediatric ward. She's a patient."

"Where?"

"Alexandria. Virginia," he hissed, his face twitching.

"The name."

"Anderson…Medical."

"Security?"

"Only one guard. In the lobby. They were told…she has a virus. One of our doctors is caring for her."

"Where is she? Which floor?"

"I…I think the third."

"Cuff yourself. You're coming with me."

CHAPTER 36

"What are you going to do with me…ungh…once you have her?" Arthur gasped as he bent over double, every neuron in his being on fire.

"I'm thinking about it. Considering the option you gave me when you pulled the trigger, I'm not feeling generous."

"I…never mind."

"No, there's not much to mitigate a bullet to the brain that failed to fire, huh? 'My bad' doesn't really cut it. Now move."

As they reached the entry foyer, she stepped back into the living room and scooped up the briefcase and the Beretta.

"Open the door. Slowly. Then we'll walk to my car. It's down the block, to the right," she instructed. Arthur fumbled with the lever and twisted it, the cuffs making it difficult.

They walked down the front steps and were on the sidewalk when she spotted movement on her right – a man with the distinctive shape of a silenced pistol in his hand. She dropped to one knee as she raised her weapon and fired two shots at the running gunman, the second shot whipping his head back as it tore through his face.

The window of the car next to her exploded in a shower of glass, and she pulled Arthur to her and twisted, firing at another shooter down the sidewalk. She could hear the *thwacks* as her slugs slammed into his chest, but he was still shooting even as he dropped. A bullet ricocheted off the sidewalk and then a round caught Arthur in the chest. She adjusted her aim and squeezed off four shots at another man in an overcoat crossing the street. He went down hard, his weapon clattering by his side as he tumbled onto the asphalt.

Jet squinted in the dim light and spotted another shooter coming around a truck by the house next door and waited till she had a clear shot, then fired three times. Two of the slugs caught him in the throat as he shot at her, his aim going wide. A second bullet pounded Arthur in the stomach.

Arthur's legs buckled, and he sank to the ground. She dropped to one knee, sweeping the surroundings with the Beretta, alert for any further threats.

The street was silent.

"You stupid asshole. You triggered an alarm somehow, didn't you?" she hissed.

Blood spread across Arthur's shirt, and he moaned. The chest wound was ugly and had punctured a lung – she could hear the air frothing out as he fought for breath.

"They'll...find you... miserable bitch..."

She studied his mangled face, twisted by pain and hate, and then stood.

"Drowning on your own blood is a lousy way to go. I've seen it. There's nothing worse...except for a stomach wound. At least your last few minutes on the planet will be your most painful. If I could make it last forever for you, I would. I hope there's a hell. You belong there, you filthy bastard."

He couldn't speak, his hands claws, clenching automatically in unspeakable agony.

"Kill me. Please." The words were a moan, barely audible.

She glanced around at the fallen bodies and shook her head.

"You earned this. Enjoy it."

She spat on his twitching face and then turned and jogged to the Explorer. Within twenty seconds, she was pulling away, leaving Arthur to expire on the sidewalk, his final moments spent in unimaginable suffering, cold and alone.

❦

The hospital service door was locked. Jet worked the picks and had it open in under a minute. She adjusted the black knit cap on her head and listened for any signs of movement. It seemed deserted. After looking around to ensure that the parking area was still clear, she pulled it open. Thankfully, there was no alarm on it. She stepped inside and, glancing through the glass window on the interior door, confirmed that there was nobody nearby. She closed the exit softly and then turned to the stairwell, taking the steps two at a time.

At the third floor she paused, listening. It was quiet.

She swung the steel door wide and stepped into the hall. The lights were on dimmers, set low for the night, and she heard a single nurse at the staff station at the far end of the wing talking on the phone in hushed tones, an occasional giggle punctuating her exchange. Festive decorations of dancing ponies and singing birds decorated the colorfully painted corridor, confirming that she was in the pediatric wing.

Jet moved silently to the doorway of the first room and peered in. It was empty. The second housed a little boy sleeping on the bed, maybe six years old, a heart monitor beeping at a low volume on a stand by his side.

The two adjacent rooms were also empty.

The next one had a small form curled up on its side, covers half off, facing away from her. She stepped into the room and approached. The child rolled over, sensing a presence.

It wasn't Hannah.

Another titter echoed from the nurse's station, and she slowly inched back into the hall, pausing to listen again before moving to the room across from her.

Empty.

She heard a rustle from the corridor and turned.

"Hey. What are you doing here? You can't go in there..." the nurse exclaimed.

Jet started to stammer an explanation and then slammed the side of her neck with an incapacitating strike. The nurse's eyes rolled into her head, and Jet caught her as she collapsed, pulling her into the room and closing the door. The woman would be out for a few minutes, but time was Jet's enemy now.

She darted from room to room and, in the one closest to the nurse's station, came across another slumbering toddler. She sidled to the side of the bed and peered down at the sleeping face.

Hannah.

Jet's nostrils filled with Hannah's essence, and a surge of adrenaline coursed through her as the little eyelids opened groggily and regarded her.

Jet saw recognition, and Hannah smiled before closing her eyes again and snuffling.

She gently lifted Hannah and held her to her breast, murmuring to her as she vaguely remembered her mother doing when she was a baby. Hannah snuggled closer, and Jet's heart nearly burst.

A part of her could have stood like that forever, but she forced herself out of the spell and moved back into the hall, then speed-walked back to the stairwell. The exit was empty, so she pushed through the door and crept onto the landing, a draft blowing up from the street level ruffling the tips of her hair. Hannah shifted against her and made a soft sound of sleepy susurration, then resumed her drowsing.

Moments later, Jet was strapping Hannah into the new child's seat in the Explorer, readying her for the short drive to where the RV sat waiting. A police car rolled by on the street in front of the hospital, and her breath caught in her throat. It hit its brake lights as it neared the intersection, slowing. Jet pulled the Beretta free of her jacket as she eased the driver's door open.

The squad car picked up speed and continued on its way.

Jet exhaled with a sigh and then climbed behind the wheel. She took another look at Hannah in the child's seat, her small head cocked to the side, eyes clenched shut as she slept, and then cranked the ignition and put the car in gear.

❧❦

"It's over," Jet said into the cell phone as she backed the RV out of the driveway, the headlights off so as not to wake the couple in the house.

"All of them?"

She described her night's activities in clipped sentences.

"And Hannah?"

"Sleeping next to me."

"What's your next move?"

"You'll be the first to know as soon as I figure it out. First thing I need to do is get as far from Washington as I can. I'll call you in another couple of days. What about you? What are you going to do?"

"I guess I need to think about that some. Can't see any reason to hide out in the jungle if the bad guys with the grudge are history. Can you?"

"Not really. Unless you're a nature nut or something."

"I'm really not."

"Then you thinking maybe you'll buy yourself an island and hang out a hammock?" she asked.

"You make it sound like a pretty attractive proposition."

"Right now, it sounds great. I envy you."

"I'll let you know what happens. You got the fifty in stones?"

"Of course."

"Then you have a good reason to come back."

She glanced at Hannah in the seat next to her, still asleep.

"I suppose I do."

CHAPTER 37

Jet sat at a weathered table across from a heavyset Latino man, Hannah by her side, watching as he took a photo with the elaborate digital camera and then inspected it on his computer.

"Perfect. I can have the passport finished within two more days. It'll pass cursory inspections, but you don't want to use it anywhere they have an automated scanner. Those are typically linked to a central computer, and it will come up as an unrecognized number," he advised.

"I need a few of those photos myself. Can you send them to this e-mail?" She handed him a piece of paper with a cutout e-mail account on it.

"You betcha. I'll do it right now." He moved his mouse around and typed in the address with excruciating slowness, then hit return. "Still not completely comfortable with these damned things. Technology. Although it's made the business easier. Used to be a passport would take two weeks, not three days. But now you just press print and the machine does the work for you." He shook his head. "But why a Mexican passport? Most of my customers want a U.S. one. If you don't mind my asking."

"I like Mexico." She smiled sweetly.

"And the name on the passport?"

She'd thought about it a long time.

"Lawan Nguyen."

"Spell it."

She did.

"Good Mexican name. You sure you don't want something like Maria Perez? Just saying…" He spread his hands wide, palms up.

"Nope."

"Fine. Now to the mundane part of our transaction…" He looked at Jet expectantly.

She removed three thousand dollars from her purse and counted it, then sat back, studying the display cases on the walls filled with stamps and obscure currencies.

"And the balance when it's done. Any problem with that?" he asked.

"No. I'll be back in three days."

She pushed back from the desk and stood, then held out her hand for Hannah, who joyfully grabbed it and slid off the chair. Hannah had decided that she hated strollers and was hell-bent on walking everywhere, her fierce determination to be independent reminiscent of her mother.

"What do you want to do now that your photo session is done, Hannah?" Jet asked.

Hannah pointed at the two-year-old Toyota Highlander she'd recently bought from a private party, parked twenty yards away in the Santa Ana sunshine. Hannah loved riding in the Highlander more than anything in the world, which was a good thing, because soon they would be doing a lot of driving.

The trip from Washington, D.C., had taken a week, and they'd slept at rest stops and campgrounds every night, avoiding the formalities of hotels. Once they'd made it to southern California, she'd put out feelers among the immigrant community and quickly found someone who could create good quality papers for her. If all went well, by the end of the week they would be in Mexico, where she planned to travel down the coast while she decided what to do next.

She placed Hannah into the child's seat and buckled her in, then retrieved a cell phone from her purse and made a call.

"How's it going?" Matt's voice was slightly distorted from the sat phone.

"Good. I got the photos and will send them on within an hour. How long to get another passport for Hannah?"

"They said a week. Only a hundred grand, seeing as we're return customers."

"And that will be another genuine one – not one that could come back and bite us later?"

"Correct. Full citizenship. But no diplomatic immunity for a two-year-old, so keep her out of trouble."

"Isn't she covered under mine?" Jet asked.

"Of course. That was a joke."

"Can you FedEx it whenever you have it?"

"Sure. Where?"

"I don't know yet. Probably somewhere in Mexico."

"Ah, Mexico. Make sure you stay away from the cartel hotspots."

"Good thinking." She paused. "What's the latest?"

"From what my sources tell me, the heroin business is up for grabs now – there's been no communication with the drug lords for a week, and the Russians and now the Yakuza are putting pressure on them to do a deal. I think it's safe to say the CIA lost that round. My contact tells me that internally it's a disaster – the associate director ran the day-to-day of the agency. So with him gone and Arthur gone missing, there's a real vacuum. And it looks like they covered up Arthur's death. Kind of figured they would. Hard to explain four dead agency gunmen and a high-ranking staffer bleeding out on the streets of Georgetown. My hunch is they had a cleanup team sanitizing the place within minutes of getting word."

"Then the group still has some game."

"Oh, sure, but only at the response level. Their top operational guys are now dead, so it's going to cause complete mayhem with their members. Everyone will be jockeying for position, and while the infighting is going on, they're losing the suppliers. That's a death blow. Literally. They've got their hands full. Maybe now, they'll have to return to doing their jobs instead of operating a global drug syndicate."

"What about you?"

"Everything's quiet. My bet is this ended with Arthur. There probably weren't many in the group that were even told about the diamond theft. Arthur would have kept a tight lid on that while he tried to recover them so the others didn't flip out and question his judgment. And anyone remaining will be scrambling to do damage control to salvage what they can of the network." Something crackled on the line, then he continued. "Besides which, they have billions in hundred-dollar bills in cargo containers – so it was never really about the money. I think it was mostly a personal thing with Arthur because I put a crimp in his plans by taking the diamonds out of play, and because I worked for him."

"I made a tape of Arthur admitting everything," Jet said.

"Hold onto it. At some point, we may want to leak it to the press."

"Think they'd use it?"

"Fifty-fifty. But I'm conflicted. I don't want to hurt the country, and this would forever tarnish its standing in the eyes of the world. But on the flip side, I don't want anything like it to ever happen again," he reflected.

"Sounds like you've got some thinking to do."

"About a lot of things."

The pause stretched to an uncomfortable length.

"You keeping my diamonds safe?" he asked.

"You bet. The bag goes everywhere with me. Got a larger purse just to accommodate it. Heavy, though."

"Got a gun?"

"Of course."

"So you're set," Matt said.

"For the time being. I figure I'll hit the road in a couple of days and never look back. And you?"

"I've been thinking about the island. I'm probably going to get a little surgery in Korea so I look different and then poke around on Ko Samui to see what property values are like."

"Get something on the beach."

"My thinking, exactly. Someplace big, so I can accommodate guests. Even if they have a kid."

Another silence.

"She's beautiful, Matt. Gorgeous."

"I would expect nothing less, based on her DNA. You know, you're a genuine Thai citizen now. Hannah soon will be, too. Maybe you should download some Thai MP3s and learn the language while you're roaming through Mexico. And then come visit. Soon."

"That's not a bad idea, Matt. It occurred to me."

They both hesitated. This wasn't the right way to talk about what was on their minds.

"All right, then. I'll call in another couple of days, before I head out. You think you'll be in Korea?"

"Probably. If you're not in any rush for the passport, I'd rather get my mug taken care of before I do anything else."

"I can understand that. I can wait a week or two. Hey – don't have them change too much."

"I'm going to shoot for younger, richer and thinner."

"I'd say you already have the rich part dialed."

"Good point."

Hannah squealed from the back seat, her way of complaining because they weren't underway yet, and Jet started the car and pulled into traffic. She had some shopping to do before they headed south, and didn't want to leave anything to the last minute.

She took side streets until she saw the distinctive outline of South Coast Plaza ahead, then pulled into the massive parking complex and found a slot near the main entrance. Hannah's favorite coffee shop was on the second level, and she delighted in people-watching while Jet used the wireless internet.

The sun warmed their skin as they strolled in the balmy spring air, mother and daughter out for a day of consumerism. Jet caught a glimpse of herself in the glass-fronted doors and saw that for the first time in forever she had an unfamiliar look on her face. She peered at her reflection for a few seconds before she realized what it was.

She was happy.

CHAPTER 38

Once the 747 had arrived in Bangkok and they had sauntered through customs with hardly a glance, Jet flagged down a taxi and took a cab to the smaller airport, where a chartered plane was waiting for the short hop to Ko Samui island.

As the King Air turbo prop taxied to the end of the runway, Hannah pointed at all the surrounding planes, laughing at some joke known only to her. Jet smiled and turned to gaze at her, never tiring of her joy at discovering something new each passing moment.

The engines increased their revs, and soon they were pulling up into the sky, Jet putting her hands up into the air and Hannah mimicking her before they both exploded with peals of glee. Once they were at altitude, Hannah seemed fascinated by the water below them and proceeded to name everything she saw.

Mexico had been a relaxed three months, drifting from town to town with no particular agenda. Hannah hadn't seemed to mind. She was a little trouper. But eventually, Jet tired of the gypsy lifestyle, and Matt's regular invitation to visit his beach house, where he'd settled into an easy-going island lifestyle, had taken on an increasing allure.

She still had his diamonds safe in her purse and had become almost used to having fifty million dollars on her arm. How many times had she walked down the waterfront streets in Mazatlan or Puerto Vallarta, Hannah in tow, wondering what any of the locals would have thought if they'd known...

Being on the move constantly made her feel like she was living in a completely different world than those around her. Which was fine – but reality exerted a strong pull, and she now longed for something more intrinsic than what she'd grown used to.

Her frequent discussions with Matt had convinced Jet that, besides her obligation to return the stones to him, she was interested in exploring the spark that had ignited during their kiss. She'd thought about it many times and always came back to the same place – it was crazy, she hardly knew him, none of it made any sense. Which was all true. But she also knew how she felt, and she wanted to give that feeling a chance, and see if it was fleeting or something more substantial.

So she'd agreed to stop in over the next week and had booked flights that avoided the U.S. system, and had left the Highlander in a parking lot in Zihuatanejo and flown to Mexico City on their first leg to Bangkok – oddly enough, through Frankfurt on Lufthansa.

And suddenly, she was back in Thailand, with all its contradictions and clamor and charm.

The plane banked and began its descent, and then the wheels were bumping down the runway, and they were taxiing to the private terminal, which turned out to be little more than a hut. She liked the place already. A warm breeze tugged at their hair as they strolled along the tarmac and approached the surrounding booths, Hannah clutching her hand, pulling her forward in her eagerness to explore new wonders.

The transaction for the rental car took longer than expected, and then she remembered where she was. Things didn't ever seem to go quite as planned in Thailand, and on an island, where the pace was even slower than usual, progress was likely to be glacial. Eventually, the always-smiling attendant directed them to a little red Nissan sedan, and after studying the map, they set off in search of Matt's new digs.

The southern side of Ko Samui was more developed than Jet had imagined, and she saw many familiar franchise names and endless rows of beach hotels with endless groups of wandering tourists milling on the sidewalks. It seemed that the unspoiled paradise that Matt had described to her had been discovered, and developer money had moved in, bringing with it the madding crowds. It happened everywhere, she supposed; there was no escaping it.

They rounded the tip and drove north, where things became much more rustic, all jungle and lush greenery, with few complexes marring the natural beauty. She checked the map again and then spotted the turnoff the clerk had marked, laughing in broken English as he'd remarked, "You're never lost on an island – just late!"

They weaved down the road towards the beach, where she could make out several compounds of newly constructed resort buildings, then turned right on the frontage road, crawling along as they admired the natural beauty of the flawless turquoise water and glistening sand. It was idyllic. Paradise found.

"Look, Mommy. Smoke," Hannah called from the back seat, pointing to an area a quarter mile away where a black cloud hung lazily over the strand.

Jet's throat tightened as they approached the site of the fire. They rolled past a gutted lot, the foundation the only thing remaining of the building, the ground scorched and still smoldering, natives ruminating the rubble as a uniformed police officer waved them by. She tried engaging him in halting Thai, asking what had happened, but he shook his head and motioned for her to continue down the road. Outwardly she was calm, but inside, her heart was sinking.

Several hundred yards up the road, they came to a little market with an attached bar. Jet pulled into the gravel lot and shut off the engine. Five tourists were loitering at the bar, enjoying their beer, looking down the road at the wreckage.

She climbed out of the car, got Hannah free of her baby seat and approached them.

"Hey. What happened down there?" she asked.

"Big fire last night. Whole place went up. We're staying right down the beach at the closest resort. I swear I heard shots, and then a big explosion, but everyone thinks I was drunk. The cops don't want to hear about it. Lazy buggers." The speaker's face was red from sunburn and decades of heavy drinking, his Australian accent unmistakable.

"Really? What are they saying happened?"

"Hard to make it out with their jabber, but from the scuttlebutt at our hotel, the owner of the house and two workers were killed. Bodies were carted off earlier," he said, then chugged half his bottle of beer.

Jet tried for a grin but felt bile rise in her throat and had to take deep breaths to keep from vomiting. She bantered and probed for any further information, but the Aussie holidaymaker didn't know anything more. Her stomach in knots, she led Hannah into the market and asked about the fire, but got the same story from the woman working the scarred register.

"He nice man. Verrry handsome for a *farang*. Shame. Maybe he piss off wrong people," she said, shaking her head.

"Why do you say that?"

"My cousin police. He say everyone shot in head. That always criminals. No accident."

"Really. You wouldn't happen to know what the address was, would you?"

The woman frowned, thinking. "I think it number nine. Don't know. Nobody use address here."

Jet paid for a bottle of water and thanked her, then pulled Hannah back outside. She looked down at the slip of paper with Matt's address on it in her trembling hand. Number nine.

Vertigo hit her, and the beach seemed to spin giddily before it settled down and her vision cleared. Her heart pounded like a drum roll as she led Hannah back to the car, where she had to force several deep breaths before taking the wheel and pulling back towards the ruins.

The policeman glared at her as she crept by, eyeing the destruction, and then she picked up speed as she returned the way she'd come, suddenly wanting to be rid of the island as fast as possible.

"Mommy. Why cry?" Hannah asked, afraid she had done something wrong.

"It's okay, honey. I was just thinking about a friend." Her voice cracked, unable to continue.

Jet dried her eyes at the intersection and pulled onto the main road, the image of smoking devastation behind her receding in her rearview mirror as she accelerated towards the illusory safety of civilization, hoping she could get the next flight out.

<<<<>>>>

Jet III – Vengeance finds Jet settled down, trying to return to a somewhat normal life of stability and safety. But fate has other plans for her when she becomes embroiled in a terrifying terrorism plot involving figures from her past, whose thirst for revenge forces her back into the kill-or-be-killed world she'd hoped to have put behind her forever.

For preview and purchase details, visit:

RusselBlake.com

ABOUT THE AUTHOR

Russell Blake lives full time on the Pacific coast of Mexico. He is the acclaimed author of the thrillers: *Fatal Exchange, The Geronimo Breach, Zero Sum, The Delphi Chronicle* trilogy (*The Manuscript, The Tortoise and the Hare,* and *Phoenix Rising*), *King of Swords, Night of the Assassin, The Voynich Cypher, Revenge of the Assassin, Return of the Assassin, Blood of the Assassin, Silver Justice, JET, JET II – Betrayal, JET III – Vengeance, JET IV – Reckoning, JET V - Legacy, Upon a Pale Horse, BLACK,* and *BLACK is Back.*

Non-fiction novels include the international bestseller *An Angel With Fur* (animal biography) and *How To Sell A Gazillion eBooks (while drunk, high or incarcerated)* – a joyfully vicious parody of all things writing and self-publishing related.

"Capt." Russell enjoys writing, fishing, playing with his dogs, collecting and sampling tequila, and waging an ongoing battle against world domination by clowns.

Sign up for e-mail updates about new Russell Blake releases

http://russellblake.com/contact/mailing-list

Made in the USA
Middletown, DE
22 September 2019